CAROLINE, CAROLINE

CAROLINE, CAROLINE

By Margaret Ritter

CHARLES SCRIBNER'S SONS · NEW YORK

Copyright © 1976 Margaret Ritter

Library of Congress Cataloging in Publication Data

Ritter, Margaret.
    Caroline, Caroline.

    I. Title.
PZ4.R615Car [PS3568.I827]   813'.5'4   75-40000
ISBN 0-684-14590-1

1 3 5 7 9 11 13 15 17 19 c/c 20 18 16 14 12 10 8 6 4 2

Printed in the United States of America

Books by
Margaret Ritter

Caroline, Caroline
Simon Says
The Lady in the Tower

CAROLINE, CAROLINE

Last night I dreamt of Caroline again. In my dream I stood on the narrow path, at the edge of the cliff, overlooking the sea. The bright moonlight caught and glittered on the waves. I stood transfixed, held prisoner by my fear of the water.

I knew, as one knows in dreams, that I could not go back the way I had come. I knew I had no choice but to go on to the end of the path. I had to go on until I found Caroline, but I couldn't move. I was immobilized by fear. I waited, hoping for a sign, for some miracle that would release me from my fear of the water. Yet all I could think of was the sea and the wet, jagged rocks gaping below like the teeth of a great sea monster waiting to devour me.

Then a cloud hit and covered the moon. I was alone in the dark. I whimpered in terror of the dark above and the water below, the way an animal whimpers in a troubled sleep before the fire. I heard from somewhere deep in the sea the toll of a buoy bell, and it seemed that surely the bell was the sign I was waiting for. The bell tolled for me. It was the hour—the time had come and I must go on or it would be too late.

I began to make my way slowly, carefully, toward the end of the path. In the dark I stumbled and nearly fell. The pebbles scattered loose from the edge and I heard them hit the rocks and splash into the sea below. Yet I went on, impelled. I began to run, wanting to have it done with. I ran and ran, faster and faster, in a sort of frenzy, to find Caroline, to see her at long last, to have it done with. I knew she was there at the end of the dark. And then, when I had begun to tire and to despair, the cloud sailed past the moon and I saw her at the end of the path at the end of the island standing on the point of the cliff.

She stood facing out to sea dressed all in white from head to foot. I saw her clearly illuminated in the silver white of the moonlight. She stood tall and proud like the figurehead of a ghost ship, a specter shrouded for a burial at sea.

I was gasping, each breath a torment, an agony of survival. Yet I managed to say her name. It seemed at first she had not heard me. Then she slowly turned. As she turned her cloak billowed out and I saw to my horror that she held Emma captive in the imprisoning folds of her white cloak. Poor Emma, such a little girl to be caught in such a terrible dream. And still I had not seen Caroline's face. She was a flame of white—her dress, her cloak, her slippers, and her face. Her face was swathed in deathly gauze. She was wound round and round by yards and yards of bandaging.

She took one step back and then another until one step more and she and Emma would have been over the edge and into the water. I had no choice. There was only one thing for me to do. I reached forward and wrenched Emma from her grasp. As I pulled Emma free I cried, "Run, Emma! Run, run!"

And she ran but I could not follow her, for when I had reached out to pull Emma free I had myself been caught in the white cloak. It held and enveloped me. I was overpowered by Caroline and, because she willed it, we were over the edge and falling, falling toward the sea.

In the long, long fall I began to scream. I heard myself

scream, but as the dreamer I knew I made no sound. The scream was a part of the dream. No one could hear me in this, the final, fatal moment of the nightmare.

And then, as I had known we must, we hit the water and went down and down and down. We were drowning, Caroline and I together. I struggled against it. I knew it was a nightmare and that surely I must wake from the dream. For I knew that Caroline was already dead. She had drowned before I had come to Fanner's Island.

One

There is a time, I am sure of it, when one can turn back. A time when disaster can be averted. For me that time was the moment I stepped from the dock at Fannerstown, Massachusetts, over to the deck of the boat that was to take me to Fanner's Island.

At that moment I looked down and saw the narrow stretch of water between the dock and the boat. I knew then it was the exact point of no return. I was leaving my native element of land and going to the fearful and unknown one of water and I was terrified. Even the kind and weathered face of Captain Fairley, as he reached out a hand to help me aboard, could not dispel my fear. He saw my consternation and grinned broadly.

"Welcome aboard, Miss Raynor. Not much water where you come from, I'll be bound."

"Not any," I said, and it was true. The Indian Mission school where I taught was in a sea of arid desert. It had been assigned to a defeated tribe by a victorious government, and at the time the tribe had not been in a position to complain of the gift.

"The Fanner Foundation must think a lot of you," Captain Fairley continued, "to send all that way for you to teach one little girl."

In fact the Fanner Foundation had not so much sent for me as they had summoned me. They had felt within their right to do so because, before his death, they had supported my father's work at the Mission and because they had paid for my college education. I was in their debt.

"Is this all you brought with you?" Captain Fairley asked, looking at my luggage.

"Yes." I hadn't known what to bring. I had never spent a summer on an island before.

"Well, travel light, travel fast," Captain Fairley remarked more to himself than to me. He called out for a dockhand to cast off our line and took me along with him to the wheelhouse of the cabin cruiser. The Captain started the motor and we were away. I looked back at the shore with regret. I was now committed to the voyage unless I cared to swim back, and I could not swim.

I looked at Captain Fairley. I think I had expected anyone named Captain Fairley to be a taciturn, seafaring man. The Captain looked very much like an old salt. He was white-haired, red-faced, about sixty-five, and he proved to be a nonstop talker. Captain Fairley was a dab hand at asking questions and then answering them himself. I didn't mind. It was oddly comforting to have to make no reply. It gave me the opportunity to orient myself to my new situation and to think about what lay ahead of me.

"You know the trouble with the Fanner Foundation?" he asked.

I could think of several and was about to select the most appropriate when he continued.

"They think money can mend anything. Well, it's not so. It can't bring back Emma's mother and father, can it? What kind of Christmas was that, I ask you, to have her mother and father killed in a skiing accident?"

It had been a terrible accident, three years ago at Christmas.

There were pictures in the papers of the ski chair fallen from the lift cable into the snow. The papers seemed to regret not providing their readers with pictures of Sara and Edward Hand lying broken and dead beside the shattered chair. The tabloids had to content themselves with an account of Sara Fanner Hand, one of the richest women in America, who had died a few minutes before her husband, Edward Hand, philanthropist. The papers offered instead the gruesome thought that now their daughter, Emma, four, would inherit tragedy along with her fortune. I didn't think even the cheaper papers could have imagined that tragedy would come again quite so soon.

"Poor little mite," Captain Fairley went on. "Then she came out to the island to live with her Uncle James and her cousin Caroline, where she learned to feel at home, and now her cousin Caroline has drowned."

I looked out at the bow of the boat cutting through the water, slicing and dividing the sea. This boat must have cost many times my yearly salary. One would think nothing could go wrong with such a craft, but at Easter Emma and her uncle, James Hand, and her cousin, Caroline, James's wife, had been out in a wonderful, splendid boat and it had blown up in the water. Emma and James had been saved but Caroline had drowned, or so they had said.

"They say she drowned." Captain Fairley might have read my thoughts. "I don't believe that. I say she blew up in the boat. Her body was never found. I was on the island when it happened. I heard the explosion and I went out to have a look-see and when I got there what a sight that was. Emma was bobbing in her life jacket like an orange cork in the water and Mr. James was holding onto a bit of timber. His head was cut and bleeding and all around them was the debris and the wreckage. It was something wicked. I got Mr. James and Emma over the side. I looked for Caroline but I couldn't find her. I didn't know what to do. Mr. James was hurt bad and so I took him and Emma over to the mainland to Fannerstown to the hospital." Captain Fairley sighed. "I didn't think to take them to the island. Maybe it would have been better if I had. What would you have done if you were me?"

I didn't answer because I didn't know what I would have done.

"I meant to do the right thing." Captain Fairley shook his head. "But I didn't count on the newspaper people and those photographers. I didn't know people could make such animals of themselves. They crowded in like sea wolves. I would do anything for Mr. James. I've worked for his family for a long time. I only came to these parts after Mr. James and Caroline Fanner married. I didn't have any idea people anywhere could act like those people in Fannerstown did during the inquest. They all acted like Mr. James was guilty of some crime. Of course it was Caroline's place. Mr. James was the stranger. The island was Caroline's. She was the Fanner but then I guess you knew that because you knew Caroline."

"No," I said, taken aback. "I didn't know Caroline. I never met her." And it was true. Caroline Fanner had taken what I had wanted most in life but I had never met her.

"Caroline Fanner was the most beautiful woman I ever saw." Captain Fairley looked ahead as if, before him, he saw Caroline, more beautiful than the Lorelei. "I've been in a few ports of call in my time but I never saw anything like her. They said she was Sara Fanner's poor relation but it seemed to me that she wanted for nothing. She had the island and she had Mr. James and she had beauty."

Captain Fairley looked at me. "I thought you knew one of them. Thought someone told me that. Must have been Sara Fanner that you knew."

"Yes," I said. "Sara Fanner was my friend."

Sara had been a dear and good friend to me. She was my senior sister at college. I never forgot her kindness to me that first day when I arrived in the East for school. I was a thousand and more miles from home and so homesick I thought I might die of it. I felt like a motherless child. My clothes were all wrong and I was all wrong. I was painfully shy. Sara made me feel welcome. She stood in the doorway of my dormitory room; a short, round dumpling of a girl, her brown eyes were very serious and dark. Then she smiled at me and her smile was warm and welcoming.

"Hello," she said. "I'm your senior sister, Sara Hand. You're lucky to get me. I'm married to Edward Hand and we have an apartment off campus where you can come when the dorm gets too much to bear."

Sara got me settled into the dorm, she showed me the campus, and then she took me to meet her husband, Edward. They were both very young and very earnest. We sat over tea and then over dinner. We talked halfway through that first night.

Perhaps we were so close because Sara, like me, had little real family. Her mother and father were both dead. Sara had distant cousins, Miles Fanner and his sister, Caroline, but she didn't know them very well. I gathered that they were as poor as Sara was rich and that Caroline was very beautiful and that they lived on an island off the Cape. Sara seemed to find Caroline's life, which was so different from her own, exotic and almost enviable.

That first year at college was a success for me because I had Sara and Edward to lean on. They were graduating and I was just a freshman, and all three of us had to work to keep up our grades, but still we managed to see a lot of each other. Because of them it was a happy year.

In late October Sara suspected that she was pregnant and by Thanksgiving she was sure enough to celebrate.

"Listen," she said to me, "you can't go all the way out west for a Thanksgiving weekend, come home with us to Boston."

I accepted eagerly. I was looking forward to a New England Thanksgiving. It seemed historic and fitting, almost as if I might dine with real Pilgrims.

I was glad we'd become friends before I saw the house in Fanner Square and began to have some idea of Sara's background. The house in Fanner Square was as far from my home as imagination and distance could make it. It was more than the multiple fortunes Sara had inherited, it was the heirlooms that were rightfully hers from generations past.

Sara didn't seem to notice that the house intimidated me; she was too polite. If one of us was a snob it wasn't Sara.

It was a good Thanksgiving, just the three of us. Edward hoped his brother James would come but James, who was pre-law at Harvard, had opted for skiing in Vermont. So it was just the three of us, Sara and Edward and I. We drank our toasts to the coming baby.

It was not until Emma was born that I met James and fell in love with him.

"Yes," I said to Captain Fairley. "Sara was my friend but I never met Caroline."

Captain Fairley nodded. While I had been remembering times past he had not once stopped talking.

"How long does it take to get to the island?" I asked, looking out into the glare of a brilliant Turner seascape.

"Not long, it's about an hour from the mainland to the island, depending on the tides and the wind. You can't see the island from the shore but it's there just beyond easy view. In the old days the first Fanners were whalers out of Fannerstown. Then they went to live on the island. In those days a captain could be gone at sea a year or more. But the Fanners kept their wives and children on the island. Poor lonely creatures."

"I think I can see the island now," I said, pointing ahead to a shape that might be mist or low cloud or land. I watched, fascinated, held in a spell, as we came nearer and nearer to land, not land as I knew it, but land surrounded by the sea. I had lived for a long time isolated from the main of society but this island was remote and detached, vulnerable to all conditions of wind and weather.

The island was smaller than I had imagined it would be. It was about a mile long and the shape of an imperfect, irregular crescent. Dead ahead of us was the bay and a landing jutting out into the water. To the left of the landing was a wide, smooth beach that ran to the end of the island and tapered off and disappeared at the edge. Above on the highest point of the island, on the left, was a lighthouse.

On the right of the landing was a shale-and-shingle beach going along the water's edge toward a small inlet in which I could see a boathouse partially hidden by trees. Above the inlet was a thicket of scrub oak and pine.

Straight up from the landing ran a path to the house which was sheltered in the protection of a hollowed plateau. It was a compact, two-storied house built of weathered timber which had become a grey-green color that must change with the mood of the sea.

The house was fashioned like the inverted hull of a ship. The windows and front door were set flush with the siding. Any extraneous architectural fancy had been avoided. The house gave the impression of having been battened down against the storm that was always expected and that must surely come. Above the second story there were six tiny attic windows like the slitted eyes of a grey kestrel.

I turned to Captain Fairley. "Is there more of the island beyond that ridge?"

"No, it's a sheer cliff face and beyond the cliff the open sea."

Well, this was it then. What I saw before me was Fanner's Island, the island that had been Caroline's domain.

As we came toward the landing Captain Fairley cut the motor and we drifted alongside the landing.

"While I make fast you go on up to the house. Mrs. Fairley is expecting you. I'll bring your bags up when I come."

I thanked the Captain for a pleasant crossing.

He smiled. "My pleasure to bring you over."

As I started up the path for the house, I knew I went so slowly because I was of two minds. I wanted to see James Hand again but at the same time I was afraid of my feelings. I had believed I no longer loved James. I had been sure that my wounded pride had healed with hardly a scar to show for the injury, but when the letter had come from the Fanner Foundation and I knew I was to spend a whole summer with him, I found I was not so sure after all. I didn't know how I would feel when I actually met James face to face again.

I had sat looking at the letter, remembering the letter Caroline had written me telling me she was going to marry James, and I found to my dismay that I had forgotten nothing. I remembered every word he had ever said to me. I remembered the entire affair with painful clarity.

I didn't meet James my freshman year. Sara and Edward tried to introduce us but it never worked out. It became a joke. When he was with them I was not, and when I was there he had gone or he returned too late. He even missed their graduation because he was away.

Sara, who by then was enormous, said she should have gotten a cum laude for being the year's most pregnant graduating senior. In that summer she and Edward went to Boston to wait for the baby and I went west to help my father at the Mission. When Emma was born I was the first person Edward called. I went back to school early and stopped in Boston for her christening. It was then I met James at last. He was bending over Emma's crib. He stood up and turned to me and said, "How do you do? I'm Emma's Uncle James."

It was such a ridiculous introduction that I laughed. I liked everything about him. He was tall and elegantly made. He had a fine head and eyes that snared one fast as a trap. He was a hero from Henry James, a painting by Sargent. He was a Bostonian, a New Englander. No western man ever managed to look distinguished at twenty-two but James did. I liked everything about him.

"And I'm Martha Raynor," I said.

"Yes. You're the friend Sara and Edward talk so much about. Look at her," James said proudly, showing me Emma wriggling in her basket. "Isn't she beautiful?" It was not true. Emma was far from beautiful but James thought her beautiful. Emma's beauty was in the eye of her beholder.

Sara and Edward and James and Emma and I all drove off to the church in a limousine. James held Emma, smiling into her as yet unfocused eyes.

Sara turned to me. "He's an idiot, isn't he?" But you could see she was pleased to have her baby so adored. She said she had asked her cousin Caroline to be Emma's godmother but Caroline's brother Miles had died suddenly so I was going to stand deputy for Caroline. "I wish you could have seen Caroline," Sara sighed. "She is absolutely and totally beautiful."

"Not," James said, smiling at Emma, "not as beautiful as my niece Emma."

It was ridiculous to watch James with Emma. He was besotted with love for her. She could spit up on him, she could wet on him, she could cry until she was as red as her toothless gums, and still he loved her.

It was early autumn when he first telephoned me at school. I didn't expect him to call but vaguely hoped he would.

"Hello," he said. "I've taken some photographs of Emma and I'm coming down this weekend to show them to you."

After that James came every weekend. Or we went to Boston to Sara and Edward's to see how Emma was coming on. When Sara and Edward went to Asia on a Foundation project and took Emma with them we came to Boston on our own and stayed at the house in Fanner Square. We played chess, we talked, we ate, we made love, and when we were alone our dreams were all clear and bright and sure to come true. James would get his law degree and he would go into a good firm and take up civic causes and in time he would be an ambassador, and I would be his lady. Other Hands had been ambassadors before him. When we were alone everything was sure to happen just as we planned.

But when we went out it was a different matter. Then we met the sort of people James had known all his life. When we went to Fanner Hall or to Fanner Center for the Performing Arts or to the Hand Library Concerts I knew I was an outlander. I felt my lack of social grace.

My father had tried to do his best by me but it had been hard to bring me up motherless. Social graces had not been easy to acquire in the hard country where I had lived. In my subculture we didn't run to Lapsang Souchong or Pekinese or string quartets. Instead we had windstorms and sudden cattle fevers and the drought. The distance between James's world and mine was as wide and deep as a canyon.

And yet I had been so in love with James that my heart was a valentine with his name written on it for the world to see. I must have been an object of pity and scorn for having had such an engraved heart.

Even now as I walked up toward the house I felt as if the very windowed eyes of the house were staring at me in silent reproach for having been such a loving idiot.

I stopped for a moment about halfway up the path, and as I looked up toward the house, suddenly along the ridge of the island to the left, toward the lighthouse, I saw something sharp and bright glitter, reflected in the sun. Someone was there, I felt sure of it, someone who was watching me, someone who had been watching and waiting for me to arrive.

But that was fancy. I must be more raw and vulnerable than I thought if I was going about thinking the world was watching me. Except when it came to James Hand I was a very reasonable and sensible person.

I squared my shoulders, took a deep breath, and went on resolutely toward the house. Since it was inevitable that I must see James I might as well see him at once and get it over with.

I hesitated only a second before the large carved oak door. I was about to raise the brass ship's knocker when the door opened. A woman stood framed in the doorway. I knew without any trick of fancy that she had been there watching, waiting for me to arrive. She gave me a long appraising look and in that one glance she observed me thoroughly. She took her personal assessment although how I rated I couldn't tell.

"Well," she spoke at last. "So you've come. I am Mrs. Fairley."

I hoped I didn't betray my astonishment. This woman was such an odd match for Captain Fairley. I had expected Mrs. Fairley to be a motherly woman of mature years like the Captain. This woman was at least thirty years younger than he. She was slight, short, and very dark. She might be Welsh or Cornish. There was something remote and removed about her. I could not imagine how they had met and fallen in love, let alone married. It was as if some strange exotic misalliance had taken place. For it seemed certain to me that she had always been here on this island. She belonged here in this house. I could not imagine her in a life other than this one. She was far from pretty but she was striking, a handsome woman but without any trace of softness. She was weathered by hard usage as some of the Indian women I knew were weathered by the life and the climate in which they lived.

"Come in," she said. "I'll show you up to your room so you can freshen up before you see Mr. Hand. He is waiting for you in the library." She stood aside from the doorway and I entered a small panelled entrance hall. It was a functional place in which to take off one's coat, a place for cold drafts to warm and lose their chill before they found their way into the other rooms of the house. There was a huge spiney coat rack, an umbrella stand, a portion of a faded Turkey carpet. The paintings were floral, of the Spanish school. Beneath the stairs was a closet. The door was slightly ajar. Mrs. Fairley closed it hurriedly as she told me something of the house.

"The library is that door on the left. The parlor and dining room are on the right. Through the door beyond the stairs is the kitchen and our apartment, Captain Fairley's and mine. You'll soon get used to the house, I expect."

She was being polite but nothing over cordial. I could not help but wonder if she resented my coming. She started up the stairs and I followed after her. Mrs. Fairley continued speaking as if it were her duty, a set speech which she had rehearsed for the occasion.

"There have been a lot of improvements made in the house in the last year. Mrs. Hand—Caroline—had it restored to its original design but she put in all the modern improvements. We have a new generator and new plumbing. The kitchen is as up-to-date as anything on the mainland. We have a freezer and a dishwasher and a garbage disposal unit. I couldn't ask for anything better."

As we came up the stairs to the second floor I saw that there was a long hall running along the length of the front of the house. Off this long hall was a series of rooms.

"This first room was Caroline's room." Mrs. Fairley paused by the door at the head of the stairs. I thought she was about to open the door and show it to me but she did not. "It's a beautiful room," she said sadly. "But since the accident at Easter it has never been used. Mr. Hand sleeps down in the library. He's had the library turned into a bed-sitting room. I suppose this bedroom brings back memories. Mr. Hand adored Caroline, of course. Everyone loved Caroline."

Mrs. Fairley went on down the passage and I followed, somehow wounded by the knowledge that James mourned so deeply for Caroline.

"You are here." Mrs. Fairley stopped at the next door. "Your room connects with Emma's by a bath, which you will share if you don't object."

Mrs. Fairley opened the door and stood aside waiting for me to go in before her. It was a spacious room. The windows were hung in floral chintz and looked out over a garden behind the house and up toward a circle of trees on the hill beyond. In the trees I could see the faint outline of a summerhouse.

"I hope you'll be comfortable." I heard Mrs. Fairley close the door softly and I turned to her.

"I'm sure I shall be. It's a lovely room."

It was indeed a lovely room, full of lovely things. There was a four-poster bed with a hand-loomed coverlet. There was a Newport highboy, which might have done honor to a museum, and a Philadelphia wing chair covered in green brocade. There were pretty Persian carpets lying next to beautifully worked rag rugs. There was a Georgian silver bowl full of fragrant potpourri and a Bristol mug filled with garden flowers. It reminded me of a little vase my mother had brought with her to the Mission as a bride. It was a relic of her brief life, a proof that had she lived our spare adobe house would have been a more comfortable and gracious home.

"I'm sure I shall be comfortable," I said.

"This is the bath." Mrs. Fairley opened the door to the bath which connected with Emma's room. It was a delight of yellow tiles and luxurious towels. Caroline had spent a fortune to make this house perfect in every way.

Mrs. Fairley didn't offer to show me Emma's room and I didn't ask. Time enough for that later. We came back into my room, and all the while Mrs. Fairley showed me closets and extra blankets and how to light the oil lamp in case the generator went on the blink, I knew there was something more, something else, that she wanted to say. At last she gave a self-conscious, nervous cough.

"The room beyond Emma's is Tibba's. Tibba," Mrs. Fairley rushed on, "is an orphan Caroline, Mrs. Hand, brought from the mainland to help out and to be a playmate for Emma. Tibba is very sweet and no trouble. I am sure you will find her useful and willing to do whatever you ask."

"I see," I said. But I did not. Why should I have to be convinced of Tibba's usefulness?

"Well, then." Mrs. Fairley coughed again. It seemed to be a nervous habit of hers. "I'll leave you then. You can find your way back down to the library on your own, can't you?"

"Yes. I think so."

Still Mrs. Fairley did not move but stood looking intently at me. Then she said sharply, "You were a friend of Sara Fanner's weren't you?"

I felt instinctively that her previous coolness was because she could not decide just how I fit into the Fanner Foundation family structure. It seemed she was asking for some proof of my status, for a category into which she could conveniently put me.

"Yes," I said. "Emma's mother and I were at school together. I was on a scholarship given by the Fanner Foundation."

Mrs. Fairley considered my answer for a moment and then, seemingly satisfied, nodded. "Oh, so that was it."

I had made a suitable answer. I too was an employee. I might rank her in the pecking order but I was an employee all the same, just as she was.

When Mrs. Fairley had closed the door behind her and was gone, I heard her footsteps on the stair and I stood for a moment looking about me, taking my bearings.

This would be my room for the summer. Everything had been done to make me comfortable, yet I was uneasy. There was something not right about this house. Or perhaps it was I who was not easy and would not be until I had seen James.

I washed my hands and face and combed my hair. I looked at myself in the mirror. I had nice, straight, brown hair and nice, straight, white teeth. My eyes were a clear brown. James had told me I was pretty and I had believed him but I was not a beauty, the fact was evident.

I opened the door and started down the stairs. The house was cool and silent. I wondered if I could really hear the sea or if I imagined it. It seemed to me that in this house I was in a shell, a chambered nautilus, surrounded by the sea. I wished I had a protective shell against the force of my own emotions.

Outside the library door I hesitated. When I was younger I always hated going into rooms for fear I would be noticed and singled out for attention. I was always ill at ease, fearful I would not measure up. Perhaps I liked teaching the children at the Mission because they were themselves too deprived to notice my failings and inadequacies. I wished I could run away from this encounter, but I had no place to run to, so I knocked.

James Hand's voice called out for me to come in. My heart

began to beat in a most irregular manner. Trembling, I opened the door and went in.

Two things surprised me. First the room was so dim. The blinds were partially drawn so that even now at high noon this was a twilight room. The second and less welcome surprise was that James was sitting by the window facing out toward the landing. He must have seen the boat arrive. He must have seen me coming up the path to the front door but he had not come to meet me nor answered the door himself. He had sent Mrs. Fairley to do that.

It told me more than all the volumes that lined the walls. It charted the way for me more clearly than the globes and maps of foreign seas and past voyages that were everywhere about the library.

Once James had run to meet me. It was on an autumn, academic day. He ran across the campus, his hands outstretched, but that was before he married Caroline. Even now when she was dead she held him. Caroline, who was everything I was not and never would be. It didn't matter that she was dead. She might as well have been alive, standing beside him in the room. Her memory had made James withdraw to this darkened room and make his bed in a curtained alcove. The loss of Caroline kept him to himself in the dark in the middle of the day.

Only when I closed the door did he make any move. He rose; still he did not come toward me but stood by his chair. He was as handsome and as distinguished as ever, taller than I remembered. There was some grey in his hair but it suited him. James stood remote, his fine eyes hidden behind dark glasses.

"Won't you sit down?" He indicated a chair opposite him but separated from him by the safe distance of a round table.

So then if he would not come to me I must go to him. I walked to the chair and hoped he could not see my shaking knees.

"Did you have a good journey?" His voice was tired but his manner was as polished and as impeccable as the diplomat he had once wanted to be.

"Yes, thank you."

"You were met in Boston at the airport?"

"Yes," I said, "the car was there." I didn't tell him I had asked the chauffeur to drive past the house in Fanner Square. It was in that house that I had last seen James.

After graduation I had a year of teacher's training, then I had to go home because my father was ill and needed me at the Mission. James went into his proper law firm. When I said goodbye to him I was sure that it was only for the moment. I was sure I would see him again soon. He called me and I called him. We wrote long letters. Just then it was all we could do. Nothing could be settled. My father was dying and it was obvious it would be soon.

But as it turned out it was not my father who had died first, it was Sara and Edward. At Christmas James called. At first I thought it was to wish me a Merry Christmas but it was about Sara and Edward and the accident. James said he had called because he didn't want me to hear it on the radio or see it on television. "I wanted to tell you," he said, and he was crying.

I could not bear to think of his being there alone but I couldn't leave. I could not go to him, it was impossible. "Listen," I said, "I can't come now, but soon."

"It's all right," he said, "I understand. Don't worry, Caroline is here with me. She's been wonderful. She's taking care of Emma."

"Who?" I asked.

"You know, Caroline, Sara's cousin Caroline. She was skiing with us. Caroline Fanner."

I was glad he had someone to help him. I didn't think of her again until I got her letter.

Life has a way of dealing out its blows in bundles. I got
Caroline's letter when I returned home from the cemetery.

The letter was quite plain. It said that Caroline was going to
marry James. She knew that I had cared for him, but she was
sure I would understand. They were marrying for Emma's sake.
Because James was Emma's guardian and because her affairs
were so complex, James had left the law firm to attend to them.
Emma was a disturbed child and needed care at home. For
Emma's sake she and James were going to marry and take her to
Fanner's Island. They had talked it over, she and James, and she
had promised she would write to me. She knew it was difficult
but she knew I would understand.

I understood that Caroline was beautiful, that Caroline was a
poor relation, but Caroline was a Fanner. And I understood that
I really had no choice. It had all been arranged by Caroline.

"Yes," I said to James. "Everything was perfectly arranged.
A car was at the Boston airport and Captain Fairley met me at
the dock in Fannerstown."

"I ought to tell you," James said, and I felt a chill in his tone,
"that I didn't want you to come."

Well then if he was going to be blunt I saw no reason not to
be as painfully honest in return.

"I didn't want to."

"I thought you might not." He turned his head away. Was
the very sight of me so distasteful to him?

"When the Foundation wrote to me," I said, "I felt I had no
alternative but to accept. I am obligated to them as you know."
James seemed not to hear me. When he at last spoke it was as if
he were talking to himself.

"I thought you might be married."

"No."

"Or engaged."

"No," I said, angry that I should have to make any

explanation. "I enjoy my work. I like teaching. This is my vacation. I don't have to start classes again until the middle of September."

"This will not be much of a holiday for you," James said roughly. "Life in this house is not very pleasant. Emma is a very difficult and complicated child."

"Do you think I'm not qualified, professionally?" I asked. My pride in my work was my one sure security. "Is that why you didn't want me to come?"

James shook his head wearily. I knew it had been a tedious question but I couldn't help myself.

"No one is qualified to deal with Emma's kind of tragedy. What can you or anyone teach her that will compensate for what has happened? Her losses were too great."

"I agree that her loss has been very great, but she must learn to go on living." I meant to sound encouraging but all I said sounded false and hollow.

James sat with his head tilted at a strange angle. Again it seemed that he had not heard me. He seemed to be listening only to his own words in the hope that if he paid great attention he could make some sense of a difficult riddle.

"Three years ago, at Christmas," he said, "when her mother and father were killed in the skiing accident she was in a state of shock. She says that she doesn't remember the accident or them."

"Did she have amnesia?"

"Not really. It was merely a handy device. She was protecting herself by not remembering what was painful. Then after the accident she went back to nursery school but it didn't work out so Caroline . . ." James had paused before he could say her name. "Caroline decided to take her away and bring her here to the island. After we came here Emma seemed better.

She felt safe here and she transferred all her affection to Caroline. She adored Caroline."

Hearing him say Caroline's name made me ache. "And she had you too," I said, my throat tight and dry. "Emma had you."

"It was Caroline that she loved. You never met Caroline, did you?"

"No," I said. "I never met Caroline."

"Then you cannot know the effect that she had on people. She could cast a spell over them. She wove a web of magic that put them in thrall."

"What is it that you want me to do for Emma?" I began to doubt that I could be of any use to her. "Am I to teach her her lessons?"

"The Foundation thinks it would be a good idea if you were here to watch over her while I am gone."

It was like an unexpected blow from behind. "I didn't know that you were going away."

"Yes. I must be away for a part of the summer. I won't be going until after the Fourth of July. I'm sorry but it's unavoidable."

I bent my head and reached out to some pretty objects on the table. I moved them about as if to study them. I didn't want James to see my disappointment. I was a battleground of rage and shame and hurt. What sort of fool was I to mind whether he came or went? I was here not for James Hand but for Emma's benefit.

"The Foundation hopes that you can win her confidence. Of course if you can teach her anything as well they would be grateful."

"And what if she will not be won?" I felt we were two stiff, cardboard actors in a set piece. I looked up and out toward the bay. On the beach I saw a small figure walking along the sand.

"Is that Emma?" I asked. "Down there on the beach?"

"Probably." James seemed not to care if it was Emma or not. "She goes down there every day for hours on end and looks at the sea."

My throat grew tighter. I was afraid that I could not keep my face from showing my feelings. I didn't want James to see my pain. It would embarrass both James and me.

"So," he went on, seemingly unmindful of my predicament, "at Easter when Caroline died it was a double blow for Emma. A compound injury."

"Yes," I said, as evenly as I could. "It was a terrible thing to happen twice over but she is young."

"Don't be a fool." James spoke sharply. "I told you it was complicated. You see, Emma blames herself for Caroline's death."

I gasped. "But that's not possible."

"Believe me she does, and her guilt is sometimes too much for her to carry."

I was horrified. "But it's not reasonable. Emma is not guilty, why does she feel that she is?"

"She believes," James spoke very slowly, giving each word a weight of its own, "Emma believes that if I had not saved her Caroline would still be alive."

I had a sudden rush of sympathy for Emma. I understood, at least in part, her feeling of guilt. I had always felt that if it were not for me my mother would have lived and my father would have been happy. I said, "Surely you've taken her to a therapist. What do her doctors say?"

James gave a short, harsh laugh. "They say that in time she will be all right. But then that's what all doctors say."

"Is it safe to let her go to the beach alone?"

"Oh, it's a shallow cove and old Pompey is with her. He is Caroline's old black Labrador. He is ancient but loyal to the death. And Tibba usually goes with her too. They play together. They build castles in the sand and tear them down again."

I knew it was partially my own distrust of the water but I didn't think it was the best thing for Emma to go alone. I remembered what Captain Fairley had told me about reporters and photographers. It would not do Emma any good to be questioned and pictured by the press. Just as I had decided to say as much to James I saw something flash and glitter. It was coming from the rise just above the beach above Emma.

"What is that?" I asked James.

He didn't answer.

"Up there," I said. "Surely you must see it."

"No."

"There along the rise. There it is again."

"No." His voice was sharp as a knife. "I cannot see it. I am blind."

And the knife turned in my heart as James turned to face me. He took off his dark glasses and sat staring blankly in my direction. It was as if he thought I was capable of looking at his sightless eyes and making a diagnosis or giving a prognosis. Since I could offer neither he put his glasses on again and we both sat silent save for the sounds of the clock ticking and the buzzing of a bee outside the window, small sounds that seemed magnified to a deafening decibel.

When James spoke again he was in perfect control. "I have to go to the hospital in Boston for treatment. I am sorry to go just now but in any case I am not much use here. If something were to happen to Emma, if a monster were to come to carry Emma off into the water, I couldn't see it."

No wonder James had found my suggestions tedious and irritating.

"I didn't know you were blind," I said. "There was nothing in any of the papers."

"No." He smiled but it was a bitter mockery of the smile I remembered from years ago. "No, I didn't want my condition to be common gossip."

"I'm sorry."

"I have found that I dislike pity." James hit at me with his words.

"I didn't say that I pitied you," I said. "We were friends once." Oh, why had I said that? It was a bid for sympathy and pity for me, for my state of unrequited affection.

"I didn't want you to come," James continued, relentless and uncompromising. "I didn't want you to find me like this."

"And what do the doctors say?"

"They say," he smiled again and his mouth was a straight, tight line, "that in time my condition may right itself."

"You mean there is hope?"

"There is always that possibility. In the meantime this is not a happy house. It is not a happy island. Captain Fairley takes care of me for I am a dependent and need to be taken care of. Mrs. Fairley runs the house. Tibba helps her and spends the rest of the time with Emma. But Tibba is only a child herself, and Emma needs someone who is responsible."

"What makes you think Emma will accept me?"

"I don't know that she will."

"Does she know that I'm coming?"

"She has been told, but what Emma thinks, what ideas she has in her head, I don't know. We were close once." He said it sadly. "But since the accident Emma has had little to do with me."

"Where shall I begin?" I would try to win Emma, protect her if I could, but I would need all James's advice and counsel.

"Why not go down to the beach and have lunch with her?

She takes a picnic basket down with her. Have a swim. Talk to her."

"I'll go down and meet Emma," I said, "but I don't swim." Already my deficiencies were evident.

Suddenly I saw James's face contort as if in pain. "Caroline was a wonderful swimmer. She could swim for miles in a strong sea."

And because I could no longer bear being compared to Caroline, because she was the perfection, the paragon that I could never be, I stood and asked, "Is that all then?"

James seemed surprised. "You'll stay?"

"Yes," I said. "Of course I'll stay. After all it is my job. It's what the Foundation brought me here to do."

❦ *Two* ❧

I managed to get from the library to my room before I let the tears flow. It was shattering to see James again. To find that he was blind was not so difficult for me to have to accept as the fact that he still loved Caroline. As far as James Hand was concerned I was an unwelcome intruder, an interruption to his mourning for Caroline. I knew that against all reason and much against my will I still cared for him. Just how much I would try to avoid finding out.

In my absence Captain Fairley had brought up my bags. I opened the large case and took out my swimsuit, beach robe, and sandals. I gathered a beach bag and stuffed in dark glasses, sun cream, and Kleenex. I was unsure of what I might need but this ought to do for today. I wanted to get down to the beach and meet Emma as soon as possible. I left the rest to be unpacked and dealt with later in the evening.

I thought I ought to stop in the kitchen and tell Mrs. Fairley where I was going. I went past the library door quickly as one passes something hot. I wanted to see Emma but I also wanted to get out of the house away from James so that I could think properly.

Mrs. Fairley was standing at a long kitchen table chopping

celery. The room had indeed been given every new conven-
ience. It was an advertisement for the kitchen of the future. The
only feature of the old room which remained was an open
fireplace.

Across the table from Mrs. Fairley, seated on a kitchen stool,
was a little girl about seven. She was shelling peas and she wore
an old-fashioned pinafore with ruffles over her thin shoulders.
She looked up as I came in and then quickly looked at Mrs.
Fairley. It was as if she were asking Mrs. Fairley's permission to
see me. It was obvious that my coming into the kitchen was
unexpected.

"I'm going down to the beach," I said. "I thought you ought
to know in case you had counted on me for lunch."

"No," Mrs. Fairley said. "I sent lunch down with Emma.
There's more than enough for the two of you."

I thanked her. She hesitated, then put down her knife and
went round the table to Tibba. She put her hands on Tibba's
shoulders. The ruffles fell beneath her touch. She coughed, then
cleared her throat.

"This is Tibba. Tibba, say how do you do to Miss Raynor."

Tibba did as she was told. She was a pretty little thing. Dark
hair and a pale face were eclipsed by extraordinary, large china
blue eyes.

"How do you do, Miss Raynor?" Tibba said in a breathless
voice.

Then she looked to Mrs. Fairley for approval.

Mrs. Fairley nodded and Tibba seemed as pleased as if she
had received a blessing. Something about Tibba's manner
reminded me of the look some of my pupils had when they came
to the Mission school for the first time. They were dislocated,
deprived, bereft of home and all things familiar. They lived in
an aura of fear lest they do something wrong and for their
punishment be sent even farther away from their family circle.

"You shouldn't go down to the beach without a hat," Mrs. Fairley said. "The sun is stronger than you think down by the water."

I was sure she was right but I didn't have a hat. It hadn't occurred to me to bring one.

"Tibba," Mrs. Fairley said, smiling at her kindly, "run and get Miss Raynor a hat from the hall closet."

Tibba set down her bowl of peas and ran off and came back almost at once with a wide-brimmed straw hat. It was very pretty with an unusual braided ribbon around the crown.

"Thank you, Tibba," I said. "That's very kind of you." I smiled at Tibba's serious face. For a moment I thought she would smile back at me but she returned to the stool by the kitchen table and went on with her work. As a child I had been like Tibba. I would have done anything to please.

As I walked down the path from the front of the house toward the beach it occurred to me that this was what I was going to be doing for most of the summer. I would be in a swimsuit wearing a beach robe for cover against the sun. I would carry a beach bag crammed with sun lotion and paperbacked easy reading, and I was not sure I didn't find such leisure a little sinful. The rich never knew how they offended the poor by having the option for leisure.

Midway down the path toward the landing the path divided and branched out toward the beach. I felt ill at ease and exposed. The world outside the house was harsh. The sun was hot and merciless. The patch of green grass before the house was replaced by sand and tufted plumes of sea grass which looked sullen. It seemed as if it had been uprooted from somewhere else and put here for decoration. I knew that thousands of people would consider it a dream come true to have an island of their own. But for me there was a kind of naked horror in the cloudless sky and the wasted crescent of land.

I half turned back toward the house to see it from a new angle and there for the third time up along the high ridge I saw a light flash. It was the reflection of something metallic glinting in the sun. Then as quickly as it had appeared it was gone. I was sure that there was someone there, someone I could not see but someone who could see me.

I didn't like the sensation. I turned and hurried on down the path over the dunes toward the beach. Over the next dune I looked and I saw Emma sitting on the beach. Her back was to me. She was carefully and methodically shoveling sand from the beach into a painted toy pail. She was wearing a sunsuit and a Christopher Robin hat. Her back was bare and brown. As she shoveled she sang to herself, more of a chanting than a singing; over and over she sang her little wordless tune.

Beside her was a large picnic hamper and against the hamper sat a doll propped up facing out to sea, a lookout, a guard, and a chaperone all in one. Beyond the doll and the hamper lay a very old black Labrador. He had been resting, his head down on his paws, his eyes closed against the sunlight. He must be a little deaf because I was quite near before he heard me.

He opened his eyes, unwilling to give up his sleep. He lifted his head and then, intent on doing his duty, rose unsteadily to his feet, made his arthritic stand, and began to bark. The bark was feeble and intermittent. It sounded as if it were powered by a battery that was running low.

Emma turned her head, the shovel midway to the pail, and when she saw me standing, waiting to see how she would receive me, she jumped to her feet and ran eagerly toward me, her face shining and smiling.

Then she stopped short and the smile disappeared. She was obviously bitterly disappointed. I might be expected but I was not who she wanted to see. I was sorry indeed to have disappointed her but I seemed to have pleased Pompey. He sank down again to his rest. His tail gave a twitch and one wag. Then he slept again, tired out by his great exertion.

Emma stood regarding me. There was no further sign from her of how I was to fare. She was a pudgy little girl of seven going on eight. She had sun-streaked blonde hair cut short in a classic Buster Brown style. The fringe of her bangs showed a thin line beneath her hat. Her eyes were round and brown. Her two front teeth were newly in and were larger than their small pearl-sized neighbors. They protruded slightly, which made me think that she sucked her thumb for her comfort and that the orthodontist would have a turn of the screws in the future.

Emma was a very ordinary looking little girl, and it was with a pang that I realized it was just how her mother must have looked at that age. Nothing at all unusual, a little girl like a lot of others unless one recognized her as the Fanner heiress.

Then this pudgy little girl became ships and forests and mines and oil fields. She became the reason grown men sat in board rooms all over the world and earned themselves substantial salaries managing her assets. Firms of lawyers waxed fat and maintained their partnership keeping the skein of her legal affairs out of tangles.

She was by birth and by inheritance the princess of an industrial kingdom, the empress of an empire. But it seemed that unseen at her christening an evil fairy had pronounced a curse, cast a spell over Emma, so that she was condemned to lose that which she loved the most and be sentenced to spend her summer alone on a remote island set in a sea of glass beneath a cloudless sky.

The tragedy that had already come to her was too great and searing for one human to cope with, let alone a little girl. Yet it was expected that she become a woman who, like her mother, would lead a life dedicated to duty. She would have to live all her life with obligations laid out and contracted for long before she was born. If she had been cursed with tragedy and great wealth perhaps there was a store of blessings in her future, but they were harder to see.

"Hello," I said. "I'm Martha Raynor. I've come to spend the summer."

Emma said nothing in reply. She kept on looking at me, her mouth slightly open to allow for the teeth. The white tips were visible as her small sigh was audible.

"You look like your mother," I said.

There was a flick of the eyelids and her gaze wavered. "My mother is dead."

"So is mine."

We had begun a game of orphan's snap and while I knew that she would ultimately win if we played it out, we might make some contact between us.

"And my father's dead," she said.

"And so is mine."

Another blink of the eyes. "I don't remember them very well. I was there with them. It was an accident and I was there but I don't remember it."

Emma held the high card. I hadn't known that she had been with Sara and Edward when they were killed. James had not told me that. Perhaps it was Emma's fantasy. I made a mental note to ask James when I saw him next.

"Then I went to live with Caroline." Emma half turned and looked out toward the water, as if she looked for Caroline to rise from the sea, and when she looked back to me her round brown eyes were as testing, as penetrating, as her mother's had been. Sara had learnt to test out the honest from the deceitful men at an early age. It had been a necessity for her self-preservation.

"Did you know Caroline?" Emma asked.

"No."

"They say she drowned in the sea," Emma said, in a flat,

small voice. From somewhere in the distance I heard the tolling of a buoy bell. It rang back and forth in a sort of mockery.

"You still have your Uncle James," I said. Emma had not mentioned James at all.

Emma looked at me for another moment, but she didn't reply. Emma had tuned me out. It was another form of self-defense I had seen her mother use. Sara had been able to tune out the world when she could not cope with a situation. I didn't know why Emma would not speak to me about James but she would not and that was plain.

I wanted to reach out to her, to take her hand and tell her it would be all right. I wanted to say that I would be her friend because her mother had been mine. But I stopped myself. We had the summer and whatever was to be between us must grow slowly and from solid ground.

"I feel," I said, "like a fish out of water."

Emma looked startled. It was not what she had expected to hear.

"I've never been on an island before. I've never spent a summer by the sea."

"You've never been to the ocean?" Emma said, incredulous. I had caught her attention and I meant to hold it.

"No."

"Where do you live then?"

"In the desert."

"But if there is no ocean where do you swim?"

"I don't," I said. "I can't swim."

"Doesn't anyone swim where you come from?"

"Yes."

"Where do they swim?"

"In a cattle tank."

"What's that?"

As I told her a little about my world and what went on in it she gave me her hand and we walked over to her pail and a pile of shells. It was a very small damp hand.

We sat on the beach together, the four of us, Emma, Pompey, the doll, and I. The doll was no older than Emma but she looked a hundred. She had been battered by love and affection, but she was a good audience and listened, like Emma, with rapt attention.

From time to time Emma gave the doll a reassuring pat or glanced at her to share a part of the story. No matter what had happened to Emma in the grown-up world she intended that no harm should come to her doll.

"What is your doll's name?" I asked.

Emma thought for a moment. She had given me her hand but the doll's name was another matter. Then Emma decided in my favor.

"Miss Baby," she said. "She's shy with strangers."

"Perhaps she'll get used to me in a few days," I said, not looking at Miss Baby, the way one ignores a shy and moody child. "We'll give her time."

"I hope," Emma said earnestly, "you won't think me rude but I don't think I would like to live where you come from."

"No," I said. "I don't suppose you would."

"Do you?" Emma asked.

"I've gotten used to it. It's my home. My work is there."

"What do you do there?"

"I teach." I saw that with my honest answer I had lost ground.

"I don't go to school." Emma might as well have slammed a door in my face.

"I don't teach in the summer," I countered.

But she did not wholly believe my answer. I had to find a way to start us off again in a happier direction.

"Do you swim?" I asked.

"Yes, I do," Emma answered promptly and then she smiled. It was a short, brilliant smile that went almost as soon as it had come. "I don't swim very well. Caroline is teaching me."

I shivered as if a chill wind had blown across the hot sand. What Emma had said was in the present tense. She had said, "Caroline is teaching me." Perhaps it was wisdom, perhaps cowardice on my part, but I chose not to correct her grammar or to question her about her meaning. I let it go. I ran away from it to a safer subject.

"I may not be able to swim," I said, "but I have a terrific appetite. Do you think we could have some lunch?"

"Of course." Emma gave me Miss Baby to hold while she opened the hamper and unpacked a marvelous lunch. I was hungry but my true reward was the custody of Miss Baby. My spirits were on the rise.

The lunch did even more for the inner woman. It had been a long time since I had tasted anything as good as the brown bread and cold ham. There were baked beans in little pots and the lemonade was ice-cold from the thermos.

There was something for everyone. Pompey had his own thermos of water and a variety of dog biscuits which he pulped against his aging gums.

"Pompey only eats one real meal a day," Emma said. "He is very old and he's getting dreadfully fat."

Pompey gave her a mournful look and sank into an ongoing state of sleep. Once he must have pursued game as he now pursued his nap.

"He is Caroline's dog really," Emma said. "I am looking after him for her."

It came like an arrow out of the blue. And embedded in her next question was another barb.

"If you knew my mother, why didn't you know Caroline?"

"I never met her," I said. "I wish I had." And it was true. If I had I would have seen for myself how she was able to cast a magic spell over everyone who knew her. "I knew your mother and your father and your Uncle James," I said. "But I never met Caroline."

Emma considered my answer but she made no comment. She put away the lunch things and for an after-lunch amusement we walked up the beach toward the end of the island looking for shells.

"I paste shells on boxes," Emma confided. "They can look very pretty on boxes."

The heat rose up from the damp sand. The sea went in and out, making its balance from tide to tide. We left our footprints for posterity only to have them wash away. The seaweed caught in rocks and hung, jellied, drying like eels at a badly catered party. I wouldn't ever feel at home on the shore or by the sea but it was just possible I might make some peace with the island.

"Do you ever go exploring over the rest of the island?" I asked Emma.

"Yes," Emma said. "Tibba and Pompey and I go for long, long walks."

"Would you take me sometime?"

"Yes." Emma was delighted with the suggestion. "We'll go tomorrow."

It was something to look forward to. For the rest of the afternoon I sat on a beach towel, wrapped in my robe, sweltering under the straw hat. I watched Emma. Her energy was enviable. She tidied up the seashore with great zeal. She might be rich but she was far from idle. She brought water in her pail to the shore from the boundless sea. She took sand from the shore back to the ocean. She made and unmade castles in the sand, their turrets packed round and rising in the shape of paper cup molds. I knew that a heat rash and the bites of sand fleas would be what I would have to show for the day. I was used to the heat of the desert, not this humid, steaming Turkish bath.

Surely in the future I must introduce some lessons if only to relieve the tedium. If I did it gradually, a book here and a pencil there, a fact or two thrown in the air, they might bear some fruit.

Perhaps I was one of those people who cannot endure pleasure. I thought of all the advertisements in glossy and colorful holiday brochures of the brilliant sun shining down on brown, bikinied bodies lying on smooth, isolated beaches. People saved up a whole year for holidays like that. To keep Caroline's island running must cost a small fortune.

I sat in the afternoon sun feeling that I should be grateful for the opportunity of sitting there at all. The afternoon passed with nothing to mar the tranquillity of the day. The water came and went, hypnotizing me into a stupor. From time to time old Pompey stirred and sighed in his sleep. I could not keep my eyes open. I put my head down on my arms, resting them on my propped-up knees, and I joined Pompey in a dreaming sleep.

"I think we ought to be going," I heard Emma say. "This is the first day out for you and you'll be as red as a lobster if you don't take care."

I knew it was something she had been told and was repeating in the way children repeat the dictums of their elders, but I was more than willing to let her take me away.

"It's the glare off the water that does it," she added, and she packed us up, organizing the return to the house with the same efficiency and dispatch she had used to tidy the seashore. Whatever her wounds Emma functioned very well. I could not imagine what had happened to make Caroline decide to take Emma away and bring her to the island.

I was allowed to carry the picnic basket and the beach towels. Emma carried Miss Baby in a casual, motherly way. Weary, loyal Pompey made up our rearguard. He came along slowly, limping a little. His hindquarters were stiff with arthritis and the going was hard for him. We were an odd-looking party but a congenial one. We were beginning to make a real bond, Emma and I, and I wanted to spend the rest of the day with her alone, strengthening and cementing the relationship. I didn't know what the rules of the household were about meals. I wondered how I could ask Mrs. Fairley if Emma and I could have our dinner alone together without appearing impolite.

I was running the thought about in my mind when suddenly I saw it again. There, above us on the rise, something flashed and glittered, a light reflecting from a metal object.

"What is that up there on the ridge?"

We stopped and Emma looked up in the direction I was pointing.

"I don't see anything," she said.

"There is someone or something up there, I know it. I keep seeing a flash of light. It's there and then it's gone again. But I know it's there."

Emma didn't answer. I looked down at her. She had her face tilted up toward the ridge and on her face was the oddest expression. She was transfixed, removed to another realm, one that was past my understanding.

"Sometimes," she said softly, "you don't see something but you know it's there all the same. That's so, isn't it?"

"Yes." I had to agree with her but she frightened me a little. It was the first time I had seen the other side of Emma, the more complicated and perhaps the darker side of her nature. Then the mood broke and we were no longer alienated. She smiled and said, "It's probably only Mac. He lives in the lighthouse and he's always looking for birds."

"Birds?" I repeated stupidly.

"Yes," Emma said. "It's something to do with ecology and conservation."

"Oh, I see," I said. I didn't see at all but it made me feel much better to know that if I was being watched it was by someone who was not only real but someone who had a legitimate reason for being on the island.

As it turned out I need not have worried about having Emma to myself for dinner. Mrs. Fairley solved that problem for me almost the instant we got back to the house. While she took my hat and put it in the closet for me she explained that if I did not mind she'd serve Emma and me our dinner in the dining room.

"You see," she said, "Captain Fairley has his dinner with Mr. Hand, and Tibba and Emma and I usually have ours in the kitchen, but as you are here I thought you'd like to dine with Emma."

"Yes," I stammered, unable to believe my good fortune. "If that's not too much trouble."

"No," she said. "No trouble at all. I enjoy Tibba's company."

Emma and I went up for our showers and to dress. At the head of the stairs Emma suddenly asked me, "Do you know why Captain Fairley eats his meals with Uncle James?"

"No," I said.

"It's because Uncle James is blind and he can't feed himself. He doesn't like to have us see him dribble."

It was a hard thing to hear and it must be even harder for James, fastidious James, who had loved good food and good wine and playing the genial host. Why had Emma felt she must tell me that? Had it given her satisfaction? Did she really dislike James as much as that?

So then it seemed we were to live in the house divided, two by two—James and the Captain, Mrs. Fairley and Tibba, and Emma and I. And somewhere out on the point at the end of the island in a lighthouse was a man named Mac who presumably shared his crust with the birds.

After dinner, which went along well without any particular

incident, Emma came up to my room with me and sat on the edge of my bed, Miss Baby in her lap, and they watched me unpack. Emma said nothing but I saw her observing my meager wardrobe. Much of it had come from a mail-order catalogue. It was polite of Emma not to mention my lack of fashion sense.

I was growing increasingly fond of Emma and Miss Baby. It was a quiet evening, the house silent, settling in for the night. Through the window of my room I could look out onto a heather twilight dimming out above the trees. Up beyond the garden I could see the outline of the summerhouse. It would be pleasant if I could get Emma to exchange some days at the beach for some days in the summerhouse. It would make a change and keep me from total sunstroke. I didn't have a sunburn, thanks to the hat, but I had spent hours in the damp heat and I was drained in both body and emotions. As soon as I thought it was a reasonable hour I asked Emma if she wanted me to come and tuck her in bed.

"No," she said. "Thank you, but Tibba and I usually play games before bedtime, but I'll see you first thing in the morning and we'll go for a tour of the island."

"I'm looking forward to seeing your island," I said, not paying attention to my words.

"It's not my island," Emma corrected me. "It's Caroline's island."

And so it was. It was Caroline's island. Caroline might be dead and gone but if she had been here still she could not exert greater power over the people she had left behind her.

I was tired but when Emma had gone and I got into bed I found I couldn't sleep. I heard the girls in Emma's room. Emma and Tibba were laughing and giggling. I heard the library door open and close. Captain Fairley had given James his supper and put him down for the night. I didn't want to think about James; it was too painful. I preferred to listen to the laughter of Emma and Tibba. It, at least, was some relief to the mournful sadness of this house. On the whole I felt I had had a successful day with Emma. Any day must be counted as a success that ends in laughter.

I slept, I had no idea how long, before I was awakened by laughter. But this was not Emma or Tibba. This laughter was as cold and mirthless as Siberia, as heartless as the Snow Queen's sliver of glass. It transformed what had seemed good to evil.

The laughter was from somewhere in my room. I sat up, startled into wide wakefulness. As I sat up I saw the door of my room slowly and silently close. I knew I saw it. The blinds were not drawn and it was a bright night. My eyes did not deceive me or play tricks. I reached out to turn on the bed lamp and then I decided against it. I got out of bed and walked in my bare feet toward the door.

If I had put on my slippers I probably wouldn't have noticed it, but in my bare feet I felt the damp patches on the carpet and by the door itself there was a large patch of damp. There was no mistaking it. It was as if someone had come from the shower or the bath and paused on the way to look down on me as I slept.

Someone from the bath or the sea. I bent down. There was something caught at the bottom of the door. I opened the door and just over the sill, draped like a silken ribbon, was a long piece of damp, vile seaweed. The moment my hand touched the slimy thing I heard Emma's voice saying, "Just because you can't see someone it doesn't mean they aren't there, does it?" And I heard again the laughter cold and mocking in my mind.

If this was a joke I didn't think it was funny. If it was a girlish prank I did not find it amusing. But even as I started toward Emma's room to see if she and Tibba were huddled under the covers trying not to laugh I knew it was not their doing. Just as I knew that if I was not mad there had been someone in my room, someone who had observed me while I slept.

I got back into my bed. I was trembling violently. I told myself it was because of the chill night air, but I knew it was because I was afraid. I lay awake a very long time before I could fall asleep again.

~ Three ~

I might not have awakened before noon if Emma hadn't come to get me up.

"Come on, sleepyhead," she said. "You'll be late for breakfast. I'm taking you on a tour of the island, did you forget?"

"No," I said. It was absurd to see her round face there by my bed. For one moment between waking and sleeping I had the sensation that I was back at school and Emma's mother, Sara, had come to wake me up for class.

We had our breakfast in the kitchen with Mrs. Fairley and Tibba. The sun was shining. It was well into another clear, hot day on our summer island.

Tibba sat on the kitchen stool where she had been sitting yesterday. This morning she was stringing and snapping beans. She made a still life study, the basket on the table, the pan in her lap, as she sat with her neck arched over the pieces of green. She was really quite beautiful but very quiet and withdrawn.

Emma chattered on and on about this and that. Mrs. Fairley busied herself serving up the breakfast. On impulse I said, "I wonder if Tibba would like to go with us on our tour of the island."

Tibba didn't answer but I saw her eyes move to Mrs. Fairley.

Mrs. Fairley, it seemed, was the arbiter of all Tibba's behavior.

"Not today." Mrs. Fairley shook her head. "Today I need Tibba to help me in the kitchen."

I saw the look of disappointment that Tibba could not conceal. Her eyes went from Mrs. Fairley's face back to her work. I felt drawn to Tibba. She was an old-fashioned child with manners that were almost antique. Emma seemed fond of her, yet somehow she took Tibba for granted as if Tibba had always been a part of her life and indeed as if all the time Emma had been on the island Tibba had been there. Tibba was one of Emma's reliable creatures like Miss Baby or Pompey.

Emma seemed fine to me. Perhaps the Fanner Foundation and James over-reacted to Emma's whims and moods. And yet, and yet, there had been the water and the seaweed and the laughter in my room last night. There was something wrong in this house. Whatever it was was there just beyond my reach, there but unseen.

Mrs. Fairley had packed us our lunch. She handed it to me as we were about to go off on our ramble and then suddenly Emma said, "Wait, I'll get your hat for you." She ran out into the hall to the hall closet. While Emma was gone I saw Tibba looking at Mrs. Fairley.

"May I go with them tomorrow?" Tibba asked. It was almost a whisper.

"Yes, tomorrow you may go," Mrs. Fairley replied, and Tibba looked as pleased as Pompey when he was given a biscuit.

When Emma came back she handed me a hat. It was a wide-brimmed straw but it was a different hat from the one I had worn the day before.

"I brought you another hat," Emma said. "The one you wore yesterday was Caroline's. When I saw you coming down from the house in it I thought you were Caroline. I thought she had come back."

It was no use to stammer out some lame excuse. It would mend nothing for me to say that I was sorry, that I had not known. I could only be thankful that we were on our way out of the house. Otherwise I might have said something I would have regretted to Tibba or Mrs. Fairley. Surely Mrs. Fairley had known it was Caroline's hat. Or had she? My head ached with unanswered questions. I was relieved to be out into the garden, into the fresh air.

I carried the picnic basket and a string bag full of books and papers and crayons. The books were for me to read and the crayons and paper were for Emma. I thought I might get in some small blow for education today.

Emma had a pail, a shovel, and a ball in a large reticule. She carried Miss Baby in her arms. Miss Baby was totally indifferent to the day and to us. Her unblinking eyes saw everything with impartiality.

I was very pleased to be going off with Emma. I had been prepared to do my job but I found I was looking forward to the day with Emma and our outing. It was like being with a slightly diminished and askew version of her mother. Perhaps Emma's father's portion in her had even improved the mixture. Sara had cared passionately about helping people and causes. Edward had quietly spent his time trying to find some reasonable way of helping them to help themselves.

The garden was lovely and green and quite small. It smelled like a potpourri. There were many plants that I didn't recognize.

"This is the garden," Emma said so seriously I could not laugh at the obvious statement. "It is planted between the house and the rise because that shelters it. It's the best location, but it doesn't get as much sun as most gardens. The flowers for the house grow best by the kitchen wall. But here you can grow

Bible Leaf and Jack in the Pulpit, all sorts of things that usually grow in the woods."

Emma paused and her brow furrowed. "You can grow a lot of things on this island when you think about it. We've got wild beach plums and berries. If we were cut off from the mainland and had salt and flour and stuff like that we could live here a whole year. Caroline says they used to do that in the olden days. Or if not a whole year they had to stay the whole winter without seeing anyone from the mainland. Caroline used to live here in the winter. She says the waves came up almost to the top of the cliff. You haven't seen the cliff but it's very high, and Caroline says she felt like the sea was going to come right up and cover the house."

We walked through the garden and started up a path toward the summerhouse. I smelled the pine. The odor was pervasive and insistent, a drug to the senses.

"I like the smell of pines," I said. "Do you?"

"Oh yes." Emma turned to me and beamed. "I love it when the sun hits them and you feel like you are floating, half asleep, in a feather forest."

The path that ran to the summerhouse was steeper than it had looked from my window. The island was deceptive. It was larger and not at all the shape I had first thought it would be. The first Fanners had chosen their location to suit their purposes. They had built the house and planted their garden in exactly the best of all possible locations.

Even the boathouse in that little cove away from the bay was in just the right place.

The summerhouse was made of a wooden frame around glass and screened windows. It was an octagon, a rustic kind of bubble. It was sturdy enough so that one could come here during the bad weather and someone, Caroline more than likely, had put in a stove and an electric light.

"What a wonderful gazebo," I exclaimed.

"What a wonderful what?" Emma asked, perplexed.

"It's another name for a summerhouse, gazebo."

Emma still looked bemused. "I've never heard this called either one."

"What do you call it then?" I asked, wondering if I had made a regional blunder in usage.

"It's the Widow's Look."

"And I've never heard of that."

"Caroline says that most of the houses in this part of New England had Widow's Walks built on top of the houses, but here on Fanner's Island it would have been too cold and too low to see the sea so the first Captain Fanner built a Widow's Look for his wife. She could come up here and look out to sea and wait for his ship to come. Of course, if he didn't get home she was going to be a widow and that's how it got its name."

"I see."

"There used to be a spyglass and a little box of ladies' handkerchiefs in case the captain's wife wanted to weep."

I laughed. "That's terrible," I said. "But it is a pretty place."

There were chairs and a table and a camp bed. There was a nice rush matting on the floor. Two open chests contained cups and saucers. Emma was anxious to show me everything.

"We could spend a day here," I said, "quite comfortably." I was thinking what a grand thing it would be to spend part of our afternoons up here instead of at the beach.

"Yes," Emma said. "Caroline uses it as a guest house. Caroline and I are going to come up here this summer and we're going to spend the night and have our supper and everything."

I felt sickened. There was something about Emma's bland usage of the present tense and Caroline that made me queasy. It was as if the car door had just slammed on my finger.

"I am glad," I said as evenly as I was able, "that if Caroline were here she'd gladly bring you up here to spend the night. But Caroline isn't here."

"She will come. Caroline said so. She told me we would." Emma's lip began to tremble dangerously.

I was suddenly depressed. I had read somewhere that depression was a rage that one couldn't express. I was depressed and I knew I was enraged. I was in a great rage against Caroline, always Caroline—her island, her beauty, her ability to control all our lives even when she was dead. Caroline, who had been loved by Emma and loved by James, Caroline, who could marry James for Emma's sake, Caroline, who had had so much, why could Caroline not have left James to me?

I looked down. Emma was tugging at my beach robe. She had been saying something to me and I hadn't heard one word of it.

"I'm sorry, Emma," I said. "I was wool gathering." Emma's near tears had vanished. She seemed quite herself again. She said, "I was asking you which way you wanted to go next. You see there is a problem."

"And what is the problem?"

"Well," Emma said earnestly, "do you want to go down to the old boathouse and then along the beach and then back up to the lighthouse or to the lighthouse and then the beach and then the old boathouse? You see, no matter where we go from here we've a little bit to do over again."

Dear Emma was trying to organize our day so that we would be totally happy. Perhaps total happiness is always impossible.

"Well?" she asked. "What do you think? Two heads are wiser than one."

And this time I did laugh to hear Emma repeat her elders. "Tell me," I asked her, "what is this old boathouse?"

"Oh," she said. "It's where Captain Fairley keeps the cabin cruiser and there's a small sailboat and sails and things and then up above is Caroline's studio. Only we can't go there."

"Why not?"

"Because it's hers. Her private place and nobody can go there, not since . . ."

I felt sure Emma had been about to say not since Caroline died but she caught herself up and instead altered it to, "Not since Easter."

I wasn't going to challenge her again, not today.

"And between here and the boathouse what would we see?"

"Just the woods and an old well." I could tell from the way Emma dismissed the woods and the well that her preference was for the lighthouse.

"Then let's go to the lighthouse," I said. "I've never seen a lighthouse."

Besides, I hoped that if we went to the lighthouse I could perhaps see this bird watcher for myself. I wanted the comfort of seeing the sun catch something bright and make a reflection. I wanted to see just what and who it was that had distressed me so yesterday.

I got a good deal more than I had bargained for. To get to the lighthouse we climbed up above the Widow's Look to the very top of the ridge to the highest point of the island. I climbed, puffing and panting, along behind Emma, and when we came to the cliff path I stopped and stared in awe. I saw for the first time the full force of the Atlantic Ocean, the cruel sea, the sea which drew people to it, the sea more powerful than the Sirens' call. I stood very still trying to take something of its power and majesty into my consciousness.

The cliff face beneath us from here all the way along to the left of the island was a sheer jagged drop, down, down to the sea which churned in upon it, furious as a warring assailant. Day and night the sea came toward the mainland. The island was an obstacle and one day the sea would wash it away.

From where I stood I could see the whole of the island. A

path disappeared into the trees to the right and must end up at the boathouse. To the left a path ran along the very edge of the cliff straight on to the end of the island and the lighthouse.

The whole of the island was isolated in this angry, killing sea. Why on earth would anyone ever build a house here? Why try to survive in this lonely harsh place? My Indian Mission was placed in paradise in comparison.

I followed after Emma who was completely at home. She went skipping down the path totally unconcerned for the drop down to the sea which was on her right hand. She was without fear. But then I was fearful enough for both of us. Some latent, terrible vertigo came to full flower. My vitals contracted. Looking down from the cliff to the sea made me faint with fear. What was the old prescription? Don't look down. I raised my eyes from the sea up to the path and to the figure of Emma running before me and I followed after her with Pompey bringing up a lame and halting rear.

The lighthouse was my true north, my guide pole. It was, in its way, a pretty little lighthouse, banded round near the top with a wide red band of paint just below the beacon. The days of lighthouse keepers were over. Now the lights were electronically programmed.

Emma stood in the open doorway of the lighthouse and hallooed up the tunnel shape, calling out for Mac. There obviously was no answer because she hurried around the lighthouse and to the end of the path at the edge of the island. Much as I did not want to I felt compelled to follow her. She was in my care.

When I saw the little narrow way at the end of the island behind the lighthouse I saw nothing but certain disaster. It was not safe, but there, sitting as unconcerned as if we had discovered him in his own parlor, was a man. His legs dangled over the edge of the cliff. There were binoculars in his hand which glittered in the sun and he was looking intently out to sea.

He was a young man. I am very bad about ages but he was not much over thirty. He had a shocking, bushy head of shiny brown hair and a full beard. He was wearing a pair of blue jeans cut off at the thighs and no shirt. He was as brown as sun and wind could make him and it was obvious, looking at his powerful shoulders and muscled arms, that he had led an active, athletic life.

Emma ran to him and gave me a further panic by throwing herself onto his back. If she had had a little more force she could have pitched the two of them off the cliff and into the sea.

"Hi Mac."

"I feel I have company," Mac said. His binoculars dropped from his hand and hung swinging from a cord around his neck. In a skillful maneuver he pushed back and away from the edge of the cliff and rose to his feet. Then he turned, scooping Emma up into his arms. It was a single consecutive movement performed with the graceful balance and precision of a dancer or an acrobat.

"Say now," he grinned at Emma. "I've got a lot of company. You and Pompey and Miss Baby and a stranger." He walked toward me holding Emma in his arms. He was taller than I expected, almost as tall as James, but whereas James appeared slight and reed-thin Mac was, without being heavy, a solid, massive man. When he came up even with me he put Emma down and said, "Aren't you going to introduce me?"

He was speaking to Emma but he was looking at me. His eyes were a really startling blue, dark as the sea in a storm. It was hard to tell just what shape his face was because of the beard, but I supposed one would have had to call him handsome. He continued looking at me and I felt myself flush. Why was he intent upon adding me up, taking a sum total of all my parts?

Yesterday he had observed me magnified. He had seen me arrive. He had seen me come and go to the beach. I should be no stranger or surprise to him.

"Mac," Emma said in her most mannerly way, "this is Miss Raynor." I wondered if Emma called all grown-ups but me by their given names. I remembered to have a little chat with her about that and also to advise her that a man was always presented to a lady, not the other way around.

"How do you do?" Mac held out his hand to me. I paused for a moment before I accepted it and in that instant Mac perceived my discomfort and grinned.

"She's never seen a lighthouse," Emma said rapturously to Mac. "Or been on an island." She might as well have told him I was green and flew with gossamer wings.

Mac continued to grin. He made me feel that he was looking at something hilarious taking place just behind me. I couldn't see what was going on but he could, just there, over my shoulder.

"Well, we must do something about that," Mac said, grinning away.

"Emma tells me you are a bird watcher," I said. I felt it was a bad opening gambit but it was my move and I made it.

"In a way," Mac grinned on. "Actually I'm a spy."

He had an exasperating way of seeming to tell you something and in actuality saying nothing at all.

"I'm interested in all life forms. Human and animal. It's all part of conservation," he said. Then he leaned his head to one side and studied me as if I might be a new and interesting life form. "Are you interested in birds?"

"I'm afraid I don't know much about them." Somehow I felt embarrassed by the admission.

"I'm always happy to lecture on the subject. Whenever you feel like listening I'll be here." It was almost as if he spoke in a code which he was sure I knew.

"How long have you been on the island, Mac?" I asked. It seemed to me a perfectly reasonable question but he grinned again.

"Since early spring. I came for the first migrations. And you, Miss Raynor?"

"I came yesterday," I said. It seemed to me that he was laughing at me and I had no idea why. Then he let up in his amused interrogation and bent down to Emma.

"How is Miss Baby today?"

"She is a little hungry," Emma said with feigned innocence. "She liked the cookies you gave her last time we were here very much."

"Emma," I protested. But Mac did not seem to find her forward or bold.

"Why don't you come in and we'll see if we have any left."

"We don't want to interrupt your work." I glanced at Emma but she seemed determined on staying.

"Nonsense. Birds will wait. Besides you can see the lighthouse. It's mechanically operated now. A crew comes out from the mainland once a month to check it out. The days of the old-fashioned lighthouse keeper are gone. Still, it has been an experience living here."

Mac hoisted Emma, who held fast to Miss Baby, up onto his shoulders.

"Pompey, you stay," Mac commanded. Pompey was delighted to lie by the door and guard Emma's ball and pail.

"Too bad I can't carry you as well, Miss Raynor," Mac said agreeably. He really was the most outrageous man. "It's quite a climb."

The stairs were spiral and steep. They made me think a little of fire drill at school.

"How are you doing?" Mac called down at me from above.

"I think I can manage," I answered tartly.

"I'm sure you can. You seem to be very capable."

Now why did he irritate me so? It was not what he said as much as the way he said it. He had done it again. He had made me feel uneasy as if he had made a capital joke at my expense.

The metal steps wound round and round and up and up. Mac had been right to warn me to expect a climb. The treads were narrow and I was glad of my sneakers. They gave me just that bit of purchase on the slick metal. As we went round and round we passed by windows and it was startling to look out on the island and the sea from this height. It was a perfect view of both. Still, I was more than grateful to come to the top and the entrance to Mac's apartment. It had been the lighthouse keeper's home but now was considerably altered to suit Mac's personality and requirements.

"Please sit down and catch your breath," Mac said, depositing Emma and Miss Baby. "I'll get us some coffee to go with the cookies."

"Please don't go to any trouble."

"Oh, it's no trouble. I enjoy it. I don't have much company. I'm afraid I'm not very tidy." He looked about him.

"It's charming," I said, and I meant it. The room seemed very tidy to me and it had been made attractive and liveable. Mac had some nice prints and travel posters. The area around the bed-divan was hung with a good Indian cotton. The record player was an expensive one and his selection of records was large. I was surprised to see Herodotus and John Donne next to Simenon on the bookshelf. There was also a large selection of books on birds and a sampling of marine studies. He had a tank full of pretty fish swimming and diving in a warm, artificial light.

I wandered over to have a closer look at the records and saw Mahler and Stockhausen. Mac was a man of many tastes.

On a long bench next to a typewriter and notebooks was a

large radio. "If you ever want to use the radio phone it's very easy. Just come in any time." I thanked him, and while the coffee was brewing Mac took us up another spiral staircase to see the light.

What a strange thing it was to be capable of saving so many lives. An enormous bulb with an enormous reflector, an eye of God beaming out to the voyager. It was circled by a narrow catwalk and covered by a dome of glass. Walking around the light one saw all the island and the sea and on a clear enough day I was sure one could see the mainland. But directly below there were the rocks, and again the sight of them and the water brought on a return of my vertigo. I felt as if I might plummet through the glass down to the rocks below and disappear into the sea.

"You're as pale as a ghost," Mac said looking worried. "Something the matter?"

I nodded weakly. "I'm afraid of heights."

"Then look up," Mac said sensibly. Mac was as logical as one can be when one is not afraid.

"And I'm afraid of water," I went on, staring below me. My lips were stiff. I felt as rigid as the rocks.

"I don't imagine you see a lot of water coming from the desert."

"Who told you that?" I asked, looking at him instead of the sea.

"A little bird told me." Mac grinned. He had diverted me and now, pleased with himself, he took us back down to his apartment and gave Emma an Orange Crush and plenty of cookies for both herself and Miss Baby. He and I drank hot, strong coffee from huge mugs.

Mac made very good coffee. We all enjoyed ourselves. I found that in a matter of a few minutes Mac had me grinning back at him. I even found myself reluctant to go.

"I don't know your last name," I said.

"It's MacKenzie, but you can call me Mac."

I now knew his last name but not his first. I actually did not know much more about him than I had before.

He grinned. "Let's see if I can guess your first name." Mac did manage to have his little jokes with me. He put his head first to one side and then the other and then he said, "I think your name is Martha."

Emma clapped her hands in delight. "It is Martha," she said. "However did you guess?"

"There is a story about Mary and Martha," Mac said to Emma but he looked at me. "Martha was shy and retiring and stayed in the kitchen while Mary sat in the parlor." Then he took my hand and held it for a moment. "Well, Martha Raynor, I look forward to seeing you again very soon."

His words seemed to have a double meaning. I knew Mac could see me almost any time he cared to focus his binoculars in my direction. That gave him the advantage over me. But how he had come to know my name I couldn't guess.

Mac went all the way down the spiral staircase with us. He was a proper host seeing us to his doorstep. He hugged Emma and gave Miss Baby a fond pat. He seemed genuinely fond of Emma. But still I felt there was something more, something I could not see with my naked and limited eye. I felt as if he knew all about me and that I knew next to nothing about him. He turned to me, saving me for last.

"I hope you will come to fear the water less."

What a strange remark and what a strange day it had been. "Thank you," I said politely, and Emma and I set off on our way down to the beach. We had seen all of the island but a bit of woods and the boathouse and the well between the two.

"You like Mac, don't you?" I asked Emma.

Emma nodded. "Yes, he's very nice. Miss Baby likes him too and Pompey."

That was the supreme accolade. Then Emma frowned and shook her head.

"What is it?" I asked.

"Funny," Emma said. "But Caroline didn't like Mac to begin with. She said he was always snooping and spying but then she got to like him and they were always together. He spent a lot of time at the boathouse." Emma sighed. "Caroline didn't want me to come to the boathouse when Mac was there." Emma looked at me and waited for my reaction.

And I asked the question. "Why ever not?"

"I guess," Emma spoke slowly, "I guess that she was painting his picture."

And on we trudged, Emma with Miss Baby and her reticule and I with my hamper and beach bag and Pompey and his old bones.

Today I was able to be a bit more positive about the sand and the beach grass and the sand fleas and the shells, and I congratulated myself about my reaction to the water. I didn't mind its being there as long as it minded its own business.

I spread out the beach towels, found a locker set back into the dunes, and produced a large umbrella and some flat canvas chairs. I was beginning to make the beach a little more habitable for myself. It was not all that unpleasant at the beach when one had shade. Of course one could not ignore the fishy odor. I knew the fish had to live somewhere but must they smell so?

Emma wandered off on her eternal quest for more shells and I was left to mind Miss Baby. I considered it a mark of trust to have Miss Baby in my care. I stretched out on the beach towel under the umbrella and lay face down and relaxed. Across my folded arm I could see Miss Baby watching me with her open blue eyes. She was not in mint condition, our Miss Baby. She was chipped and cracked and battered by love. Perhaps she might enjoy a holiday at a doll's hospital.

Was it possible I was beginning to enjoy myself? I had not had a vacation in years. First there was college, then teacher's training. When I left Fanner Square and James I arrived at the Mission to find my father very ill. It was like him not to have told me how ill for fear he would worry me. Now I found I was lying perfectly still in the warm shade, seriously considering the health of a doll and wondering if I had enough energy to eat lunch before my nap.

And if I was absolutely honest I was also avoiding thinking about James Hand. The James Hand who sat in the library of the house at Fanner's Island was not the same James Hand I had been in love with. We had both changed. He was not the same any more than I was. It was too bad but our time had passed and in its place were two other people. Time had done its work, and pain and loss. Far more than blindness afflicted James Hand. He was as consumed by an impossible love for a lost Caroline as I had been consumed by an impossible love for him. The pain I still felt was mercifully lessened by the anesthetic of the heat.

I dozed off thinking of times past and the dream we had had of what life would be. I slept, dreaming of poor battered Miss Baby and I both patients in a doll's hospital. She turned to me, her blue eyes wide, and asked, "Why are you here?"

And I said, "I was battered by love."

And she said, "Oh."

Then old black Pompey came in in a doctor's coat and said, "In time everything will be all right." Because that was what doctors always said, and I slept until Emma woke me up for lunch.

I felt so guilty at dozing off when I was supposed to be taking care of Emma that I ate two helpings of everything and the moment lunch was finished and the hamper packed away I got out paper and crayons and pencils and said to Emma, "Why don't we play some games while our lunch digests?"

We drew and wrote and did small sums. We read over what we had written. Today I was only trying to find out what Emma already knew. I spent my life teaching children more emotionally at outs with the world than Emma and I prided myself that I was a good teacher. I was surprised and delighted with Emma's evaluation score. Emma was as bright as a button. Emma should be a joy to teach, and she seemed willing to learn. She did everything I asked of her and didn't grumble. It seemed she was anxious to please by giving the right answers. I couldn't see why she had had any trouble in school. When we finished she asked politely, "Is the game over?"

"Yes."

"Then I think I will go into the water. Are you coming?"

"No," I made an excuse. "The water's too cold."

Emma smiled. "It's warm enough for me." And she ran, her little pudgy legs churning up and down, toward the sea as if she were the happiest of children running toward a happy experience. I felt ashamed of testing her without her knowledge and consent. It seemed somehow slightly dishonest.

When Emma came back from the water she had goose bumps and her lips were blue. She sat shivering beside me and I wrapped her in a thick towel and rubbed her back. She was willing to be rubbed down like a tiny pony but she began to suck her thumb for the first time since I had been with her.

"I thought you told me it wasn't cold," I said in mock severity.

"I was fibbing." Emma took her thumb out of her mouth and gave me a look. It was a look I had not seen from her before. "How did I do on my test?" she asked.

"What?" I was caught by surprise.

"It was a test, wasn't it, to see if I can read and write and add?"

"Did you mind it?" I asked.

"No, but it was sort of a fib not to tell me."

"Yes." What could I do but agree? I must not try to hoodwink her again. It would not be honest and besides Emma was too bright and too wary.

Emma gave up her thumb and nodded. She had won her point. "I like reading and all of those things," she said. "I like you. I don't mind if we do them this summer."

Emma made me feel very emotional. She liked me and I was touched. Somehow Emma had put a mark on me and the mark would not wear off.

"Will you be here for the Fourth of July?" she asked.

"Yes."

"Will you be here after that?" Her earnest round face looked into mine. She was becoming a little dependent on me. I was beginning to win her.

"Yes."

"Then you'll be here for my birthday," Emma said, pleased with the information. "It's in July right after the Fourth."

"Yes, I know when your birthday is. I'll be here." I almost reached out and hugged her. It was a little triumph to be wanted by Emma.

"Then," Emma said with deliberate coolness, "you can see Caroline."

I wasn't ready for it. She hit me a terrible blow. She meant to. Emma set me up for it. Emma meant to wound me here and now perhaps in retribution for the test.

"Emma," I said, suddenly cold in the sun, "Caroline won't be here for your birthday."

"Yes, she will." Emma's jaw grew hard. "Caroline promised

she would be here for my birthday and she always keeps her promises."

I wanted to say, "Emma, Caroline is dead," but I didn't have the courage. Instead I asked her, "What if Caroline couldn't come?"

"She will. She'll be here." Emma was staring out to sea. "Sometimes I think she is here now only I can't see her."

"What?" Again Emma had caught me off guard.

"You know." Emma continued staring ahead. "You know the way it was with you and Mac. You knew he was there, you just couldn't see him. But he was there all the same."

It was more than what she was saying, it was the way Emma looked to the sea—waiting, watching for Caroline—that put the chill to my heart. It was pure terror I felt and I couldn't cope with it, at least not here and now. I was in out of my depth.

"Well," I said, "the Fourth of July comes before your birthday. We must celebrate that first. What do you want to do on the Fourth?"

"Caroline says they always have a beach party." Emma took her eyes from the sea and looked back to me. I was weak with the strain. I tried to remember just how often Emma had mentioned Caroline in the present tense. But I couldn't think properly.

To Emma, Caroline was not dead, could not be dead, for if Caroline was dead she, Emma, was guilty. James had said that Emma could not carry such guilt. It was too great a burden for her. For Emma the only salvation was for Caroline to be alive. If Caroline was coming then it would be all right in some future time. Emma could hang onto her balance just so long as there was the hope that Caroline was alive. I could not take that hope from her. But after the Fourth there would come a day that was Emma's birthday, a day of reckoning. Life on this island was a time bomb ticking away. I'd have to try to build a defense, open a campaign against that evil day, but before I could do that I must talk it out with James.

After dinner, when Tibba and Emma were safely settled upstairs in Emma's room playing a game of Parcheesi, I went down to the library and knocked on the door.

"Who is it?"

"Martha."

There was a short pause and then James said, "Come in."

James had to prepare himself to be seen by those he could not see. He was sitting at his desk. The lamp was lit and the light fell onto an open book. The book was large and leatherbound. If I hadn't known better I would have assumed that James had been reading just before I came in. Pompey sat beside him. He raised his head and then seeing who it was settled down again.

"I hope I'm not disturbing you," I said.

"No." James gave a wry and painful smile. "I wasn't doing anything. In fact if you hadn't come I would have sent for you."

James was being polite, nothing more. I didn't think any misfortune could make James forget his manners.

"How are things going with you and Emma?"

"She is very like her mother."

He frowned. "Do you think so?" James seemed genuinely surprised.

"Do you think she's more like Edward?" I asked.

"No," James said. "She is nothing like Edward and I do not think her very like her mother. Emma seems to me to be herself, unique."

For some reason it irritated me that he should not have observed in Emma a continuation of her parents. I began my list of questions.

"You said yesterday that Emma doesn't remember her parents or the accident."

"No." James frowned. I had cast a shadow over him as dark as his glasses.

"Was Emma with them when it happened?"

"Yes. They were all together on the ski chair lift." James spoke as if the words had been projected from him by force. He did not speak loudly but it could not be easy for him to go back over that time. It had been the first event in a reign of terrors.

"We had rented the ski run for the day. There was a large party of us, a private party. Sara and Edward got into the chair and just then, just before they went up, they scooped up Emma and put her between them."

I hadn't really believed Emma had been with them on the lift. I felt stiff with horror. Emma had been telling me the truth. No wonder she was traumatized.

James covered his eyes with his hand as if that would blot out what the glasses and his blindness could not erase.

"Yes, she was with them. Emma had been with Caroline but Emma wanted to go with her mother and father and Caroline let her. I heard Caroline call out to them, 'Wait for Emma.'"

He stopped. The room was as silent as space. The sound of his voice was washed away by the impact of what he was saying. Then James went on.

"Yes, she was with them. When they got about three-quarters of the way up the mountain, over a gorge, the cable broke. First one strand and then the other. After the first break Sara and Edward had a few seconds and they put Emma between them and their arms around her. Then the other strand broke and down came Sara, Edward, ski chair, and all."

I couldn't think about Sara and Edward. It was too terrible. I could only think about Emma.

"How badly was Emma hurt?"

"A mild concussion."

"But not amnesia?"

"No, not really. She just blocks it out. She pulls the curtain. I know she remembers but she won't talk about it. You see Sara was killed instantly and Edward lived only a few minutes. Emma was there, born out of their death."

"I am sorry to ask you all this," I said. "But it is important for me to know, if I am to help Emma."

James turned his head away from me toward the warmth of the fire. It was strange to need a fire in summer. He said, "There were a lot of questions asked at the time. I became executor of Sara and Edward's estate. I am Emma's guardian."

"And Caroline inherited nothing from Sara."

"But she did." James seemed astonished that I should think otherwise. "Caroline got a legacy from Sara. It was certainly enough so that Caroline would never have to think of herself as a poor relation again. Besides, I was able to keep my wife."

I knew that James and Edward were comfortably off, though far from Fanner rich. Nobody was as rich as Sara had been, for all the good it did her or Emma.

"And Emma went back to Boston with you and Caroline and went back to nursery school?"

"Yes, but she had to be taken away."

"Why?"

"She would do nothing all day. She sat looking out the window. She was like a shellshock case. One of the walking wounded. Caroline did everything she could to help."

"And so you came here?" I asked, dreading to hear the answer.

"Caroline thought it would be better for Emma if we were married." James had turned his head away from me. "It was like beginning again for Emma. She gave all her trust and all her love to Caroline."

Pompey stirred. He got up and circled around and around and then settled again by James. James reached out his hand and stroked Pompey's back. All creatures on this island had been Caroline's. Even Pompey was bereft without her.

"Is there something wrong?" James asked me. "Is that why you are asking all these questions?"

"I'm not sure," I said, and I wasn't. "It's just that I feel if I know exactly what happened I am better prepared to help Emma."

"What else would you like to know?"

I didn't like to ask him but since I had begun this line of questioning I went on with it. "At Easter," I said, hesitantly, "when Emma was in the water, was she injured physically?"

"No." James shook his head from side to side as if trying to shake loose from the memory of that day. "I got Emma off the boat before the blast."

"But not Caroline." That was a statement, not a question.

There was a silence then so long and so deep I thought it might never end.

"No. I couldn't get to her. The last thing I saw before the explosion was Caroline. She was inside a plastic dome that covered the cabin. The flames were all around her face."

I would have given anything if James had not had to tell me that but I had asked and I had gotten my answer. I felt it was important to know. Out of nervousness, in a sort of wild filibuster, I began to talk about Emma.

"Emma really is like her mother, you know. She is good at her studies. I gave her some tests today and she reads well ahead of her age group. She writes well and has been well-grounded in math. Her word rate is most impressive. She is very well organized about her time. She is thoughtful of others. Today she took me on a tour of the island. She was the perfect guide. We went to the garden and to the Widow's Look and over the cliff path to the lighthouse. We saw everything but the well and the old boathouse."

"You mustn't go to the boathouse," James cut in sharply.

"So Emma said. She said that Caroline's studio has been shut since she . . ." And there I was back again to Caroline and her death, that which I had run a verbal race to avoid.

"There is nothing to see," James said. "Captain Fairley keeps the boat there but the studio is shut and locked." My feelings were hurt by James's attitude but I felt I deserved it because of my clumsiness.

"We had a very interesting day. I met Mr. MacKenzie and we saw the lighthouse and he gave us coffee and cookies." James nodded.

"Mac is a very nice fellow. He comes in and plays chess with me when he has the time."

"Emma seems to like him. She seems to go there often. I had the impression that she's a regular visitor."

"Do you think she's making a nuisance of herself by going there too often? Is that what this is about?"

"No, no." I hastened to deny it and then I realized what it was that was niggling and gnawing away at the back of my mind. If Mac had been on the island at Easter, why hadn't he heard the explosion? Why hadn't he gone out with Captain Fairley to see what had happened? I heard Emma's remark echoing in my memory. "Caroline didn't like Mac at first, but later they got to be great friends."

"Martha."

It was the first time James had called me by my name and it made me jump.

"There's something on your mind, something important. It's about Emma, isn't it?"

"Yes," I said. I had to tell him now. There was no way out of it. "It's something Emma said today. It upset me very much."

"What was it?"

"Emma told me that Caroline will be here for her birthday.

Emma says Caroline promised her she would be here and Emma believes that Caroline will keep her promise."

For a time James said nothing and then he sighed. It was the saddest sigh I had ever heard.

"Has Emma ever told you that Caroline would be here for her birthday?"

"Yes." His answer was almost inaudible.

"And what did you say?"

"I said nothing. I am a coward, I know, but I said nothing."

I too was a coward. I had said nothing today. "Emma can't really believe that Caroline is alive?" I asked him, but I knew I was clutching at straws.

"People believe what they want to believe. Children more than the rest of us," James said quietly.

And it was true. I had believed James loved me. That was just as foolish as Emma's believing Caroline would come back for her birthday. James looked tired and drawn. I had pressed him hard and I was truly sorry for that.

"You must try and understand," he said, "how difficult it is for her. I told you when you came that Emma is very complicated. She has layers and layers of guilt. Any sudden wind could shatter her into a thousand pieces."

"But James," I protested, "unless something is done, Emma's birthday will come and Caroline will not be here. Won't she break then?"

"There is a little time. Perhaps you can think of something."

"Me?" I was dumbfounded.

"Sara believed you could work miracles with children. So does the Foundation."

"Teaching perhaps," I said, "but Emma needs more than a teacher."

"I know that."

"She needs someone to love and you are going away."

"Emma doesn't love me," James said bitterly. "Sometimes I think she hates me."

"Must you go?" I knew the answer before I asked.

"Yes. As I am, I am more dependent than Emma. Captain Fairley feeds me and shaves me and dresses me. If Caroline were to come back now and stand in this room I couldn't see her."

It was his true motive for going. James wanted to see so that if Emma's miracle did occur and Caroline came back he could see her. I felt I was caught in a vise.

"Will you be back by Emma's birthday?"

"Yes. I'll try to be back by then."

"But if you aren't?" I said. I had to be practical since I was going to be in charge. "What if you aren't back?"

"You'll have to deal with the situation."

"I can't," I said. "I can't be responsible for shattering her sanity. I can't do that."

"Please," James implored me. "You know I'm proud but I'm asking for your help. If not for me, for Emma."

"All right," I said wearily. "I will try."

While we were talking Pompey had moved to the fire. He shifted and whimpered in his sleep. His paws fluttered. He was in a dream and in his dream he was running for his life. It was like an augury, a shaking of sacred bones, or a portent of disaster. In an instant the prophecy was made fact. The lights went out and the room was in darkness save for the firelight.

I gasped.

"What is it?" James asked.

"The lights," I said. "They've gone out."

"There's an oil lamp on the desk. Don't worry, it's only the generator. It does this from time to time."

I lit the lamp and James thoughtfully suggested that I take the lamp to light myself up the stairs.

"What about you?" I asked.

"There's another lamp by the bed," he said.

I had spoken without thinking and I was ashamed of my words. James had no need for a lamp. It seemed I could not accept the fact that James was blind.

As I passed through the hall on my way to the stairs, I heard the faint sound of a radio coming from the Fairleys' quarters. The battery radio was a modern blessing. From the radio came the ghostly disembodied sound of canned laughter for a comedy show. Then I heard the laughter from the top of the stairs. I had heard it before. I had heard it last night in my room. It was like the sharp shards of splintering ice, a wind in a crystal cave.

A door opened above me and I heard the sound of feet running down the hall. Tibba and Emma must be running because they knew I was coming and would catch them at some prank.

But at the top of the stairs there was nothing, no one. Nothing suspicious at all until I saw in the dim and flickering light of the lamp that the door to Caroline's room was open. Perhaps because I had a Pandora complex and partly because curiosity unsatisfied killed the cat I opened the door still farther and went inside.

Even by this poor light it was an exquisitely lovely room. It was a shrine to Caroline's beauty. And as I wondered why I had chosen that exact word I smelled the incense, the odor of musk. I saw on the small table two candles in silver candlesticks. They had just been snuffed out and the wicks were still smoking. Between the candlesticks was a silver salver and a portion of the incense that had turned to ash.

Beside the salver was one Tarot card. I knew little about the Tarot. This card was the ten of pentacles. The picture was of a patriarch surrounded by a family and a dog. There was an arch behind them which opened onto an impressive house.

Each card has two meanings, one positive and one negative. The positive meaning of this card was inheritance, property, honor.

The negative meaning was the loss of inheritance, family misfortune, and loss of honor. Some people took the Tarot seriously. To some it was only a game, but I knew with a terrible certainty that it was not a game for children. Not a game for a child as fragile as Emma. She could mistake cardboard magic for reality.

~~◦◦~~ *Four* ~~◦◦~~

Next morning Emma and Tibba were in the kitchen before me. They were as bright and shining as the morning sun. They had planned all sorts of extra treats for the picnic basket, blueberry pie and lobster salad in iced containers. It seemed impossible that these two little girls could have anything to do with Gypsy cards or secret ceremonies, but someone had dropped the card and someone had been in Caroline's room. I had heard the sound of running feet.

Miss Baby and Pompey sat like double patience on a monument waiting for the expedition to set out. I told the girls, who were eager to be off, that they might go on down to the beach without me. I said I wanted an extra cup of coffee and out they ran like little wild things without a backward look.

I really wanted to have a chat with Mrs. Fairley. I had done nothing last night about my discovery of the candles or the Tarot card. This morning I had looked into Caroline's room and they were gone. The candles had been replaced with new ones and the incense ash had vanished. The Tarot card was nowhere to be seen.

When we were alone I said to Mrs. Fairley, "Thank you for letting Tibba go today. Are you sure you don't need her?"

Mrs. Fairley went impassively about her morning chores. "No, I don't need her. To be plain I've been keeping her home because I thought you and Emma ought to have a chance to get acquainted."

"That's very thoughtful of you, Mrs. Fairley." Then I went on slowly trying to sound offhand. "Last night did your lights go out?"

"It's the generator." Mrs. Fairley shook her head. "The Captain had to go out and tinker with it. It was one of Caroline's improvements. It's never been all right. The old one worked fine. It had been here ever since I was a girl, but then Caroline got this new one. It's never been any good, always on the blink."

I was diverted from both the generator and the Tarot card by Mrs. Fairley's information. "You've been here since you were a girl?"

"Oh, yes." She seemed to enjoy my surprise. "I've been on the island since I was not much older than Tibba." She wiped her hands and said, "I hope you found the oil lamp in your room."

"Yes, thank you, but I thought Captain Fairley had always worked for Mr. Hand?"

Mrs. Fairley nodded. "That's right. We didn't marry until after Mr. Hand and Caroline did. When they came to the island it seemed like a sensible arrangement."

Marrying as a sensible arrangement was too prosaic to suit me. But she seemed to find it a compatible arrangement. However I had not stayed behind to talk about Mrs. Fairley's private life but to find out if she knew what had become of the Tarot card and the candles.

"I don't know how you manage to keep the place running so smoothly," I said. "You must have to get up early to get so much done before breakfast."

"Lands' sake no." Mrs. Fairley clearly rejected the notion. "I like to have everybody out from under foot before I begin."

So my theory didn't stand up to examination. If Mrs. Fairley had not been upstairs this morning she couldn't have moved the card or replaced the candles. So then I must concentrate on the girls, find out what they were up to, and I think, even then, I dreaded the answer.

I got a hat for myself from the hall closet. Caroline's hat was there on a peg. It seemed a long time since I had fretted over whether Mrs. Fairley had given me Caroline's hat with some malice aforethought or not. That seemed a simple problem in comparison with the ones I had now.

I went out of the house. The cabin cruiser was lying down by the landing. Captain Fairley had made his morning run to and from the mainland. I could not get over the fact that he and Mrs. Fairley were newlyweds. I couldn't help but wonder what a marriage based on sense, not sentiment, must be like. I had had offers of marriage in the past few years, all sensible proposals, but they did not appeal to me. I yearned, it seemed, for true love.

It was another day of sun and blue sky, but somehow in the glare of bright light there lurked a few discreet clouds. I was so dazzled by the present weather that I ignored the clouds and what they could mean. Outside the front door I half turned to put on my hat and I saw, through the windows of the library, James sitting with a towel around his neck. Captain Fairley was shaving him. Poor James, to be dependent must cost his pride dear.

I walked along so caught up in my own thoughts that when I heard a voice above me saying good morning I jumped like a cat on a hot brick.

"I'm sorry, I didn't mean to startle you."

It was Mac, all brown and naked to the waist and of course

festooned with binoculars. He was grinning at my fright. I wondered with some bitterness if he had startled me on purpose.

"Good morning again," Mac said.

"Good morning," I said, nothing over cheerful.

"You're late." Mac looked as if he expected some explanation. "The girls have already gone down to the beach."

"My, you are being a good spy today." It was cheap sarcasm but Mac seemed not to notice it. I supposed what rubbed me the wrong way about Mac was that his health and his vitality contrasted so vividly with James's sitting in the house having to ask for the simplest thing.

Mac continued grinning. It was the one thing I knew he did superbly.

"I've been watching for you."

"Won't your bird count get off?" I should have been ashamed of my rudeness but I was not. To be honest I was rather enjoying it. I had the sneaking feeling that the glasses and the beard were only a disguise, a false face Mac presented to me for inspection and approval. At any moment he might expose his true identity.

I started away on down the path. "I mustn't keep you," I said, but Mac was too fast for me. He was down from the dune blocking my path before I could get around him.

"These glasses are a useful device," Mac said. "You can see quite a lot through them. You'd be surprised." He swung them off his neck and around mine before I could protest. "For instance," he went on, "you didn't get to the boathouse yesterday. With these glasses you can be there in no time." Mac stood behind me and, like a golf pro patterning my perform- ance, he turned and swung me in the direction he wanted me to look. "Do you see the boathouse?"

Indeed I did. I nodded. I saw the boathouse clearly and also a little portion of the path leading from the house to the boathouse and on the path I saw Mrs. Fairley. She was not doing her housekeeping this morning.

"You can't see the well," Mac said matter of factly. "It's hidden by some trees. The well is the only really hidden place on the island. You ought to go to see the well sometime. It has quite a history."

I was about to thank him for his suggestion and return the glasses when he swung me gently and firmly away from the boathouse toward the direction of the beach.

"And if for some reason you can't be down on the beach and you want to know what the girls are up to you can find out by looking through these magic glasses."

He swung me from one direction to the other and now he lowered my eyes and the glasses and there, sure enough, were the girls, the two of them on the sand, caught and magnified. They were sitting on the sand huddled together like two witches in a grade school *Macbeth*. They were facing out to sea and were bent over the sand. Tibba was drawing something on the sand with a bit of stick. Slowly, slowly, as the binoculars came into better focus I saw that what she was drawing was a pentacle, just like the one on the Tarot card.

It was a five-cornered star drawn in one line and used in the practice of magic. Mac must have felt me stiffen with the shock. He let go of my shoulders. The glasses fell from my hands and swung crazily on their string. I wanted to run away to escape from the idea that Emma and Tibba were playing at magic but I was paralyzed with foreboding.

Mac stepped round to face me. He was no longer grinning. "Have you seen enough?"

"Quite enough."

"Sure?"

"Yes. I'm sure." I handed back the glasses. I had seen more this morning than I had expected to see. Mac had been a puppeteer. He had maneuvered and manipulated me into discovery and I could not say at that moment whether I was grateful or bitterly sorry. I had seen what he had wanted me to see, Mrs. Fairley on her way to the boathouse and the girls at their games.

"Thank you," I said, my lips numb.

"Not at all. If you would like a pair of binoculars for yourself, I have an extra pair."

"No." Anger replaced my shock. "I'm sure you won't let me miss anything of significance."

Mac nodded. He knew perfectly well what I meant. I was sure of it, and now since he had brought the situation with Emma and Tibba to my attention I would have to deal with it. Just how to go about it I didn't know. I did not want to surprise them. It might give them the impression I was sneaking up on them and I did not want that, but since they were intent on playing games I decided on a ploy of my own. I called back to Mac who was climbing up over the dunes. I shouted, "Good-bye, Mac," loudly enough to wake Pompey.

I saw the girls' heads come up and turn in my direction. I waved and signaled to them. I couldn't have let them know I was coming more plainly if I had fired off a cannon. Then I watched to see what they would do. I didn't like the results. Emma stood up and backed away as if disclaiming her part in the affair. Tibba quickly began to move the stick back and forth to erase the pentacle.

I now had an advantage over them. I knew something they didn't know I knew. Or did I? It would be best to keep my wits about me, to go slowly but not to accuse them of something without proof. I came on down to them as if it were an ordinary morning and we all had an ordinary day before us, an ordinary day in the sun by the sea.

We ran and walked and picked up shells and put them down

again. We had our lunch and after lunch I set the girls to schoolwork. We sat under the big umbrella and worked with full attention. To my surprise I found that, bright and quick as Emma was, Tibba outshone her.

If I did not keep on my toes and think of new ways to teach old tricks they would both be bored soon. We began to tell stories. Each one told a paragraph. They liked doing it because they got to participate and because it made them use their imaginations.

It was because of the storytelling that I said I thought history was so much fun to learn since it was a continued story without any ending. They wanted to know what I meant, and thinking myself clever I told a little about the Pilgrim Fathers and why they had come to Plymouth and the first Thanksgiving. I ended with the thought that right here in this area there was a lot of local history that they could learn if they liked.

And Tibba nodded solemnly and said, "Oh, yes. Like the story of the witch."

She saw at once I didn't know what she was talking about.

"There was once a witch," she went on, "who came here to this island in the olden days. She came over from the mainland and asked the Fanners to give her shelter. She thought she was safe with them but they sent her back to the mainland."

I didn't like the direction of the story but I asked, "And then what happened?" as if I were the pupil and Tibba the teacher.

"Oh," Tibba said, "when she got back to the mainland they burned her, but before she died she cursed the Fanners and ever since that day the Fanners who have lived on the island have had bad luck."

"What a terrible story," I said weakly, looking at Emma who was held under the spell of Tibba's words.

"But it is history, isn't it?" Tibba asked innocently, and I had to agree that it was. I was glad after that to let the girls go into the sea for their afternoon swim. Someone had told Tibba the story just so she could repeat it and Emma would hear it, I was convinced of it.

I felt oppressed. I had been so pleased with the lessons and yet now I felt defeated. Emma would believe Tibba about anything before she believed in me and if Tibba believed in witches and spells and Tarot cards Emma would take her word that they had power and existed, power enough to bring Caroline back again.

Perhaps the island *was* under a spell. The tension, the stress, the pressure, was always there just beneath every surface. The heat was close and the air heavy. Even the weather was against me. The storm was coming and the clouds had begun to gather. I could not ignore them. Pompey lay, his tongue hanging out, his breathing short and shallow. Only Miss Baby seemed unaware of the barometer.

We got back to the house, the three of us, well before the rain, but by the time we went inside the sky had turned black and the clouds bubbled and boiled like the bottom of the sea, and then in a flash the lightning struck and the thunder rolled like a great timpani and the rain came down, wave after wave of rain in imitation of the cruel sea.

We had our supper in the kitchen, Emma and Tibba and Mrs. Fairley and I. It was close and my nerves were stretched by the storm and the unremitting sound of a pounding boom that came from the sea striking at the cliffs at the back of the island. It would have been a pleasant supper if it had not been for my state of nerves. With the first rain the generator went out and we sat around the table by the light of kerosene lamps, eating a delicious chowder fit for Norse gods.

After supper, when Captain Fairley had fed James, he went out to see what he could do about the generator. Mrs. Fairley sat and sewed and Tibba and Emma held Miss Baby between them looking at a picture book. From somewhere in another part of the house a shutter broke loose and banged on and on. Outside was the storm wanting to get in to destroy and lay waste the humans who sheltered here.

I looked at Emma and Tibba, a double portrait of innocence, their blue and brown eyes focused on fairy tales and knights of old. They were only vulnerable children. Or were they?

I said goodnight to Mrs. Fairley and bent down to Emma to give her a kiss. She accepted it without returning one to me. The kiss she took to be her due. I saw Tibba, her face upturned, waiting to be kissed as well. And so I kissed her too, and she put her arms around my neck. There was nothing calculated about Tibba's gesture. Tibba only wanted to share, to be a part of a family in a warm kitchen safe from the storm.

"Do you want me to come in later?" I asked Emma.

"Why?"

"I thought you might be afraid of the storm."

"No, I like the wind and the rain. Are you afraid?"

"No," I lied.

As I went past the library on the way upstairs I saw a thin line of light under James's door. He was alone and in the dark and the storm. No lamp could light such a night for him. The house bent and groaned, the creaking boards seeming to wail and to cry. Or was it an unearthly laughter, the sound that the wind made tearing at the old building?

Like a child frightened of the dark I ran past Caroline's room and into my own. I lay in bed in the dark. I imagined noises in the attic and on the stairs and in time I heard Emma and Tibba come up the stairs, and each went into her own room and closed her own door. They were both braver than I.

For no sensible reason I thought of Mac in his lighthouse. I felt in danger of personal shipwreck and I wondered whether I would feel more secure if I could see the beacon. Salvation always seems possible if there is a light.

I got up and looked out at the island shrouded in mist and rain and there, sure enough, the light shone out in the midst of the storm. It came and went, rounding its way in a regular cycle, a never-failing sign of hope for all the souls at sea. And then, just there before me above the garden I saw a tiny pinprick of light that looked as if it was coming from the Widow's Look. It must be an illusion. There could be no light in the Widow's Look if the generator was not working.

For the first time in years I said my prayers. My lips moved and I heard myself say: Please, in the morning let the storm be over.

But in the morning the storm was not over; if anything it was blowing even harder. In the kitchen I was surprised to find Captain Fairley, his feet up on the fender of the fireplace. He sat in an old rocker filling his pipe.

"Morning," he said. "I thought I'd have a smoke before I went out to have another look at that confounded generator."

"How long is the storm going to last?" I asked.

"Could go on for days but I reckon it will blow itself out soon. Too much sound and fury in it."

I poured myself some coffee.

The Captain sat smoking, looking into the fire while I drank my coffee. Then unexpectedly he made a suggestion that surprised me.

"This generator is going to keep me busy for most of the afternoon. Why don't you go in and visit with Mr. James?"

"I don't know if he'd like that." The Captain looked at the fire and I peered into the depths of my coffee cup.

"I know he'd like a game of chess. I'm not much use to him." The Captain spoke gently as if trying to coax a child. "Cribbage is my game."

I said nothing.

"I remember one time," the Captain put his head back as if

about to tell a sea legend, "one time, oh, years ago, Mr. James told me about this wonderful girl he had met who could beat him playing chess."

I flushed, and try as I would I could not blame the warmth on the coffee.

"The way he talked about her I knew she was something special."

I thought of the house in Fanner Square where James and I had played chess on winter afternoons. We had sat in front of the fire and played chess hour after hour, concentrating on the game and on each other. It was a dull, chronic ache to know that time would never come again. Once the memory had hurt like being seared with a poker from the fire.

"What happened to the girl?" I looked at the Captain. He kept on puffing at his pipe and would not look back at me.

"I'm not sure," he said. "But I know he still thinks of her."

Before he could get any deeper into the subject Mrs. Fairley and the girls came in from the pantry. They had smoked ham and dried beans, some turnips and carrots from the root cellar, and mason jars of homemade relish.

The minute the girls saw me they descended on me begging permission to go up to the attic where, they assured me, there were trunks and trunks of old clothes and shoes.

"Please, please, let us." Emma and Tibba begged in chorus. "We can play dress up and everything."

It seemed like a very suitable rainy-day thing to do. "I don't object if Mrs. Fairley doesn't," I said. "But mind you tidy up after yourselves."

"We will, we will," they shouted, and they ran away to have their marvelous day.

Mrs. Fairley went about the cooking and in a few minutes Captain Fairley knocked out the pipe against the hearth and rose. "I'd appreciate it if you'd tell Mr. James where I've gone," he said to me. "Tell him I'll bring him his tea." And he gave me a wink. "Don't beat him too badly at chess."

James was pleased I had come. I was sure of it. We sat in the library. There was a fire in the grate. Pompey dozed in front of the fire, lying on a thick fur rug. He was almost smiling. It was so pleasant to be in the warm, out of the wet and for once having a respite from the beach. Or was I projecting my own feelings to Pompey?

James and I played chess. He called out his moves to me and I made them for him. From the black blindness of his mind he could visualize the board and men. He played, if anything, a better game than he had all those years ago. But as I looked at him, grey and thin, his hands folded in resignation on his lap, too young a man to look so old, it seemed to me that the essential personality of the James I had known had been altered into another shape. He was not the same man nor would he be himself ever again. His air of sadness came close to the fatalistic. It made me sad to think that James Hand was gone forever and I would not see him again, not the James who had been so young with me.

Yet all told it was a pleasant afternoon. I had thought it must have been horrible for the Fanner women and children to be here on their own for a winter or for a year while the men were away at sea, but on the other side of the coin how wonderful to be here the whole of the winter if one was here with one's husband and children, the family all together away from the world and its cares. What then could be happier?

The thought put me into such a state of euphoria that I even saw myself in some golden future time, my family about me, and I was swimming in the sea. I could swim for miles and miles. In my daydream I had become a dolphin of a swimmer.

"You aren't paying attention," James said. "What are you thinking about?"

"Swimming," I said truthfully. "I must learn to swim. It's ridiculous not to know how. Even babies swim. I saw a picture of some infants the other day; they were in the water all on their own and they looked quite happy."

James laughed. It was the first time since I had been here that I had seen anything like his old good humor.

"Why don't we give up the chess and have some sherry instead?"

It was as if there had been a crack in time and we had slipped through it to the past.

This was the time of the storm but as we sat content, sipping our sherry and listening to the savage wind and the outrage of the rain wanting to get in, I knew the storm was only the lull before some future deluge. This was only the beginning.

"How's Emma?" James asked.

"All right," I said. "She's in the attic with Tibba playing dress up."

"Have you had a chance to talk to her about her birthday yet?"

"No." I didn't know whether to tell him that I thought before I had that conversation with her I ought to make sure she and Tibba were not trying to make contact with the spirit world. But then I decided against it. It seemed too farfetched even to talk about.

We sat, peaceful and quiet together. Pompey had come to sit by James's chair, and James stroked his head, pulling at his ears, which gave Pompey great pleasure. Pompey might have been Caroline's dog but he was now James's devoted and admiring slave.

I looked around the room. This was the first time I had been here when I had an opportunity to admire the maps and walls of books. Every Captain Fanner from days gone by had brought something of his travels home with him. The house was a treasure trove of the world. The alcove bed hung in quilted cotton was James's retreat into a room which should prepare one for adventure and far-off places.

"James," I asked, "somewhere here in this library I am sure there must be a history of the island and of the area around Fannerstown."

"Yes," he said.

"May I borrow it?"

"Perhaps you might be interested in the book that's on the desk. Captain Fairley has been reading to me in the evenings."

Before I could ask James anything about the island or the story of the witch Captain Fairley came with a tea tray and I made an excuse to leave. I knew James would not like me to see him with a napkin tied under his chin. It seemed to me that the afternoon had gone in a second. The days would never be long enough with James for company.

I took the book back to my room and began to read. There was time before supper, and above my head I heard the girls running in the attic, their feet scampering like little mice.

I had meant to read straight through the book but instead I managed only a chapter before I fell asleep. There really had been a witch named Tibba just as Tibba had told me this afternoon. The storm went on unabated but I was out of it into a dreamless sleep.

After supper, which we had before the kitchen fire, we played Crazy Eights and bobbed for apples. After the game there was popcorn and milk and for a diversion suddenly, out of the storm, Mac appeared bursting through the door in an oilcloth slicker and hat which was streaming rain.

The girls were overjoyed to see him.

"What a greeting," Mac grinned. "Which one of you ladies will give me a cup of coffee and which one will tell me what you are got up as?"

They had worn bits and pieces of their found finery to supper and had refused to take them off. They really were charming and it did no harm to see them happy. Both girls went to get Mac his coffee and both returned to tell together the joys of the day in the attic. Somewhere in between their chatter Mac managed to tell Mrs. Fairley and me that he had been onto the Coast Guard on the radio, and they thought the storm would be over by morning.

"It's already started out to sea," Mac said. I felt he had brought the news to reassure me in particular. And as if to give pledge to the promise no sooner had Mac told his news than the lights went on in a blaze of electrical extravagance.

"Wonders to tell. The Captain has gotten the fool thing going." Mrs. Fairley seemed more pleased than any of us. Most of her kitchen aids ran off the generator. It seemed strange though to see the bright lights again. It was as if it was the end of the play and the house lights had gone up.

"Are you girls looking forward to the grand and glorious Fourth?" Mac asked the giggling, wriggling ladies.

"Yes, yes," the girls agreed. They were looking forward to the Fourth especially now the storm was going to be over and Captain Fairley could bring lots and lots of fireworks from Fannerstown.

It was then we decided, I think because we had been admiring the girls in their getups, that we ought to have a costume party on the Fourth. It had always been the custom on the island to go down to the beach but no one had ever gone down in costume before. It seemed an excellent idea.

"What will you ladies come as?" Mac asked.

"It will be a secret," Emma replied promptly because she hadn't made up her mind. Then the idea grew and we all decided to come in costume and surprise each other.

"What do you think?" I asked Mrs. Fairley. "Do you think Mr. Hand will have any objection?"

"I'm sure he won't," Mac answered, "not if you ask him."

I felt my cheeks go hot. I could not hear James's name without emotion.

Mac stayed until the Captain came in full of his success with the generator.

"By the way," Mac said to the Captain after he had congratulated him, "I thought I saw a light in the Widow's Look last night."

The Captain frowned. "Might be some drain from the wiring. I'll look into it."

Then we told the Captain about our plans for the Fourth and I was lulled into a sense of security. I was so off my guard that I barely noticed Mac's last remark.

"When I saw the light last night," he said to the Captain, "I thought we might have a visitor."

It seemed harmless enough at the time but I was to remember it later and remember it well.

❦ *Five* ❦

The storm was over the next morning and the sun came up as I had forgotten it could, bright, brilliant, blazing away. It had been there all the time but I could not see it. So much for my faith. I wondered what sort of gibbering idiot I would have been, mewed up on the ark for forty days and forty nights.

And with the sun came a great activity. Getting our costumes together for the Fourth of July gave us something to take our minds off our problems. Preparing for the masquerade was a lovely game, quite the nicest game we had played yet. For the time being I didn't have to wonder what the girls were up to. And, as Emma's birthday was not until after the Fourth, I could put off my confrontation with her for the time being.

Everyone had harmless secrets. There was a lot of up and down in the halls and shrieks of "Don't come in until I tell you." Needles and thread were in short supply and there was the constant query "Who has the scissors?" It all seemed like Christmas in July.

Everyone seemed to know who they were going as but me. I could not decide. Invention failed me. I had thought of Molly Pitcher and Dolly Madison and Abigail Adams. And I had rejected them all. I could not fix on a character. It was not that we didn't celebrate the Fourth of July at the Mission but I felt constrained to outdo myself. Here I was in the cradle of the Revolution and for Massachusetts nothing but the best effort would do.

It was Mrs. Fairley who mentioned the torch. She said that in the attic there was an old carriage torch, one like those the link boys had used in the eighteenth century. The Fanners had not needed a carriage on the island but they had used it to light themselves up from the landing.

The next time I was in the attic rummaging through boxes of India cottons and China silks I looked up on a shelf above me and there was the torch. And it came to me in a burst of inspiration that I would go to the clambake as the Statue of Liberty. I knew full well that the lady had come to these shores later than 1776 but she was the heart and spirit of the Revolution. Lafayette knew that and the French knew it, which was why they sent her as a sort of revolutionary housewarming present.

I was sure that in a sheet draped in a neo-classic manner, the torch held high in hand and with a gilt paper crown, I would more than pass muster. I was delighted with the choice.

By the morning of the Fourth we were in a fever. We all worked to set the scene. Rather like actors who must build the set and make the props before they can perform, we hung the front of the house in red, white, and blue bunting. We gathered and stacked an enormous pile of driftwood on the beach for the fire. We carried down pails and kettles. We dug a trough and lined it with stones and seaweed so that the corn and clams could be roasted in hot coals and steamed by the seaweed. We wet down the corn and put it, still in the shucks, inside a giant kettle until the evening. We brought extra blankets and the ice cream freezer and coarse-ground salt. It occurred to me that a clambake was a New England version of a luau.

And along with all the old and traditional ways of making a clambake we mixed the new thermal carriers full of ice and beer. For what would the thing be without ice?

And then, our morning's work finished, we went to our rooms and collapsed for long, much-needed naps. When dark began to fall we put on our costumes and we were ready for the fete to begin.

There was some good-natured jostling and jockeying for entrances. Each wanted to be the last upon the beach. Captain Fairley came as George Washington with his teeth out. He was a caricature of a portrait by Copley. He brought his friend Benjamin Franklin. The part suited James, who was able to wear half-spectacles to shield his eyes. Mrs. Fairley came as Betsy Ross and brought along a small flag to sew upon. I, as the Statue of Liberty, made my entrance with the torch lit and shining bright o'er freedom's land.

Emma and Tibba came along mincing and prancing in high heels which they soon had to abandon because of the sand. They had fashioned cotton wool into wigs which they had liberally powdered with cornflour. Their faces were painted and patched beyond all recognition.

When we asked who they were, they proclaimed themselves to be great beauties. Emma said she was the most beautiful lady in Boston and Tibba claimed to be the most beautiful lady in Philadelphia. It seemed that they had looked into the mirror, the two of them, and recited "Mirror, mirror on the wall, who is the fairest of them all?" But as there had been no reply they had each decided to be the fairest, taking this way out of their difficulty.

We agreed that each was, in her own way, unique and in a class of her own. To make them triple perfect, Miss Baby attended as the most beautiful lady of New York, which I thought cut up the territory pretty well.

Poor Pompey was left to bring up the rearguard as a veteran of the war. He limped along in yards and yards of bandages. He looked as sheepish and foolish as the rest of us looked pleased with ourselves.

Then we waited for Mac but he didn't arrive, and just as Captain Fairley was about to light the bonfire and proclaim the clambake well and truly begun there appeared on the dunes above us a bearded apparition in a French Blue coat. It carried a banjo and when it spoke it was with an absurd French accent.

"Mes amis," it said. "Lafayette is here."

And we all knew that Mac had arrived at last. He really was funny. His fractured French caused roars of merriment. I could not decide whether his accent, his beard, or his banjo playing was the worst.

The food, on the other hand, was unbelievable. Mrs. Fairley and the Captain had produced miracles. There was the traditional salmon and peas and new-boiled potatoes which would have been enough for any meal, but there was more to follow. There were lobsters and clams, sloshed over with melted butter which ran down our chins. There was corn on the cob and more butter. There were blueberry pies and homemade vanilla ice cream. It was so rich and rare as to make me feel I had never really tasted plain vanilla ice cream before. Even James could eat without the Captain's help and never mind if he dribbled or dropped morsels to the sand, for we all did.

The fire blazed up hot and toasted our cheeks. We sat on the blankets in a circle of light. Away from the house, here on the beach, for the first time since I had come to Fanner's Island I felt that Emma and James had put aside the memories of their tragedy. They joined wholeheartedly into the celebration of life, liberty, and the right to pursue happiness.

After we had eaten until we could eat no more we packed away the victuals and Captain Fairley and Mac climbed to the highest of the dunes and when the night was the blackest and the fire banked down to a subdued glow they set off the fireworks display. There were flights of rockets and cannonades of Roman candles and a repeating whirl of Catherine wheels. I tried to describe everything that was happening to James and I hoped his memory would fill in the colors and details.

After the last and final salvo, which made a representation of the flag, Emma and Tibba begged and pleaded to have sparklers and under close supervision they were allowed to light them in the embers of the fire and whirl them round and round in circles and figure eights. The rest of us, including Miss Baby and Pompey, were an appreciative audience.

In the bursts of rockets and flares of Roman candles I observed all our faces. We were caught, held, and released with the speed of the eye and its capacity for optic illusion. We were caught in the shuttered lens, first one and then another, and because of our disguises we were all familiar strangers. We were a mixed bag of cardboard cutout figures, enlarged, elongated shadows cast against the dunes. We were out of history, out of context, larger than life, transformed into other beings.

Mac seemed quite capable of gracing an eighteenth-century drawing room. I could see him coming home to the family chateau and trying to explain what it was all about, this American Revolution, and what it might have to do with the future of France. Nowhere to be seen tonight was the bearded, binoculared, blue-jeaned bird watcher. That was the disguise and this the reality. But if he was neither bird watcher nor French nobleman, then who in reality was Mac?

James, in his half-spectacles, seemed totally sighted and wise. The wisdom of the politician and the sadness of the professional diplomat that James had once hoped to be mingled with Franklin who had been both. Poor Richard, now a rich man, who perhaps would have liked to be a boy again buying a bit of bread for a penny.

Captain Fairley, the salt of the sea, was transformed into a Virginia country gentleman on his plantation. He was a father figure extraordinary.

Mrs. Fairley was the most surprising of all. For one flashing, bright instant she was no longer raw and worn but pretty—sitting, her sewing in her lap, smiling as she looked lovingly at Tibba and Emma making patterned magic with their sparklers. She held her head high like a person of confidence and self-esteem.

I could not see myself but I knew I too could not look like myself if all the others were different. I could only hope that I did not betray the hurt and pain that were so near the surface. It was there, I couldn't deny it. I had not gotten over James, I had just put the pain out of sight and covered it with a paper-thin shell.

At last the little girls gave up playing at being beautiful ladies and were delighting in being themselves again. Only Miss Baby and Pompey looked and were forever themselves. Miss Baby sat by a hamper, her eyes round, unblinking, china blue, Miss Baby who never winked at reality, Miss Baby who, if truth be told, looked slightly damp from the sea air and Pompey who, although it was past his bedtime, was happy to be with the people he loved, for what was dear, old, black Pompey if not loyal and loving.

Ever-vigilant Pompey, though somewhat hard of hearing and failing in sight, would, if we had been threatened, have perceived the danger before any of us.

When the fireworks were all used up we sat closer to the fire and sang songs while Mac played an accompaniment on his banjo. We sang "Someone's in the Kitchen with Dinah," and

"She'll be Comin' 'Round the Mountain," and "Yankee Doodle Dandy," and several verses of "What Shall We Do with a Drunken Sailor." As the night grew colder we grown-ups held our mugs of black coffee to warm our innards and our hands.

Sometime during the singing James had moved closer to me until we sat almost like a pair apart. And so when he spoke he could do so without being overheard.

"I'll miss you," James said. And my retarded heart gave a bump and then began to pound.

"When do you go?" I asked, steadying my coffee with both hands.

"Tomorrow."

"So soon." It was a statement more than a question.

"Yes. The hospital has a room for me."

"I see." I bent my head. I didn't want to run the risk of anyone seeing my face.

"I'll be back as soon as I can," James said softly. I knew he meant to reassure me although it was none of my affair where he went or when. "I'll try to be back for Emma's birthday."

"I know you must go, I understand." I gulped some coffee quickly and it burned in my throat.

James then undid all my resolution for self-discipline. He reached out and touched my arm. His touch burned hotter than the coffee.

"Before I go there is something I want you to do for me."

He had not touched me in all the time I had been here, not even to shake hands. It startled me to find his touch like an electric shock. In the course of my life people had touched me with no reaction on my part at all, but one kind word and one touch from James and I would have done anything he asked. Perhaps he knew that and that was why he touched me.

"Let the others go on up to the house before us. Make some excuse to stay behind with me."

At least for that moment we were close again, bound in intimacy. Then the intimacy vanished. It was dispelled as quickly as it had begun.

Mac interrupted us. "Hey you two, more coffee?"

"No, thank you," James said, taking his hand away from my arm.

As it turned out I did not have to invent any excuse to stay behind. It worked out as simply as if it had all been arranged. Mac observed that Emma and Tibba looked sleepy and he offered to carry them up to their beds. They were tired, their eyes half-closed, and were enchanted with his proposal.

This left Captain and Mrs. Fairley with all the pots and pans to deal with. It seemed natural enough that I should come along with James. The Captain offered to come down again for him but I said there was no need to make another trip. I said I would walk up with Mr. Hand.

"Is that all right, sir?" Captain Fairley asked James. "Sure you don't want me to come back for you?"

"No need," James said evenly. It was almost like a command. "When we get up to the house I'll ring for you if I need you."

Mac set off with the girls, one on each hip, their arms around his neck. He carried them as easily as if they were two sacks of sugar. Then Captain and Mrs. Fairley went off laden with the household goods. Pompey hesitated for a moment, holding back in case James wanted him and then, old party that he was, he opted for home and bed.

As I watched them go I found I was keyed up. The excitement was not without an element of pleasure. I wondered what it was that James wanted of me. The others were out of sight before he spoke again.

"Have they gone then?"

I looked at him. It was hard sometimes to remember that he could not see. "Yes," I said.

"Thank you for staying." And without any more ado he told me what it was he wanted. Of all the things I might have thought of, this one would never have occurred to me.

"I want you to take me to the old boathouse."

He might as well have asked me to take him to China.

"Take you to the boathouse?" I echoed stupidly.

"Yes. I want to get into Caroline's studio. I can't do it on my own and I don't want anyone else to know I've gone there."

I wondered why James did not want the Captain to take him, but I didn't ask and he didn't tell me. He stood, and as a gesture of his helplessness he took off his spectacles and put them in his pocket. For the first time he seemed to me to be totally blind and defenseless.

"You will have to lead me," he said.

I took his arm as if it were the other way around and he was escorting me home from an evening party. We went slowly up over the dunes toward the path. We went away from the last glow and warmth of the fire. What a wonderful gift Prometheus had stolen for us all.

It was a clear night. There was a first-quarter moon, a small crescent, bright and promising. I went with care, finding our footing with caution. As we walked I tried to imagine that we were any couple out for an evening stroll. I imagined that we had been to a fancy dress ball to honor the Fourth of July.

In truth we must have looked demented or at best absurd. What would people think if they could see the Statue of Liberty and Benjamin Franklin out for a stroll?

At the junction of the paths which led either to the house or down to the old boathouse, I decided that carrying the torch was quite unnecessary. I put it behind a plum bush, thinking I could get it tomorrow. Then we walked along down toward the boathouse without conversation. I think both of us were aware of a strain in keeping our footing. The stars were as bright as diamonds. They winked in an astral conspiracy overhead.

The sound of our footsteps changed its tune when we went from sand to hard-packed path to the scattering shingle of the pebbled beach. I felt James close to me. He had once walked with his arm around me and I knew I fitted beside him as snug and tight as Adam's rib. It hurt to be so close to him and I found I was short of breath. I had great difficulty breathing properly when I was with James, some constriction of the chest. I remembered that other time as if it were a fairy tale or a dream recalled. Then we had not been able to stop talking. We had had everything to share. We had had no secrets, or so I had thought. All the clichés of lovers we had reshaped and rephrased until they were new and shining. We had had great expectations of a life together. But in the end of all it had only been my expectation, not James's. I was in pain and there seemed no cure.

The doctors said that in time Emma might be all right again. In time James might see again. But time had not made me right again. All I could say for time was that it passed.

Now tonight, in a little time, we had come to the boathouse. At the two large doors I paused. "You'll have to tell me where to go."

"Yes," James said, "I remember the way." He pushed open one of the large doors and we went into the dark. It was now a case of the blind leading the blind.

In the center of the boathouse I perceived a docking. Beyond there were two slatted doors which opened onto the cove. The boathouse was a big garage for a boat. The square in the center was filled with water. Around the water ran a three-sided walk, a space for sailors' tack.

"To the left," James whispered, as one does in the dark,

"there is a staircase. It leads up to Caroline's studio. The key is on the riser of the third step. It's hanging on a hook."

I closed the door behind us. I didn't think we had been followed but it seemed a wise precaution. It would not do for anyone to see the open door and come to investigate. We were now in the smothering heat sealed in with the damp and the smell of chandler's wax and rope and sail. The stale water in the docking was fetid and there was a clinging odor of oil and gasoline.

We went hand in hand around toward the left. I was not able to see clearly so that when a shape appeared it took a moment before the bizarre became the commonplace and everyday. Something loomed large and forbidding and only when I looked again did I see it was an oil drum. A sail seemed an angel of death, the rowboat a monster standing against the wall. In this enclosure I felt that I was inundated by the damp and the dark. The place was as bad as the desert for the making of mirages.

I bent down and my fingers found the steps. I counted them—one, two, three. There, below the rim of the third step, was the key just as James said it would be.

What he hadn't told me was that the steps running up to the studio had no handrail. From that open stair one could fall as easily as one could climb. One could fall and hit the rough planking of the floor of the boathouse and pitch into the water.

If I had been on my own I would have clung like a limpet to the inside wall, but in this adventure I was playing the role of the protector so it was I who took the open side and put James safe against the wall. It was, I supposed, the sort of thing that made his blindness so humiliating to him. James, who had always stood between others and harm, now had to be led sightless in a wilderness of shameful dependency.

And I, while I usurped his place and his function, did not relish the experience. By the time we came to the door of the studio I found I had been clutching the key in such a tight grasp that I nearly had to pry my fist open to get it out. It seemed the key was symbolic of lost hope.

I put the key into the lock and turned it. I heard the click of the sliding bolt; the door opened slowly, creaking on its hinges as if it were being violated by force, a rape of the lock. But even if Pope had been there to chide me for my misuse of title I would not have been comforted. I was afraid. We stood in the doorway, both James and I breathing quickly, not so much from the climb as from the fear and the excitement.

For that first instant I couldn't see the room before me or the stairs behind me. Then, as my eyes became accustomed to another dimension, I saw the outlines of windows and above me the shape of a skylight cut into the roof. Through the skylight shone a sliver of a new moon and the light of the new moon was augmented by bright stars.

"Can you see anything?" James asked.

"Yes," I said. "The moonlight is bright enough for that." It seemed the depth and width of sadness that I could see the moon and James could not. I wondered if he would be offended if I sat him next to the round table that was the centerpiece of the room. Before I could suggest it, James spoke.

"Now," James said, and his head moved from side to side as if he were surveying the room. "And now we must find it."

"What?" I asked.

"I don't know." He smiled a remote, thin smile as if the secret was a joke only he could appreciate. "I won't know what it is I am looking for until you see it." It was a joke but a poor one.

"James," I said, "I'm more than willing to do whatever you want but I can't help you if you don't tell me any more than that."

"I can't." James put out his hands in a wide circle of air. He

was reaching into space, into the unknown, with nothing in his
reach for him to hold onto. "Somewhere here in this room is the
answer to a riddle, the solution to a mystery. I don't know what
it is. I only know that it's here somewhere. I know it's here
because I've thought about it hour after hour, over and over ever
since the day Caroline died. I don't know what it is exactly that
I'm looking for. I don't know that if I had my own two eyes I'd
know it when I saw it, but I know it's here. I can't tell you any
more, Martha. I don't think even if I did know more I should
tell you."

"Why ever not?"

"Because if I find it it could be dangerous."

"To whom?" I was astonished by everything James had said.

"Please, I don't want to tell you any more."

"All right," I said. "You keep your secret." I knew that
whatever tortured question-and-answer game James had been
playing with himself he was absolutely sincere. He was in
terrible and true earnest. "Where am I to begin?"

James thought for a moment. "Yes," he said, satisfied with his
decision. "The best thing is to tell me everything that you see.
First the general and then the specific. Tell me everything,
don't leave out anything."

It was, I thought, a game of "I Spy." Here, in this room, there
was a hidden object. Only the game was made more difficult
because the person who had hidden the object was dead in the
sea. It was Caroline's studio and it was Caroline who had hidden
the object; and it was up to me to find it, whatever it was.

"It is a very large room," I began. "There are windows
facing out onto the harbor. If you had a powerful glass you
could see the mainland. There is a skylight. It must give a good
light for a painter. There are smaller windows on the right and
to the left there is a door going into a bath and a closet dressing

room. Along the back wall is an open kitchen and a serving counter.

"It is a room that's been faced with a wall covering and painted stark white. The roof is beamed, the original beams I should think. The floor is painted a cherry red and there are a few small rugs scattered about. There are two large armchairs and a long sofa which could be used for a bed. On it is a printed India cotton. It is obviously a studio, an artist's work place. Even though it's been unused you can smell the oil paints and the turpentine.

"In the center of the room, like the focal point in a painting, is a large round table. It has a green baize cloth on it that falls to the floor and another short round cloth on the top. On the table is a lamp and a collection of bibelots—shells, a bird's skull, and a starfish. Around the table is an arrangement of chairs and stools and alongside of them are small tables for drinks. The whole studio has been well thought out. It's all very comfortable.

"Hanging from the beams are some mobiles of seabirds and more starfish shapes. They seem to be a motif of Caroline's." I had said her name without hesitation. "They are some of her work, aren't they?" I asked.

"Yes," James said. "Caroline was very talented. Some of her paintings were quite good. She loved the sea and the island. She loved this place." He paused. "There was nothing Caroline couldn't do if she set her mind to it."

I hurried on to describe the lighting fixtures fastened on the corners of the beams. They were positioned so as to focus in cross lighting toward different points on the walls.

"Caroline," James said, "used to give herself one-woman shows. She changed the exhibits to match her moods."

It seemed to me that in this domain of hers Caroline had made up her own rules for life. I suppose there was no reason she should not rule absolute. It was her island, her boathouse, her paintings, but it made me shudder to think of holding exhibitions for oneself. It meant she was excluding the viewer, as if an audience was unimportant to her.

Yet she had not been a dilettante. She had worked and worked hard, one saw the evidence. All along the counter facing out onto the cove there was paint and canvas. The brushes and the supplies, all tidily and neatly put away, were ample for a dozen artists. I didn't think I had ever seen an artist's studio which was in such perfect order.

I wondered if this passion for order was some further extension of Caroline's personality, just as the books that filled the shelves along the right wall were a reflection of her taste.

"Caroline used to spend most of her time here." James's voice sounded rough with remembered emotion. "Before we were married and before the house was renovated this was her place of refuge. It was a sanctuary from that old house that was falling down from rot and damp. She worked here, slept here; she and her brother made this their real home."

"Did you know her brother?"

"No, he was dead before I met her."

"I never think of Caroline's having a brother," I said. "It seems that she was always on her own."

"Oh, she had a brother all right. Her brother Miles was the black sheep of the Fanner tree. And believe me they had several dark rams before him, but Miles took the honors. He was younger than Caroline and as handsome as the devil himself. She adored him as others adored her. She doted on Miles. She took care of him. She spoiled him. She got him out of scrapes only to have him go and find a new and usually worse situation to get into. They lived here on their own like Brontës on the moor, turned in upon themselves with only Mrs. Fairley to look after them.

"It was only after Miles died that Caroline came to stay with Sara in Boston. That was when we met." James was silent for a moment, his face turned dark, his mouth working. Something in James went out of control when he mentioned Caroline. Then all his emotions were too near the surface, too exposed. His memories were too painful, they boiled hot and scalding, and when he said her name they overflowed and passed the rim and bounds of his discipline.

I said nothing. It was hard enough to have to watch and to know that he had not forgotten and would never forget Caroline, that she was there between us. I could not compete with Caroline alive and I could compete with her even less now that she was dead.

"She used this studio as her refuge," James went on. His voice was hoarse and his words slurred together. "She came here even after we were married and she would stay here hour after hour painting. She was a good painter, I think. You have seen some of her work."

I couldn't remember if I had.

"In the library," James said.

I thought back to the library and looked about the walls in my memory. Then I saw it in my mind's eye. Yes, of course, that painting would have to be Caroline's. "The seascape," I said. "The ship in the fog."

"Yes."

I felt as rudderless as the ship in Caroline's painting. I was lost in the dark. I felt I had lost my way forever in a sea of mists created by Caroline. "Well then," I said briskly, to hide my feelings, "that is the general outline of the room. Where shall I begin on the specifics?"

James thought for a moment. "The kitchen. Begin with the kitchen. There is a flashlight in the drawer by the sink."

I hesitated a moment. "James, can you tell me nothing? I don't have any idea of what to look for."

Then he reached out for me. His hand found my arm and then my hand. "Believe me, I don't know what I am looking for. I can only see with your eyes. Look for something ordinary, something deceptively simple. Look for something that is so simple it could be overlooked."

"All right," I said, but it was not much to go on. I took the flashlight from the drawer by the sink and I began my search. I looked in the kitchen cabinets, on the shelves, in the drawers, in the storage space beneath the sink. I gave a sort of running commentary throughout.

"It is well stocked, one could live here for months without going to the mainland for supplies. There are stores enough for a winter. Meat in tins and fruits and vegetables. There's powdered milk and coffee and flour and jams and tea and spices and cartons of cigarettes." They were all Gitanes; I didn't have to ask if they were Caroline's brand, I knew they must be.

"Caroline bought in quantity," James said. "She liked to order by the case or by the gross. It was a reflection, I suppose, of a time when she had been so poor and had had to count the cost of everything."

I didn't feel it was my place to comment but I did wonder just why Caroline was the poor relation. I remembered Sara had told me some story about two Fanner brothers of long ago. One wanted to leave the island and go to Boston to seek his fortune, while the other had been sure the thing to do was to stay at home on the island. It was at a time when whaling was over but the one who stayed could not accept that the old days were done. Families were strange and quarrels ran deep. Obviously the Fanner who had gone to Boston had done well and the one who had stayed home had not. Perhaps it was pride that had prevented Caroline from asking Sara for money. But after

Caroline's brother Miles had died, then for some reason it had
been easier or at least possible to accept Sara's hospitality and
help.

Certainly when Caroline began to spend the money she had
gotten from Sara and from her marriage she spent on a grand
scale, first on the house and then on the appointments.

From the kitchen and the cupboards I went to the linen
cupboards. Here there were linen sheets and the finest towels
and blankets, all folded in beautifully lined and scented drawers.
And in the bath the supply of soap and toilet paper and bath salts
and beauty aids was more than adequate for a short stay. This
was enough for a siege. I looked in the medicine cabinet. There
were toothbrushes and toothpaste and jars and jars from a local
chemist.

"Here's something," I said, unscrewing a lid and smelling the
contents. "Here, I'll let you smell." I held out the jar to James.
It was a distinctive medicinal odor but I didn't know what it
was.

James smelled and thought for a moment, then he said, "Yes,
it's for burns."

"But why are there so many?" I protested. "You'd have to be
badly burned to need all this." And I could have cut my tongue
out. I remembered what James had said about Caroline. The last
time he had seen Caroline her face had been in the flames.
Surely even though I wished Caroline had never existed I had
not spoken out of pure malice. I preferred to think I was merely
thoughtless.

"Caroline had a fear of being burned." James spoke without
emotion.

And I accepted it as reasonable. It was as reasonable as my
fear of heights or my fear of water. It was only coincidence that
her worst fears had come true.

James continued evenly and factually. "I remember once

Caroline got a small burn at the kitchen stove and she put almost a jar of ointment on it and bandaged it with yards and yards of bandaging."

"Well," I said, "that's all in the bathroom." I didn't think it necessary to tell James there was a carton of bandages there now. I went on to the closets in the dressing room. Neatly hanging in perfect order were slacks and shirts and a transparent container of sweaters. Her robe and nightgowns and lingerie were in quilted satin compartments, every item placed with care. The only flaw to be found was a rim of grease on the neckband of her dressing gown. I looked at it wondering if it was of any significance and decided it was just some night cream generously applied after a day by the sea.

"What next?" I asked James.

He thought for a moment. It seemed that we were at the end of places to look. But I could not have been more wrong.

"Tell me," he asked, "what is your impression of the studio now you've had a chance to look at it?"

"It's all in perfect order," I said, and then I faltered.

"Go on."

"It's as if Caroline were still here. It's as if the studio had only been shut up while the owner was on holiday." I waited to see how James would react.

"I'm sure that's a fair description," he said. I felt him longing to see the studio for himself.

"After it happened," James said, "after the accident and Caroline was dead, Mrs. Fairley came down and tidied it and locked it up. I couldn't bear coming here. I couldn't face the truth. There were too many memories. Can you understand that?"

I nodded dumbly. I couldn't answer. I felt the tears well up in my eyes and my throat was tight with pain. He would never get over Caroline. He would never forget her.

"I suppose," he said thoughtfully, "that I put it off because I had hoped to see for myself what it might be that was hidden here. You see this blindness of mine is hysterical. Or so the doctors tell me. There is no reason, no medical reason, why I cannot see. The physical damage was mended months ago. Still the fact remains that I cannot see and so I must ask you to look now wherever I tell you. No matter how foolish it seems to you."

I swallowed and felt my throat relax and I blinked back the tears. "Where shall I look next?" I asked, and I tried to sound cheerful and willing.

"Behind the mirrors."

I looked around the studio. "But there are no mirrors."

James frowned. "That's strange, there were two. I distinctly remember a large oval one on the right wall between the windows and another by the door."

I looked and I saw the outlines of where they had hung, an oval outline and a small square. Then I went on to hunt for the missing mirrors. At last I found them in the back of the closets covered with blankets.

"Mrs. Fairley probably put them away for safekeeping," I said, but I did not altogether believe my explanation. "Why don't you ask her?"

"No," James said slowly. "I think not. No one but you must know we were here tonight."

"All right," I said. "Is that the end of it?"

"By no means." James smiled and it was a smile of grim determination. He asked me to look under the rugs, in the vases, and around the moldings. Then I pulled out the paintings that were stacked by the wall at the end of the long counter. As I pulled them out I described each one as I came to it.

I was no critic, no proper judge, but I knew that they were all most original. Caroline had had a style of her own, her own view of the world. The colors were harsh and bright and pure. Some were almost brutal. There were stark bits of driftwood set on a solitary beach. The sea and the sky and the birds were all creatures of her landscapes. Then suddenly, after so many canvases full of sea and air and birds and sand, I turned round a large canvas and I gasped. It was the first portrait I had seen. It had no face but the outline had been sketched in charcoal and a few colors had been put on as an experiment. There was no doubt who it was, or rather who it would have been. It would have been a portrait of Mac.

"What is it?" James asked. "What have you found?" He was so eager, so hopeful I had found his hidden object.

"It's the portrait of a man," I said. "It's not finished but perhaps you can remember the painting." I couldn't lie to James, but I didn't want to tell him it was Mac. I was not sure why but I was reluctant.

"Tell me more," James demanded. "Tell me all you see."

"I think," I said, because I had no choice, "that it may be the beginning of a portrait of Mac." And I waited for his reaction.

"Oh." James did not sound nearly so surprised as I had thought he would. "Perhaps it was something Caroline had just started before Easter. When Mac first came to the island Caroline did not take to him. She felt he was an intruder. She was used to the other man who did the bird watching. He was a dear old duffer and Mac's manner jarred her. She said she felt Mac was some sort of spy. Then after awhile Mac so charmed her and they got on better and he started coming down here in the afternoons. I suppose he must have been sitting for her."

"I see," I said, but I did not. Emma had been at great pains to tell me Caroline had not liked Mac and now James had said as much. Both seemed to accept that they had become friends but it did not ring true to me, not from what I knew of Mac or had been told of Caroline. I could not believe that they would ever get on very well. I went on turning through the paintings until I came to the last and the largest. It was a double portrait of a man and a woman. The woman was in the foreground and the man stood behind her, his hands on her shoulders.

Her face was so beautiful it took my breath away. It made me feel as if I had had the wind knocked out of me. The features were not perfect; they were, if taken separately, something askew and at odds, but added together in her face they made perfection. Around the face, framing such rare beauty, was a mane of tawny hair. It made me believe that Caroline was some creature from time unremembered. The man also was of another time and space. He might have been the other side of her coin, the mirror image of the woman. They were elementals, spirits materialized to seduce and ensnare the world.

"You're very quiet," James said softly.

I cleared my throat and tried to speak but I felt their four eyes burn into me. Then I said, "The portrait is of a man and a woman. They are young and very beautiful. Their eyes are their most extraordinary feature, almond-shaped like Mongol raiders from the north. The eyes seem to follow one about the room.

"His hair is dark but hers is a tawny blonde. It catches the light and changes hue. They are enigmatic, inscrutable; they are like a pair of Giocondas smiling because they know something that the rest of us do not. It is their secret and theirs alone."

Her shoulders were bare and the hands of the man were on them. What I did not say to James was that the man held her in an embrace so intimate, so full of knowledge of her body that they might have been performing some ritualistic act before me and I could not have been more shocked. Nothing could have been more revealing than what I saw before me now. Their relationship was no secret at all. At the bottom of the portrait there were the words "Tibba and Dickon." I stared in disbelief. The witch and the devil.

I had only seen polite society photographs of Caroline before, posed in elegant clothes for the Sunday papers or for *Vogue*, but I knew this was the Caroline that James had seen and who had done as she pleased with him. And, as surely as I knew the woman was Caroline, I knew that the man was her brother Miles.

I said nothing for a long time. I could only stare at the portrait. There seemed nothing more that I could say.

"Something has upset you," James said. "What is it?"

I couldn't answer.

"Tell me what it is," he said insistently.

"The portrait of Caroline and Miles. It is seeing the two of them together like that."

"Yes," he said. "I remember the portrait well." He carefully betrayed nothing of his emotions. I could not imagine how James must have felt the first time he had seen it.

"You're frightened," James said insistently. "Why?"

"I don't know." I hesitated and then blurted out, "I feel I shouldn't look at them. I feel as if I had violated some secret ceremony. It is as if they had banded together to exorcise the curse they knew was put on Fanner's Island and the Fanners. I feel that they were always in communication with each other. Even after Miles died I feel Caroline made contact with him in some spirit world."

"But that's nonsense," James said. "Caroline never believed in seances. It was a joke. It was a joke, I assure you." James obviously thought I was being foolish but I persisted.

"What was a joke?"

"It was a joke when she pretended to be clairvoyant. Oh, you know, cards and Ouija boards and dim lights and all that sort of thing but it was only a put-on. It wasn't real. It was a great joke and it passed the time and amused her. She'd come out here with Miles and Mrs. Fairley when they were all living on the island and they'd sit around that big table, hands pressed together, and have mock seances. It was something to do on wet, cold afternoons. They amused themselves and they didn't do anyone else any harm. Caroline laughed when she told me about those seances. She threw back that great mane of hair and she laughed and said it was a magic table."

And then James stopped short and his hand went suddenly to his head. It was as if he had been struck with a thunderbolt of the gods. He was now as pale as a spirit summoned from another world.

"Of course," he said. "That's it. It's the table, something to do with the table." He took my arm and held it hard enough to bruise.

"Please," I said, "you're hurting me."

"I'm sorry." He let me go but his mind was not on my injury. "Take the lamp and things off the table."

I did as James asked. I took the lamp and put it on the floor and I removed the objects and put them beside the lamp. Then I took off the cloth. It was no magic table from what I could see of it. It was a large, round, golden oak table like thousands of others.

"Well," James demanded, "what do you see?"

"A table," I said. "Nothing more."

Still undaunted he said, "Look underneath, look at the base."

The base was a tri-legged affair. It didn't match the table but it was nothing unusual.

James was not to be put off with that. "There is something else," he said, "there must be. Look, Martha, look."

I was underneath the table playing the flashlight up at the underside before I saw it. There, between the tabletop and the base, was a join and beside the join a shallow drawer.

"Yes," I said. "Just a minute. I think I have found something." I opened the drawer, pulling it out to its full length, and then I put my hand in cautiously, as if I expected to find snakes and bats and toads. In fact what I had found was a book, an old leather-bound book, and in gold letters on the face of it was written *Journal.* I stood up, pleased, hopeful that what I had found would be what James wanted. I described the book.

"Yes," he said, "that's it. I'm sure of it." But he did not look pleased. He looked very, very sad.

And I added, "There is an envelope in the book, a square manila envelope, something official by the look of it."

"Give it to me," he said sharply. "And don't look inside. Don't open it."

I had felt proud of my find and in want of praise and now James was sharp and abrupt.

"I'm sorry," he said. "But it would be better for you to forget all about the book and the envelope. Forget we were even here tonight."

"If you like," I said, and I put the cloth and the lamp and the objects back on the table trying to place them just where they had been so that if Mrs. Fairley should come to clean she would not suspect anyone had been here.

"All right," I said. "I've done. Is there something else or can we go now?" I had not been aware before of how great a strain this game of "I Spy" had been for both of us. I was ready to go just as soon as I had put away the canvases. In my haste to leave this place I had almost forgotten the flashlight. I returned it to the kitchen cabinet and quickly came back toward James. As we started for the door I saw something so unexpected that I screamed. Something white glowing in the dark like some ectoplasm from a past seance. It hovered before the door and changed shape in a ghostly fashion.

"What is it?" James demanded.

"It's right there." I gasped. "Right there before us."

"What?" James's voice was sharp.

I knew it was nothing that James could see or do anything about. It was my vision, my terror. I reached out quickly before my courage failed me and I touched at it and then I laughed.

"What is it?"

"It's a scarf," I said weakly. "It's nothing but a white scarf. That's all. It was hanging on the back of the door. I didn't see it before because we were facing into the room. It's nothing, James, just a long white scarf and my nerves playing tricks on me."

"It was Caroline's scarf," James said. "I gave it to her."

There was nothing anywhere that had not belonged to Caroline.

We went down the steps slowly in the darkness. I held James and he held the journal, guarding it as closely as I was guarding him. I put the key back on the hook below the stair. I felt safe now, protected by the dark. We left the boathouse and made our way back toward the silent and sleeping house. It must be later than I had thought, for all the lights were out.

I held to James and he held to the book and the envelope. I didn't ask him how, if he could not see, he was going to read the journal or see what was in the envelope. I didn't ask because if he had wanted me to know he would have told me. In some melodramatic way I knew he believed that this night had not been without its dangers and that he did not want to put me into any further peril.

We slipped into the house quietly. I opened the door to the library for him and whispered, "Do you want me to call Captain Fairley for you?"

"No," James said. "I'll be all right. I want to put the journal away before I do anything else. I'll ring for him if I need him."

James held me for a moment. I could feel his breath, short and warm, on my cheek and I could feel myself waiting, wanting to be drawn closer into an embrace, but all he did was say, "Thank you, Martha."

Suddenly I was chilled, standing there in the hall in my absurd bit of sheet wound round me for Miss Liberty's costume. The party was over and I must have looked as bedraggled as I felt. I was glad to say goodnight, to shut the door to the library. I knew my way in the house well enough now to find my way upstairs without turning on a light.

I was halfway up the stairs before I heard a great thud and what I thought was a cry from James, then a groan of pain. I stood on the stairs still and cold with fear. Something was wrong, very wrong. I did not want to offend James by finding him tripped over some bit of furniture in the dark but every instinct told me it was something more than that which had caused him to cry out. I ran down the stairs and opened the door to the library.

As I opened the door something out of the dark room crashed against my chest. It knocked me flat to the floor, the weight of it held me for a moment and then was gone. I did not try to follow for suddenly my entire attention was riveted on what I saw in the library.

The hangings around the alcove bed were ablaze. The fire was well along, the flames lapping up the material into deadly ash. I smelled the smoke, acrid, eating at the linings of my lungs. The final horror was that I could not see James.

Some old Girl Scout training or some past discipline of fire drill from school took over automatically. I leapt into the room and pulled first one hanging and then the other from the sides of the bed. I made them into tightly rolled balls and prayed that the flames would be contained in them while I carried them to the bathroom, dumped them into the tub, and then ran both taps and shower at full force.

I was singed and shaking with a sick fear. It was some relief to hear the hissing as the water soaked through the fabric to extinguish the fire. Then and only then did I dare to go back into the library to look for James.

I saw him dimly in the light from the fireplace. He was slumped by the desk. I bent down and held him in my arms. His head had hit the edge of the desk and there by the scar, new healed from his Easter experience, was a gash in his forehead. Blood ran down his cheek. I saw the pulse throbbing in his temple.

His Benjamin Franklin glasses had fallen out of his pocket and were shattered beside him. There was a key in the desk drawer. James must have been putting the journal in the drawer before he had fallen. But why had he fallen and how had the fire started in the bed hangings unless, and I had to face it, there had been someone else in the room.

I felt James stir in my arms. His eyes opened but it must have been of little use to him since he could see nothing.

"James," I said. "James, it's Martha. Don't try to move. You fell and hit your head. You were putting away the journal. Do you remember?"

He nodded, his head turning as if he could see and was looking about for some bearings to locate himself to consciousness.

"Please," I said, "if you'll stay still I'll get you a drink and then you can tell me what happened."

After I had given him a drink and gotten him into a chair he still seemed dazed but he picked up the thread for himself.

"I had said goodnight to you." He began slowly, carefully finding his way. "I thanked you and then I came in and I went over to the desk to put the journal in a drawer. Good Lord!" James stopped. "The key, where's the key?"

"It's safe," I reassured him. "It's in the desk drawer lock."

He sighed with relief. "Then I heard something. There was a crash, a lamp must have fallen and started the fire." He waited to see how I would accept his explanation.

"That's not good enough," I said. "The lamp was not lit. It was dark when you came in. You didn't just fall against the desk and hit your head. Someone hit you. Just as someone hit me when I opened the door. There was someone in this room who knocked you down, who set the fire and then hit me on the way out."

"That's impossible. There was no one in this room. There couldn't have been." I didn't know why James was so obstinate in his denial, but he would not admit there had been anyone here.

"Then what," I demanded, "started the fire?"

"Pompey." James seemed bent on the idea. "Pompey must have been by the fire. I startled him and he hit against me and then when you opened the door he bounded out. You know he's not steady on his feet and he is capable of knocking cinders out of the fire with that great tail of his."

"James, I won't argue with you but I am not so silly as to believe that it was Pompey. No, James. There was someone here. Someone whom you did not see and someone I did not see but someone all the same."

He made a sharp gesture and then put his hand to his head. He winced in pain. His head hurt badly, I could see that, but he would not let up. He said, "Promise me, on your honor, swear you will not tell anyone you were here tonight. You promise?"

"All right, I promise, but . . ."

"No." He stopped me. "There's little enough I've ever done for you or can ever do now." His face was pale and haggard.

"You're badly hurt," I said. "I'll get something for your head." In the bathroom I found some bandages next to some ointment like the ointment that had been in Caroline's studio. I made James as comfortable as I could. Then I asked him if he wanted me to call Captain Fairley before I left him. He shook his head.

"I'll make it right with him in the morning. Remember your promise. You'll not tell anyone you were here with me tonight."

"I'll remember."

I stood by the door not wanting to say goodnight and having no other choice and then for no particular reason I asked, "James?"

"Yes."

"How did Miles die?"

"In an automobile accident."

"Oh."

"He crashed the car through a guard rail and went over a cliff. The car exploded and he was burned to death."

I felt suddenly drained of sense and reason. It was horror that filled my mind. Miles and Caroline and the Tibba of long ago, and now tonight it might have been James dead in a fire.

I left him then more sure than ever that the fire had not been caused by old Pompey. There had been someone in James's room, I was sure of it.

~ Six ~

Next morning I went down to the landing to see James and Captain Fairley off. James was pale and drawn. He didn't mention the night before. He said nothing about the journal or the fire, but I noticed he had a package under his arm and assumed he was taking the journal with him. He looked unfamiliar in his suit. It was strange to see him in city clothes. He seemed transformed into yet another person, a prominent man, a power in the great world.

I stood on the landing, James on the deck of the boat. There was a division, a gap of water between us. He could not see me but I saw him bright and clear.

"Take care," I said.

"You too," he said. "I'll be back as soon as I can."

It was extraordinary how painful the parting was. It would have been even worse if Captain Fairley had not treated us to one of his steady streams of conversation. Bless the Captain, he was never at a loss for words. I supposed I felt so bereft because it seemed a repeat of that other parting, a sort of emotional feedback. That other time, when I had left Boston, I hadn't known I would not see James again or that he would marry

Caroline. Now I knew that even though she was dead he still belonged to her.

I stood on the landing watching after him until the boat was out of sight. And as I stood there I felt a sense of total unreality. The sun, the sea, the sky, were all bent out of shape, distorted in my vision. I knew I was tired but then it occurred to me that I was crying.

I thought about last night and all that had happened. I knew James had considered the discovery of the journal and the envelope of some singular significance, while I considered that the fire had not been an accident. He had made me promise not to tell anyone I had been with him. He had not told me why, or why the journal was so important. I knew he had not wanted me to come to the island. It had been the Foundation's idea to ask me here. At first I had felt rebuffed but now I believed the reason he had not wanted me to come here was because he did not want me mixed up in a situation which might prove too difficult for me.

I hoped that James would be back before Emma's birthday. I did not feel in any way adequate to cope with Emma's disappointment when her birthday arrived and Caroline did not. It was all confused and distorted. In my state of mind no wonder the landscape seemed warped and bent toward destruction.

I knew that no matter what James had refused to say there was a great deal going on I did not understand. It was like an exhibition of sleight of hand. Things appeared and seemed to be and then vanished, leaving me uncertain. I was sure that there had been someone in my room that first night. Just as sure as I was that there had been someone in James's room last night, someone who had set that fire. It was not an easy thought to accept, for it meant that there was someone on the island who wished James ill. I should be glad for his sake that he was gone away from the island and out of danger.

Then, somewhere in all this, there was the children's magic which might in the long run be even more harmful than some grown-up's sleight of hand. My mind was in such knots and tangles I would never get my woolly thoughts into a tidy skein.

I went, heavy-hearted and heavy-footed, back up the path toward the house. On the way I intended to pick up the torch I had left at the crossing last night but when I came back to the plum bushes the torch wasn't there. I remembered distinctly that I had put the torch beneath the plum bush. I had not, it was true, looked for it on my way down this morning; all my thoughts had been on James and his departure. But now he was gone and so was the torch.

It was getting on toward noon and the morning mists were being burned away by the sun. The sun was beating down in its brutal, unfeeling passion to dominate the earth. I imagined that I heard a ringing in my ears, an early warning system, a persistent, penetrating signal being sent out to my nerve ends. It was a message that as yet I could not decode. Was it real, this feeling, or was it a form of psychic sunstroke? It was as if the storm warnings were up when I could see no storm coming.

Did it have something to do with the disappearance of the torch or with James and the fire? I wished he was here, I needed him. It seemed a sign of weakness, a sort of sickness. Perhaps this was what my symptoms amounted to, a low fever, a base-grade infection that would not yield to treatment.

In the kitchen Emma and Tibba and Mrs. Fairley were still at the table. The girls had been worn out by their late night and had overslept their usual hour. They were reliving the marvels of their costumes and the wonders of the fireworks when I came in. Sharing the memory of last evening seemed to give them as much pleasure as the event had itself.

Mrs. Fairley glanced up from her work. "They've gone then?" she asked, "Mr. Hand and the Captain?"

"Yes," I said. "They've gone." Now we were a pavilion of women, a totally female household save for Pompey. I didn't count Mac in his lighthouse as household.

"I'll get myself some coffee," I said to no one in particular. I suddenly felt vulnerable and cast adrift in uncharted seas. I wanted for some reason to assert my own being and identity. In the misguided way one has of putting one's foot in it when one is unsure I asked the girls please to finish their breakfast and go and put their costumes away.

Their faces crumpled. From laughter and smiles they were reduced to solemn, miffed feelings. They said they had already put away their costumes in the attic. They had also tidied up their rooms. They made me feel that by speaking out unthinkingly I had spoiled the morning. They assumed the righteous air of the falsely accused.

In an effort to retrieve my good standing I sent them off to the beach saying I must stay and put away my own costume before I could come down. They were, I felt, as pleased to go off without me as I was to have them go. I was evidently not a fit companion to humans today. Even Pompey gave me a wide berth.

When they had gone it occurred to me to ask Mrs. Fairley if she would care to join us on the beach.

"You never get a day off," I said. "You haven't spent a day at the beach since I arrived."

She seemed not to mind my former ill temper. "No," she said. "Thank you but I'm not one for sitting out in the hot sun. Besides, I've got the library to clean."

I waited for some further comment. She did not mention the fire or the burned curtains, which must still be scorched and wet in the bathtub. I felt certain she knew about the fire by this time, but she said nothing. I waited. She was standing at the sink rinsing the breakfast dishes before putting them into the dishwasher. Then, just as I was about to go, she said, as if she had been saving it up like a sweetmeat, "I found your torch. It's by the library door. If you're wanting to put your costume away in the attic you can take it up with you."

I went along to the library and there, sure enough, as Mrs. Fairley had said it would be, was my torch just inside the library door. I didn't want to stay in that room. It reminded me of the night before.

Quickly I went up the stairs to my room to collect the sheet that had been Miss Liberty's robe and her bedraggled and pathetic paper crown. I went down to the far end of the hall and up the narrow steps to the attic. The silence of the empty house with only Mrs. Fairley and me in it rose all around in shock waves.

The attic was hot and airless, a tomb for rubbish of greater or lesser value. The only sound in the attic was a wasp that droned and hummed around its mud nest. In the dim light which slanted in through the narrowed windows it seemed I was in the midst of a jumble sale of history—old sea chests, high-backed Hong Kong rattan chairs, leather-bound trunks, and a peg leg hanging from a rafter—all macabre and, in my present state of mind, distasteful and upsetting. Even an empty parrot's cage caught dust and held no promise of a more lively occupant.

I saw that the girls had indeed put their costumes away in one of the trunks, but a part of Emma's skirt peeped out. They had meant to be neat and tidy but had fallen short of the mark. So much for their good intentions. I opened the trunk and began to make order of their tumbled, hasty chaos.

As I folded and rearranged the costumes my hand hit on something metallic. I lifted out the dresses and there, below the costumes, I saw a candlestick like the one that had been in Caroline's room. Then I saw the rest of the hidden store.

There was a pack of Tarot cards, candles, a box of matches, a

Ouija board, and a book entitled *Magic and Spells*, and I knew with a sick certainty that these must be the games the girls had been playing on that rainy afternoon in the attic. They had spent their time in casting spells while I had played chess with James in the library.

Now that I knew what they had been doing I could not let it go. Emma's idea of reality was already clouded. She might well believe that by magic and spells and a drawing of pentacles they would see Caroline again, that Caroline had not drowned in the sea. I knew I must deal with the situation. I had to do something to prevent Emma and Tibba's playing with these things again.

I put the costumes over the foul and evil dream I had uncovered. I closed the lid of the trunk. I put the torch on a shelf and I went downstairs to find Mrs. Fairley.

She was in the library making up the wall bed. A rug had been placed over the burned portions of the carpet and the windows were wide open. Even so I could still smell the faint odor of the fire. It hung and cloyed the air in the room.

Mrs. Fairley turned when I came in; she seemed neither surprised nor startled to see me. Her eyes were cool and brown windows to a soul I could not fathom.

"Mrs. Fairley, I wonder if I might have a word with you." I sounded stilted. Why should I be so afraid to speak to her? It had to be done.

"If you like."

"It's probably nothing but I think I should say it all the same." I had not begun very well.

She said nothing. I should have been on the attack but I had put myself on the defensive.

"You know Emma is a sensitive, suggestible child. She is certainly a very lonely child. When she lost her mother and father and then lost Caroline she lost her world."

Mrs. Fairley shook her head, as if she could not understand my words. "She has this house and her uncle and all of us."

"And you've been wonderful to her, I know." I rushed on. "I know it's been a good thing too for her to have Tibba to play with." I stopped. I felt like an old horse coming up lame.

Mrs. Fairley sensed my discomfort. "Is this about Tibba, Miss Raynor? Has Tibba done something wrong?"

"No," I said. "It's not that exactly."

"Tibba is a good child. She means to please." Mrs. Fairley sprang to Tibba's defense.

"Yes," I said, "I know that, but she wants to please so much that perhaps she may have done some things which are not for Emma's good. You see Emma has gotten it into her head that Caroline is going to be here on her birthday."

Mrs. Fairley made no reply but her eyes were as hard as stones. She resented my saying anything about Tibba, although why she should I didn't know. I felt I was being as tactful as the occasion demanded.

"Well, you know and I know that is not possible," I went on, determined to see it through. "But Emma does not."

"And Tibba," Mrs. Fairley demanded in return, "what has Tibba to do with it?"

"I think that Tibba, in order to please Emma, has been fostering this idea. I think Tibba has encouraged Emma to believe it might happen."

Mrs. Fairley bit at her lower lip. She gave a nervous cough. It was a habit of hers when she was undecided. Then she said, "Are you sure of what you are saying?"

"I think," I said, "that the two of them, Emma and Tibba, have been playing some unsuitable games." Even as I heard myself say the words they seemed slightly ridiculous. I didn't give myself much credit for doing this at all well.

"You've seen them playing games?" Mrs. Fairley frowned.

"No, I haven't seen them." If I said I had seen a shape, a diagram, a pattern drawn on the sand and then erased it would sound hysterical. If I said that I had heard them giggling and running down the hall away from Caroline's room and had discovered a card and some ash and two burnt candles it would have sounded even more hysterical.

"No," I said, "I haven't seen them playing games but just now, as I was putting away my costume in the attic, I saw that one of the trunks had not been properly closed. I looked inside and I found some Tarot cards and a Ouija board and a book about magic and spells. I know they go up to the attic. They were up there during the storm. I found candles and matches. I don't like the look of it. You can understand that, surely?"

Mrs. Fairley shook her head. It seemed beyond her comprehension. "Those things you mention, the cards and the Ouija board, they've always been here. They were Caroline's. She thought them harmless enough. It amused her to tell fortunes."

"But Emma and Tibba are children. What might be a harmless diversion on a winter's evening for an adult might be dangerous for children, for Emma especially. It would be bad for her if she thinks she can bring Caroline back again."

"Is that what she thinks?"

"I don't know but it would be bad for her if she did. Don't you agree?"

I was almost desperate for some response from Mrs. Fairley. I felt I had to make her give me some commitment. I went on pressing my point home. "Children sometimes fancy that they can see ghosts."

"But there are no ghosts." Mrs. Fairley was obdurate.

"You know it and I know it but not Emma and perhaps not Tibba."

It was Tibba's name that caught Mrs. Fairley's attention. "And you think that what Emma and Tibba do when they are out of sight, you think they play with those things?"

"Yes," I said. "That's what I think. I think they light candles and play at magic and make up little spells to bring Caroline back again."

"Then what's to be done about it?" Mrs. Fairley was being reasonable. I could ask for nothing more.

"I want you to talk with Tibba. I don't want you to accuse her of anything, I don't mean that, I just want you to tell her as plainly as you can that they must not play with magic or spells."

"You want me to take the cards and the book and the Ouija board away?"

"No, I don't want to make too much of it. Just talk with Tibba and later on today I'll have a word with Emma." Mrs. Fairley stood statue still, she gave no indication of what she might be thinking. "Will you do that?" I asked.

"If that's what you want."

"What do you think?"

"Doesn't signify what I think. You're in charge of Emma. You're responsible for what happens to her."

"Yes," I said, "I am, so I would be grateful if you would speak to Tibba."

"Is that all?" She was ready for me to go.

"No, not quite. I was wondering about Tibba; where does she come from?"

"An orphanage on the mainland."

"And Caroline brought her here?"

"Yes. Caroline said that Tibba could stay, that this was to be her foster home. It was settled, you see, but that was when Caroline was alive. Mr. Hand seems to like Tibba well enough and she does what she's told. Do you think she should go, is that it?"

"No, no, nothing of the kind. It's just the name. Is Tibba her real name?"

"Yes. Tibbatha Grey."

"I can't help but think about the legend of the witch who was named Tibba."

"Oh that." Mrs. Fairley seemed relieved. "Tibba's a common name. Lots of Tibbathas in these parts."

"I had never heard it before. Not until I read and heard the story of the witch."

"Well," Mrs. Fairley smiled a caustic smile, "there are no witches nor no ghosts neither. Don't tell me you believe in witches or ghosts?"

"No."

"Well then, it couldn't have been a real witch in the story could it? It was only a story, after all."

"Of course," I said. "But you will talk to Tibba, won't you?"

"If you say so." The conversation had come to an abrupt halt.

"Don't you think it is a good idea? Just to be on the safe side?"

Mrs. Fairley thought for a moment and then she said, "I'll say this. It is not good to play with fire."

And with that as my thought for the day I left Mrs. Fairley to the library and started on down for the sun and the beach and the girls. I had had my little conversation with Mrs. Fairley and I felt as if it had all been for nothing, as if nothing had been solved.

I felt flat, diminished; yet one thing remained constant. Emma must not wake up on her birthday and expect to see Caroline. For Caroline would most certainly not be there. If that belief was not dispelled it would surely do Emma harm. It could do her irreparable harm. If there was any chance, no matter how remote, that Tibba and Emma had been playing at the occult, it must be stopped, and the sooner the better. It would be horrible if Emma came to feel she could materialize Caroline if only she was worthy enough, and good enough, and true enough, to cast a true spell. And to that end I had acted. I had spoken out to Mrs. Fairley.

It was a long, hot day on the beach. I slept or dozed while the girls carried away the ash of last night's fire and picked up the leftover bits of fireworks. They did not want or need my help and I was tired. I dozed and then woke with starts and tremors. Again and again I sat bolt upright as if the unexpected had come and found me napping.

I would have begun to think myself mad if it had not been for old Pompey. He too knew something was not at rights with the universe. He would rise all of a sudden and give little growls and look about him with his old eyes and then, seeing nothing, the hairs of his back would fall and he would sink down to sleep again until the symptoms returned.

We all ate dinner together in the kitchen. It was a subdued meal and as soon as I could I took Emma off with me to my room and left Tibba to Mrs. Fairley. It didn't require much skill to maneuver Emma into the window seat in my room. I sat across from her. We were sorting over new-washed shells. Since it was my conversation I began it, hoping it would be as simple as my looking out the window to the green of the garden and the woods beyond.

"Emma."

"Yes?"

"Did you enjoy the Fourth?"

"Oh yes. It was a lovely party. Miss Baby thought so too."

"What did you like best?"

"The sparklers."

"It will soon be your birthday. What would you like?"

"Presents."

"Besides presents."

"A cake."

"What kind of a cake would you like?"

"Can I have any kind I want?" The prospect seemed to delight her.

"Yes."

"Angel food with a lemon icing. And candles. And ice cream."

"And for presents?" I asked.

"Well, Miss Baby needs some new clothes. She's looking terrible lately. It doesn't matter when she's on the beach all day but she needs some clothes if she is to go anywhere else. And she needs a new wig."

"You could send her to a doll's hospital."

"To a doll's hospital?" Emma's eyes were all round and brown.

"It's a place," I explained, "where they make dolls look as good as new."

"Is that where James has gone?" Emma asked.

"No." I had a sudden pang for James far away in his hospital bed. "No, he's just gone to an ordinary hospital."

"They don't always make people as good as new," Emma said, and her words were backed by her own experience.

"No, but they try."

Emma gave me a most appealing look. "I couldn't be parted from Miss Baby."

I couldn't argue with that sentiment. Miss Baby was Emma's darling and she did not have so much in this life that was dear to her. I took another tack.

"What do you think James will bring you for your birthday?"

"Oh, I know already," Emma said confidently.

"How?"

"I told him what I wanted."

"And what did you ask for? If it's not a secret."

"I want a lot of glue and some cigar boxes."

"Emma!" I had to smile. "You amaze me."

"I need them," Emma said earnestly. "I never have enough glue for the shells and I can't buy cigars by the boxful, I don't have the money."

A great heiress and she did not have the wherewithal to buy glue and boxes for her hobby. It was something that would never occur to me to consider but Emma was, in her own eyes, in dire want.

"What else would you like for your birthday?" I asked. "Besides cake and ice cream and glue and cigar boxes and a new wig and wardrobe for Miss Baby?"

"Nothing else," Emma said, "except of course Caroline. Caroline will be there and she will bring me a surprise."

So there it was then, flat out in the open. I had fished for it. I had put my line into deep and muddy waters and I had gotten Emma to rise to the bait.

"Emma," I moved the shells about trying to appear calm and casual. "What if Caroline didn't come for your birthday?"

"But she will," Emma said. Emma's faith at that moment would have moved mountains.

"Emma, you don't expect your mother and father to come."

"No, they're dead." Emma's face reflected her fury. Her jaw, her mother's jaw, was set in opposition. "Caroline is coming and you can't make me believe she isn't. Just because you can't see someone doesn't mean they are dead."

The fish was bigger than I was. I was being pulled into the sea. I was fishing out of my depth. I was in over my head.

"Caroline's not coming back," I said.

Emma lowered her head. Her lip was fixed against her upper teeth like a little animal at bay.

"I don't believe you. She's here now. She's on the island. Out there somewhere on the island. She's here. Sometimes I think I can see her." Emma's jaw gave a little quiver and her eyes began to tear.

I'd pushed her too far and I'd gotten nowhere. I could not tell her Caroline was dead. If she was put under too much stress she would break. She already felt herself guilty of all her world's tragedies. I had to think of something to say, some words that would get through to Emma without hurting her. Communication was imperative.

As I was trying to think of what to say and how to say it, I looked out of the window and there at the edge of the garden, framed and wrapped all around in the green of the trees, suddenly I saw her. My breath stopped and caught in my throat. I saw Caroline.

She was dressed all in white from head to foot. I saw her as surely as I was sitting in my own room. I had just told Emma that Caroline would not come back but she was here. I knew it was impossible but I saw Caroline. I saw her at the end of the garden looking up at the window, looking up toward Emma.

My blood froze. It was not an idle expression. The shock had turned me to ice. There were crystals in my veins and I was freezing in a vise of glacial fear. I could not speak or make a sound, I was so afraid. But then the blessing was that as I could not make a sound I could not scream. And so I sat and prayed that Emma would not turn around to look out the window. I heard Emma saying, "Caroline will come for my birthday, she will. She promised and she never breaks her promises."

I made myself swallow. My mouth was dry, my lips were as numb as if I had spent a dreadful day at the dentist's and he had gone quite mad with the Novocain. All I wanted at this moment was to get Emma out of this room and away from the window before she could look around and see what I saw. I had come into the room to convince Emma that Caroline was not ever coming back and I had seen Caroline for myself.

At last everything clicked: the water and the seaweed on the floor of my room, that first night; the sound of laughter, or had it been a crying and a wailing, from Caroline drowned and then risen from the sea.

Always in my mind I came back to water and to my fear of it. But now, at this moment, my greatest fear was for Emma.

"Come on, Emma," I said in a stilted tone. "Let's go down to the kitchen and make some cocoa."

Emma was delighted. She had been diverted as I wished I could be diverted from the fact of Caroline out there at the end of the garden.

"Would Mrs. Fairley mind?" Emma asked.

"I don't think she'd mind," I said. "Not if we wash up after ourselves."

It is remarkable what one can do with one's will against all one's emotions. I willed us up and out of my room. I willed us down the stairs to the kitchen. I poured the milk into the saucepan and I willed my hand to be steady as I made idle and foolish chatter with Emma. I was composed and calm. I was perfectly behaved until I was pouring out the hot milk into mugs liberally filled with cocoa powder and the back door opened. It was then my will failed me and I screamed.

The milk went all along the table and onto the floor. I was so sure that I would see Caroline standing at the kitchen door that when I realized it was only Mac I began to cry.

"I'm sorry," Mac said. "I didn't mean to startle you."

I sobbed and sobbed, out of control. I sobbed as if I would never be able to stop. I could not stop myself from sobbing; not even when Mrs. Fairley came out of her room in her robe and slippers and tried to convince me that there was nothing to worry about, not even when she mopped up the milk as if nothing was the least amiss could I be comforted.

"What is it?" Mac asked Emma. "What's the matter with Martha?"

"I think," Emma said, "that she's crying over spilt milk."

Seven

I was not crying over spilt milk. I was crying because I was in a state of mortal, gibbering terror. I could not for the life of me control my fear any more than I could control my tears. I had used up all of my will to get Emma and me downstairs and I was for the moment bankrupt of courage.

"I'm sorry," I sobbed. "I am so very, very sorry."

"Don't worry about it," Mrs. Fairley said, seeming not to notice my hysteria. "I'll clean it up in no time."

Mac grinned as if I had told him a capital joke.

"I didn't mean to frighten you, honest," he said. "I just came over to tell you Captain Fairley called in on the radio phone. He and Mr. Hand arrived safe and sound and the Captain is going to stay with Mr. Hand for a few days. They wanted me to tell you. They thought you'd all want to know."

Even news of James could not stop my tears. They were as involuntary as an attack of hiccups. As the sobs and tears continued unabated, it seemed to me that the scene in the kitchen was the stuff of madness. Mrs. Fairley mopping up milk, making her kitchen as neat as if it were her regular cleaning day; Mac grinning away, playing the good messenger, the bringer of good tidings; and Emma, whom I had been brought to the island to defend and protect, defending my absurd behavior like an indulgent parent defending the antics of a spoiled child.

I couldn't tell them that the reason I was behaving like such an idiot was because I had seen a ghost. I didn't believe in ghosts, not even Caroline's ghost. I was crying because I knew Caroline was alive, somewhere on the island. I had seen her shimmering like a phantom at the edge of the trees. But Caroline was not a phantom, she was real. Somehow she had survived the accident and she was here. Perhaps at this moment she was outside looking in at us through the lighted window.

But if Caroline was out there why did she not come in? It was her kitchen, her house. Why did she not open the door and come in? She had promised to be here for Emma's birthday. Then why had she come tonight? Was it some sort of preview, some psychic forecast? Or was Caroline playing a game of her own? Was she outside now laughing at my hysteria? It seemed I could almost hear her laughing, her head thrown back, her hair streaming in the wind, laughing because she was playing a joke on us all.

Perhaps it was my sanity and not Emma's that had been toppled and put out of balance. Perhaps I had projected all my fears into one instant vision. Perhaps by some mental short circuit I had fused the fragile wires connecting the real and the unreal. I feared Caroline so much because she was all that I was not. She had all that I could never have and my fear had made me a little mad.

But if my balance had been rocked by the sight of Caroline what would her sudden return do to Emma? What would become of Emma's fragile, small purchase on life if Caroline appeared out of nowhere? For I was convinced that Emma *knew*

Caroline was dead and drowned in the sea. Otherwise why had Emma played at magic? Why had she cast her childish spells if she really thought Caroline to be alive?

With that sobering thought as my goal, I took hold of my scattered emotions. I dried my eyes and sat at the long kitchen table with Mrs. Fairley and Emma and Mac. We sat as pleasantly and easily as if nothing had happened. Mrs. Fairley made some more cocoa and we drank it and talked quietly about the Captain and Mr. Hand and the wonders of the radio age which made such instant communication possible. And all the time I felt as if I must be the victim of some great plot. It was a virulent attack of paranoia, but I could not help feeling they must know something I didn't know. I felt like a child awakened from a nightmare to whom the adults promised there was nothing to fear, but I had seen the great shadows and the fangs, I had seen the ghost in my dream, and the dream was more real than being awake.

After we had our cocoa Mac left and Emma and I said goodnight to Mrs. Fairley and went upstairs, Emma to her room and I to mine. I did not doubt that Emma would go straight off to sleep but I did not go to bed and I could not go to sleep.

The house was silent and sleeping but I was wide awake. I sat in the chair facing the window. I stared out toward the garden and the trees beyond. I stared, eyes straining, looking at the spot where Caroline had stood. I must not sleep. I must stay awake, I must keep the watch until Caroline came again, for I was sure she would.

I sat staring into the dark until I became mesmerized and my eyes opened and fell, and without any knowledge or permission my eyelids fell and I slept.

When I woke the next morning I was still sitting in the chair. My muscles were cramped and aching. I was exhausted from the vigil I had not properly kept, and I was afraid. Fear should vanish with the sun but mine had only increased.

As I went into the bathroom for a quick shower I caught sight of myself in the mirror. I was a pitiful object. I looked as bad as I felt. There were circles under my eyes, not romantic dark smudges but deep circles of fatigue that would not wash away.

I showered hot and cold and then hot again. I toweled myself dry, hoping the rough friction would get my circulation going. I did a few deep breathing exercises to get the oxygen flowing toward my brain so that I could think logically and clearly and sort out fact from fantasy and put each into a neat and sane order.

I had to get some grip on the affair, for Emma was in my charge and if I continued in last night's frame of mind I'd be no good to her. I was here to take care of Emma. If I couldn't take care of myself I couldn't very well take care of her. I must do better today.

I went downstairs. The house was so quiet I felt a sound barrier had enveloped it in the night. The kitchen was empty. There was coffee on the stove, the clock was ticking on the wall, and on the table was a pitcher of orange juice and rolls and butter. I called out to Mrs. Fairley through the pantry and at her own door but there was no reply. She was nowhere to be found; nor were the girls.

I drank some coffee standing at the table waiting for some sound but there was none. I started over the house looking for some sign of life. I looked in the dining room and the parlor and in the library but there was no one. I went up the stairs into Emma's and Tibba's rooms but they were not there, and then in some desperate last measure I opened the door to Caroline's room. As the door opened a curtain billowed out, and in terror I shut the door and ran down the steps and out of the house.

I was a nervous wreck, fearful of my own shadow, terrified by clocks ticking and coffee cups and a curtain caught in a draft of wind. I was terrified because I was alone and at any moment I expected Caroline to appear from nowhere.

I ran toward the beach, wild to be away from the house. It seemed I was pursued by all the ghosts of Fanners past. I looked up toward the ridge for a glimpse of Mac. I had become accustomed to Mac's being on the cliff above the beach path. I had gotten used to his watching me through his binoculars. Today I looked toward the high rise above the beach but he wasn't there. There was no glittering reflection caught in the sun. It seemed like an evil omen.

I turned back toward the house, I looked to the sea, I looked all around in a circle, I looked for the unseen and the unknown. Then I ran until I came over the last dune and there on the beach were Emma and Tibba and Miss Baby and Pompey. They were there in their usual place. The girls were making a castle. They were laughing, looking up at me serene and secure in their usual routine.

As I came down to them Pompey did not rise to greet me, but he beat a small tattoo with his tail. He yawned, his old rusty jaw opening and then closing. His grey muzzle twitched off a fly and it was such a great exertion for him that he slept and snored.

The girls were as lively as Pompey and I were exhausted. They ran and shrieked. I could not remember ever having heard them so noisy. Or perhaps they had always been so and they had not gotten on my nerves because I had had none.

I was well aware that I must do something, take some positive action, but I didn't know what action to take or where to begin and so I lay on the beach towel under the umbrella and made what virtue I could of my lethargy.

In the afternoon, sometime after lunch, Mac came down to the beach. He had never been down to visit us before and at first I thought he was a mirage or a specter come like Caroline to haunt me, but Mac was real. The girls were in transports of delight, they ran to him and twined themselves around him. Then the three of them came to stand over me.

Mac spoke to me kindly. "You're not looking well," he said. "Are you feeling all right?"

I seemed not to be able to respond properly to his question, but the girls immediately joined in the game and were his nurses in attendance.

"What have you been doing today?" Mac asked.

"Oh," I said, vaguely casting about for some neutral activity to mask the plain fact that I was doing nothing, nothing at all. "I've been reading."

"What else?" Mac demanded an answer.

"I had lunch."

"She's bored," Emma said.

"Why do you say that?" I snapped.

"Because it's true." Emma stood her ground. "You never do anything. It must be boring never to go in the water."

"Why don't you go in?" Mac asked kindly. "It would do you good."

"She can't swim." Emma answered for me.

"You're kidding." Mac seemed shocked. "Is that right? You can't swim?"

"No," I said with some asperity, "I can't."

"Why don't you teach her?" Emma seemed artless. It was an innocent enough request.

"Sure," Mac agreed promptly, "I'd be glad to. Swimming is easy."

As the three of them disposed of my freedom of choice my

irritation grew. At least it was some diversion being irritated, a diversion from the thought of Caroline. Only Tibba had not spoken but she too seemed to agree with the plan.

"I warn you," I said with smug satisfaction, "I won't be a good pupil."

"I'm a good teacher," Mac countered. "All you have to do is to trust me." He held out his hand and I took it.

I wanted to overcome my fear of the water. I wanted to be willing, pliable, and biddable, but the moment we came to the rim of the ocean I knew I could not manage it. As I walked out through the foam and seaweed into the ripples and into the water I became hopelessly stiff legged.

"You're doing very well," Mac said and I had to laugh at his lie. It was obvious I was doing so badly.

"Have a little confidence," Mac said. "If not in yourself, in me. You don't have to overcome your fear of the water to swim. I don't expect that of you, not in one afternoon. You just concentrate on trusting me. I know my job. I used to teach swimming in a youth club in the city where the boys had never seen water. They swam in no time and so can you."

It was the first thing Mac had ever said to me of a personal nature, the first clue he had ever given as to what his past life had been. As far as I knew Mac had sprung fully clad with his binoculars from the brow of the lighthouse.

"Did you win gold medals for your swimming?" I asked.

"Some," Mac said. "But I was only a runner-up for the Olympics. I never made the team."

It was the sort of answer I had come to expect from Mac. I didn't know whether he was telling me something that was a fact or whether he was joking.

"Just do what I tell you," Mac said. "You can trust me."

I said no more and let Mac give the orders. I followed him into the water waist deep.

"Now," Mac said. "Bend over, close your eyes and put your face into the water. Just your face."

I did as he told me. I held my face in the water but not for long. I suddenly stood up shuddering.

"I hate the sea," I said. "Being in it is like being pickled in brine. Maybe I'd do better in a pool."

Mac shook his head. "No, in a pool you'd only say you hated the chlorine. No, be honest. You hate the water."

"Yes," I said sheepishly, "I hate the water." I knew it was not reasonable. Why would any sensible person hate an entire element? I had expected Mac to grin or laugh at me. Instead he was silent and I felt he was sympathetic to my unhappy situation.

"You ought to learn to swim," Mac said, his face serious. "You are a teacher. You are responsible for all your pupils. If one of them were drowning how could you save her?"

I knew that Mac meant Emma. It was Emma I was here to teach and to guard and to protect. Mac had made his point. It was a sharp reminder of my limitations.

"All right," I said to Mac, "I'll try." I gave him my hands and let him lead me. I accepted Mac as my authority. I allowed myself to float but only so long as he held me. When I felt Mac's hands let me go I thrashed about and then sank like a stone.

"You have to have a little faith," Mac said sternly.

"I do," I said. "I have perfect faith that I can't manage this."

"You have to have faith." Mac was relentless and dogged. He persisted in his belief that I could swim.

Emma and Tibba sat on the shore, their feet stuck into mounds of wet sand. They watched, both amused and aghast to think that an adult could be so silly. Clearly they had never seen such an exhibition. Nor had Miss Baby, nor Pompey who sat up and looked at me, his head first to one side and then the other.

Finally even Mac, Poseidon, king of the ocean, had to give up and admit he had had enough for one day. I agreed with him. It was enough, more than enough to last me a lifetime. But I was not to be let off so lightly.

"Tomorrow," Mac said. "We'll try again tomorrow."

"Tomorrow," I said, and we wearily started, all of us, back toward the house.

I didn't think it would be any better tomorrow than it had been today.

I was hopeless. The girls went along, their eyes downcast, shuffling their feet through the sand. I had embarrassed them. When Mac left us at the path to the house the girls ran on ahead and I was left behind to try and bolster my own ego. I tried to raise my self-confidence by thinking of the things I could do well. I could cook and sew and teach. I was usually sweet-tempered in adversity. I was just a creature of some grave, basic anxiety and one of the manifestations of that anxiety was my fear of the water. Another was eating too much when I was nervous.

I ate an enormous supper while the girls regaled Mrs. Fairley with stories of my ineptitude. It had not been a good day. I would be the first to admit that, but at least my failure in the sea had served to take my mind off the most corrosive of my fears. For a time I had forgotten about Caroline.

Mrs. Fairley listened to the girls and then looked at me in disbelief. "You mean to say you can't swim?"

"No," I said, "I can't."

"I never met anyone who couldn't swim."

"Well, now you have," I said with some feeling.

"Well, I never." Mrs. Fairley was clearly bowled over by my admission. She looked at me for a long time and then gave one of her nervous coughs.

After a double helping of blueberry cobbler and thick cream and tea in mugs we all four of us sat down to play a game before bedtime. At last the girls began to yawn and although they would not admit to being sleepy they did concede that they could lie down and rest for awhile. I myself was so tired from the stress and the unexpected exercise that I was sure I could go straight off to sleep. But when my face was clean, my teeth were brushed, and I was in my nightgown and in my bed I could not sleep. I lay, wide awake, waiting for her, waiting for Caroline. And when I could no longer lie there waiting I got up and went to the window and looked out. I half expected to see her, white and shimmering, at the edge of the trees. Instead I saw something else. I saw a light in the Widow's Look.

I had seen it before during the storm. Mac had come in the next night to tell Captain Fairley that he, too, had seen a light in the Widow's Look. The Captain had blamed it on the generator. He had said there must be a fault in the wiring but now there the light was again. I remembered with a chill what Mac had said when he left that night. He had said, "I thought we might have a visitor."

I was possessed of the notion that there was a visitor in the summerhouse now and that the visitor was Caroline. I hurriedly reached for my robe and threw it over my nightgown. Without further thinking I ran down the stairs. I had to know if Caroline was out there.

I had no idea of what time it was—my watch was on my dressing table—but the hour was late. The night was dark and the house was dark. There were clouds covering the moon and masking the stars. I made my way around to the back of the house past the library windows and then past the kitchen and through the garden. The path seemed narrower than before and my robe caught at nettles and thorns. A flimsy white nightgown and robe were hardly suitable attire for an island at night but I had not wanted to take the time to dress and I had not been sensible enough to take a coat.

It was only a short way after all and I hurried on, rushing toward the light as if I were following a will o' the wisp. When I came up to the little clearing before the Widow's Look and started toward the half-open door I stopped just for a moment and suddenly, without any warning, I was seized from behind, held pinioned by an arm. I opened my mouth to scream and I felt a hand cover my mouth.

A voice in my ear said, "Be quiet. Do you understand?" It was a man's voice, rough, low, and allowing no argument. "If you'll be quiet I'll take my hand away from your mouth."

I nodded feebly. The hand was removed and I gasped for breath and for courage. Then he turned me around to him and I saw that it was Mac who held me.

"What are you doing here?" I gasped.

"I might ask you the same question." Mac's eyes were hard, the familiar grin had vanished. His jaw was set and his mouth was a thin line of disapproval.

"I saw a light," I said, "and I came out to have a look."

"Dressed like that?" Mac clearly did not believe me.

I nodded. It was like the classic dream of being in a public place and suddenly finding I was in my nightgown.

"Then go in and have your look." Mac pushed me away from him. "By all means go in and have your look." Mac was angry. I didn't know whether his anger was for himself or for me or for the whole world in general, but I saw he was in no mood to suffer fools gladly and he plainly thought me a fool to be here. I stood for a moment staring at him stupidly and then with as much dignity as I could manage I opened the door and went into the Widow's Look.

At first the little house seemed empty. Everything was just as when Emma had first brought me here and then I saw him. It was Pompey. He was lying in front of the wicker table in the circle of lamplight. It seemed as if he were lying in white sea foam. He was lying in an awkward position, his legs bent into a grotesque attitude as if he had been running and had fallen into a troubled sleep. I stepped toward him. I was about to bend down and touch him when I heard Mac's voice cutting out at me like a whip.

"Don't touch him."

"But he's hurt." I turned to Mac, bewildered. "Can't you see he's hurt?"

Mac's face was a mask of stone.

"No," he said. "He's dead. Pompey's dead."

"Dead?" I echoed. "But how? What happened to him?"

"He's been electrocuted."

It took a moment for the meaning of his words to sink into my consciousness. "Oh, my God."

"If you'll look again," Mac said, "you can see he's lying in a patch of water. There is an exposed wire running from the light socket; it's just there beneath him."

I looked and I saw the wire, live and lethal, running from the wall socket into the damp patch where Pompey had been killed, and I saw that what I had at first taken for foam was in reality a portion of white scarf, the white scarf that had been hanging on the door of Caroline's studio. It was the same, I was sure of it.

"Have you seen enough?" Mac demanded.

"Yes," I said, and I turned away from Pompey and from the deadly pale white scarf. I had seen enough to make me want to weep and enough to heap more terror on the load of it I already carried. The patch of water made me think of the water on my bedroom floor, the first night I had come to the island.

"If you had touched Pompey," Mac said, "if you had come in and stood where Pompey is lying it could have been you dead and not him." His words were as brutal as stones from a sling.

Poor old Pompey. How could one reconcile the death of a dear old dog who had never been anything but loyal and loving in his whole long life? It filled me with a futile rage to think of him lying there and I could not touch him nor give him comfort. In my anger I lashed out at Mac.

"You asked me what I was doing here," I said. "Well, what were you doing outside? Why didn't you help him? Why did you just let him lie there?"

The questions seemed to change Mac's attitude toward me. He sighed. "I'm sorry I frightened you. I was just going to turn off the generator so I could move Pompey out of the electric field when I heard you coming, and I waited to see who it was."

"I see," I said, but I did not see why Mac should hide in the shadows and seize me as if I were some trespasser. There was something more to it, I felt sure, but he had accepted my explanation so I supposed I must accept his.

"It's a dangerous game," Mac said, looking at Pompey.

"What is?" I did not understand Mac tonight, not what he said or did.

"Playing with electricity can be as deadly as playing with fire."

I felt my face flush. What could Mac know about the fire? Did he really know something or was it just a lucky hit?

"Surely," I said, "this was an accident."

"Perhaps, but there have been enough accidents in the Fanner family—wouldn't you say?"

It seemed Mac was more accusing than questioning.

"First Caroline's brother dead in a car accident. Then Sara and Edward dead in a skiing accident. Then Caroline dead in a boating accident. It was only a lucky accident that Emma and James were not killed at Easter."

Mac's voice lashed around me like a gale.

"Now, as an ecologist I can't help but observe that the Fanners are growing extinct. Emma is the only one of them left."

"Don't say that," I protested, as if I could erase his words, but he went on.

"What if Emma had seen the light and come out here? That would have been a most profitable accident, wouldn't it?"

"Profitable to whom?"

"Oh come on, Martha." Mac sneered at my question. "You're a bright girl. It would have been profitable for whoever gets Emma's fortune. The Fanner fortune."

We stood in silence looking at each other. I could not believe what I had heard. It seemed too horrible.

Mac wouldn't leave it alone. "You could have been killed tonight. You can get badly hurt in other people's accidents."

"Who would want to kill me?" It was ludicrous. "I don't have any money. I'm as poor as a church mouse. I don't have anything of value."

"Don't you?" Mac asked me as if I were ignorant of rich and hidden assets. "I think," he said, "you may know something of great value."

"What?"

"I think you know something. You know something that frightens you very badly."

"That's ridiculous," I protested, but Mac had scored a direct hit. I knew more than was comfortable at the moment. I knew about the fire in James's room. I knew about the journal he had found. I knew about a patch of water in my room. I knew the girls were playing at magic, and I knew that Caroline was here on the island. And I knew it was her scarf from the boathouse that was under poor Pompey.

"Listen to me, Martha. Last night you were scared out of your wits. Why? If you know anything, anything at all, no matter how irrelevant it seems to you, you must tell me."

I was trapped. Pompey was behind me and before me stood Mac asking me to tell him things that were not mine to tell. I had promised James I wouldn't tell anyone I had been with him at the boathouse. I did not want to tell Mac I thought I had seen a ghost.

"Please." Mac went on beating and hammering at me. "Tell me what you know. Tell me while there is still time."

I stood silent.

"All right." Mac stood back away from the door to let me pass. "All right. If you won't, you won't. I think you had better go. It's late and staying here won't do either of us any good."

I hesitated. "I don't want to leave Pompey," I said.

"There's nothing you can do for him. Go on. I'll wait for you until you get back to your room."

"How will you know when I am there?"

"Because," Mac said patiently, "you will light a candle. If you could see the light here you must know I can see the light in your room. Or hadn't you thought of that?"

"And what about Pompey?"

"After you are safe in your room I'll cut the generator and take Pompey out and give him a decent burial."

"Where will you take him?" If I could not stay at least I wanted to know where he was to be buried.

"I'll bury him at sea."

"Oh, no!" Suddenly I could not bear to think of Pompey really dead and in the sea.

"Pompey was an old island dog, an old sea dog. It's fit and proper to bury him at sea," Mac said.

And if I was honest I saw that Mac was just as moved by

Pompey's death as I was. Against all my good intentions there were tears in my eyes.

"Go on," Mac said gently. "But remember if there is something you know you should tell me. You must know you can trust me."

I ran out of the Widow's Look. I ran away from death and fear. I ran all the way home like a child afraid of the dark and in my room I lit a candle and held it in the window until I saw the light in the Widow's Look go out.

I had lit a candle for poor old Pompey and so I said a prayer for him as well, a prayer for Pompey who had been loyal to the death. Poor old Pompey, who would never have gone out in the night to the Widow's Look unless there was someone there whom he trusted; poor old Pompey, who had not died by accident.

The wire had not been there by accident, nor had the white scarf. They had been put there by someone who meant to kill. I thought about it until my head ached with the thinking but I didn't know who would have made such a death trap or for whom it had been made, and when I could not think about it any more I got into bed and put the covers over my head.

Eight

But I couldn't keep my head under the covers forever. I had to come out sometime and when I did I had to face facts. Mac was right. I did know something that frightened me. I knew several things. I made a list of them, last to first.

I knew Pompey was dead. I didn't think that his death had been an accident. If his death had not been an accident then someone had put the live wire in the Widow's Look and Pompey's death could have been my death or Emma's.

But who had done it?

Pompey knew who it was in the Widow's Look last night, someone he trusted or he would have barked. But there the matter became more difficult because Pompey had trusted everyone. He had trusted me and the girls and the Fairleys and Mac. Pompey had obeyed Mac's command to stay, I had seen him do it that first day at the lighthouse. Pompey had trusted James. I had a mental picture of Pompey before the library fire, James's hand on Pompey's head. But in the end of all Pompey had been Caroline's dog.

It always came back to Caroline. But why would Caroline want to kill Emma or me? Mac said it was for Emma's fortune, but Mac thought Caroline was dead. Surely he could not suspect James.

I knew no matter what Mac said that James could not kill anyone. Besides James could not have put the wire in the Widow's Look because James was in the hospital in Boston. I knew James had not set the fire in the library. James had said he believed it was Pompey's fault.

But suppose Pompey knew who it had been in the library that night of the fire. That's why he had given no warning. James hadn't wanted to put me in danger, but it seemed that I was in danger and certainly Emma was in terrible danger because Caroline was not dead. Caroline was here on the island. My thoughts raced around and around like kittens chasing their tails.

Emma's birthday was the tenth. This was the seventh. Three days. James had said he would try to be back for Emma's birthday but he was not here and might not be here. I had to handle things myself. The sooner I found Caroline the better for Emma and for me.

And where was Caroline? James had said that the key to what he was looking for was in the boathouse, in Caroline's studio.

I sat bolt upright in my bed. Of course, how stupid of me. That was where Caroline was. It was where she had always been. How she had gotten there I didn't know but that's where she must be. The scarf under Pompey had come from there. It was the ideal place for her to hide. There were enough supplies for a siege. Now that I knew where she was hiding I must find and confront her. I wasn't sure how I would manage it but I would find a way.

I dressed quickly. It was early in the day but there was not a minute to squander. When I had dressed I went in to wake up the girls. Emma was in her bed fast asleep. Her mouth was open, her teeth protruded slightly. She looked like a little chipmunk; not pretty, not beautiful, but she was going to be a handsome enough young woman and a great dowager if she lived long enough. I had to face the fact that she was always going to be in danger because of her money. Emma was the Fanner heiress. I had not been thinking of her as an heiress but as a troubled child who did not have the wherewithal for glue and doll clothes. Her fair hair was damp against her forehead, her brown eyes closed tight. She held Miss Baby clutched to her for safekeeping. I was touched by Emma. I had come to love her dearly.

I went across and opened Tibba's door. She was as serene and beautiful as it was possible for a child to be. Her eyelids, shut over her extraordinary blue eyes, were like satin. Her dark hair curled and fell into a picture of a fairy tale sleeping beauty. I had come to love Tibba too, a sad, strange child in whom I saw myself as a child, bereft.

"Wake up, you two," I said. "It's a beautiful day and we ought to be out in the sunshine."

We went down to the beach singing a three-part round, Emma and Tibba and I. We were to all intents and purposes a congenial, carefree threesome. Halfway down the path Emma stopped and looked at Tibba.

"Have you seen Pompey this morning?"

"No," said Tibba. "Have you?"

"No," Emma said. They both looked at me but I made no answer. I was not going to tell them about Pompey. I could do a lot today but I would rather face Caroline than do that.

So we went on singing and it gave me an odd pang to consider that in the autumn I would be gone and I would not see Emma and Tibba anymore. I had gotten used to seeing them every day and I would miss them. I wished there was some way I could stay. I would like to see them the whole year round. I would even like living on an island in the sea if they were there.

In some sort of defiant gesture to fate I ran out to the sea and put a toe in the water. I wasn't ready for a channel swim but I had made my gesture to the gods.

We spent a busy morning. We sketched and had a math review; we ate a happy lunch.

"Why," I asked, "does Mrs. Fairley never come down to the beach? She sends all this marvelous food but she never comes herself?"

Tibba considered the question, her eyes downcast. "I think she is always busy with the housework."

"We should make an effort to help her more then," I said. It had been thoughtless not to divide the chores more evenly.

About an hour after lunch Mac arrived for my swimming lesson. The girls were at the far end of the beach shelling. Before they could get back to us he gave me an appraising glance and asked, "How are you today?"

"I'm okay," I said, and I was. I had made up my mind to a course of action and it had done wonders for me. I was almost in a state of euphoria.

"Have you told them about Pompey?"

"No," I said. "I hoped you'd do that."

Mac frowned. I hadn't left him much choice.

When the girls arrived out of breath they wanted to show Mac their finds. He bent down to look at them, gravely admiring each shell, and then while he was still on their eye level he said, "I'm afraid I have some bad news for you."

They stood, not knowing what it might be that he had to tell them.

"You must be brave and face up to it," Mac said.

"What?" they chorused. They could not see what was coming.

"Pompey is dead," Mac said flatly.

I hadn't thought that he would tell them straight out like that.

It seemed brutal, but they took it better than I could have hoped. No tears, no fuss; they just stood there and after a moment Emma said, "He was very old."

"Yes," Mac said. "Very old."

Tibba said nothing. There was no expression on her face to give me a clue how she might feel.

"Will there be a funeral?" Emma said.

"No," Mac said. "I buried him at sea, but I think Pompey would like us to give him a memorial service."

"Do we have to wear black and sing hymns?" Emma wanted to know.

"No."

Emma took this all in and then came over to me.

"Pompey is dead and we are going to give him a memorial service."

"Do you think that's a good idea?" I asked Mac, looking at him over Emma's shoulder.

He nodded. "You have to mourn a little when something dies or grief grows and mushrooms in the dark."

What a curious man Mac was. I had not expected him to deliver a sermon on mental health. Still, the girls seemed to accept the idea, and for my part I did much better at my swimming lesson. I floated on my own without support from Mac. I allowed him to tow me out into the deep water, his hand cupped beneath my chin. I accepted him as someone capable of saving me from a death by drowning.

"Good girl," Mac kept saying over and over. "Good girl," as if he were training a substandard parakeet to speak a foreign language.

When we came back to the beach the girls applauded, high praise indeed. I urged Mac to take a bow but he insisted the credit was mine. While we were toweling ourselves dry Emma said, "Mac, what is a memorial service exactly?"

"Oh," Mac thought for a moment. "I expect it's anything you want it to be. I thought we might all go up to the lighthouse and have some lemonade and cookies. I thought that would be a fine memorial service."

"Yes, please." Emma smiled one of her flashing smiles. If she had feared something solemn and depressing that fear was gone.

We gathered up our things and put the umbrella and large towels back in the locker. I had been looking for a way to get down to the boathouse and into Caroline's studio without having to leave the girls on their own or letting anyone know what I was up to. This seemed to be a made-to-order opportunity.

"Look," I said, "I'm sorry but I think you'd better go on without me. I have a terrible headache and I think I ought to go back to the house and rest for a while."

Mac frowned. I saw he was not pleased. He looked at me sharply.

"I thought," he said, "that you were feeling better. You were fine in the water."

"Oh yes," I agreed brightly. "I've just had too much sun, that's all. Don't worry about me."

"But it's for Pompey." Tibba took my hand appealingly. "It's a memorial." I suddenly felt like a traitor to Emma and Tibba and most of all to Pompey.

"Never mind," Emma said cheerfully. "She didn't know Pompey very well." Emma was adept at taking grown-ups' clichés and turning them to her use.

"You be good girls," I said, and I asked Mac if he would bring them back in time for supper.

"Sure," Mac said. "Sure." But if I had fooled the girls I was not so sure about Mac. There was no time for him to discuss it further. The girls were pulling him away, bearing him off like Lilliputians carrying off a giant.

They pulled him up over the dunes and I started up the path

for the house. When they were well out of sight I cut down toward the shore and the boathouse.

The sun was startling in its brightness. The day was burning hot, a haze floated around the trees, and the sea distilled up a summer, seashore fragrance. I went quickly, almost running over the crumbling shale. Now that I had the opportunity I must take full advantage of it.

The boathouse door was hard to open. It was swollen with the damp heat. Once inside I was able to find my way without difficulty. It was still not a pleasant place; the water inside the docks was sluggish and green with algae. The light that filtered through the slits of the bay doors made a strange pattern on the oil-slick surface. At least today I did not imagine that sails were ghosts or that barrels were devils waiting to do me harm.

I went easily and confidently around to the studio steps. This afternoon I could keep to the safe wall as I went up the stairs. I had only myself to consider. I bent down to take the key from the riser of the third step and stopped short. It was not there. The hook was there but not the key.

My heart gave a little bump. I had hit the first setback of the day. I stood for a moment. At first all I could hear was my own breath which seemed loud as a bellows, and then I heard the music. It was the sound of a penny whistle, a child's toy. Whoever was playing it was a skilled musician. The notes of the old tune spilled out like precious beads.

I wanted to run away. I had a choice—I could run or I could stay. I stayed, drawn up the stairs by the unseen pied piper. I went slowly, my hand against the wall. A splinter from the rough wood stuck in my finger. The small pain became my companion and made me feel less alone.

At the top of the stairs I stood on the landing and stared at the door. It was open, not wide, but enough. It served. If the music had had color and shape I could have seen it escaping from the little sliver of the open door.

I didn't need a key, only the will to open Pandora's box. I hesitated because I knew full well that the story of Pandora had not ended happily, but the music was as insistent as a snake charmer's call. I swayed in thrall and I went in.

Inside the room there was no one, only the sound of the music. I looked all around and I saw the music was coming from a tape recording machine. The reels wound round and round. I smelled an odor as pungent and harsh as a rasp, the odor of the strong Gitanes. There was a cigarette burning, stuck in the indent of an ashtray on the green table, burning as if the hand that had left it there would pick it up in the next instant. The smoke curled up and up, dancing to the tune of the penny whistle.

All along the surface by the window there were tubes of oil paint laid out in a neat array. An easel was set up beneath the skylight and the palette had been prepared. On the easel there was a fresh, untouched canvas. But there was no one, no living human being.

In the kitchen the refrigerator clicked on. I heard it hum. I knew the sound, I recognized it from my last visit, but it made me jump all the same. I went to the kitchen. There was a glass by the sink. I felt inside, there was moisture against my fingertips.

Then, from somewhere above me, I heard a faint scratching. My nerves began to snap like threads. I looked up. Outside on the skylight I saw a seabird had come to rest. He looked down at me curiously, first with one eye and then with the other eye. His head moved from side to side. I must have been a strange sight for the creature. He sat perched, waiting for some happening, but there was none. There was only me for him to see.

A draft caught at some wind chimes, nothing more. My reaction was as violent as if it had been a poltergeist flying about the room. Caroline was here; she must be. I went to the bathroom and opened the door. On the washstand was an open box of white gauze bandaging, some scissors, and a jar of the ointment, but no Caroline. As I stared at the gauze and scissors, wondering what she could possibly want with them, I heard the outside door slam and I cried out. My first thought was that I had been shut in, made Caroline's prisoner here in the studio. I ran from the bathroom across the room to the door. I seized the knob and pulled, turning the handle with all my might but I might have saved myself the effort. The door was not locked. It opened easily and I fell back stumbling a little in an equal and opposite reaction to my act.

In an instant I was on the landing looking down the stairs. At the bottom, standing near the door looking back over her shoulder, was Caroline.

She was all in white from head to foot. There was a shadow from the door across her face which made a blur of iridescent white. She looked up and she saw my face but I still had not seen hers. As if it were a great cosmic joke she began to laugh. The laughter was as ghostly, as brittle, as the wind chimes. The penny whistle notes might have been crystal prisms shattering in the wind.

And then, as I looked, she was gone.

I ran down the stairs. I had never been a great one for physical exercise but some of my Indian boys were swift runners and I had been known to beat them in a flat race. No thought now for the lack of a railing, I was too intent on catching up with Caroline. I didn't know how she had gotten out of the studio without my seeing her but it didn't matter, what mattered was the pursuit and the capture.

When I came out of the boathouse into the blazing sun it was a form of instant blindness. The world seemed out of focus but as it returned and took shape again I saw, or I thought I saw, a flashing of white ahead of me in the green trees and I ran as fast as I could after Caroline.

I ran, my heart pounding a percussion, above which I imagined I could still hear the tune of the penny whistle playing on and on, the notes floating, flying out above me.

I was the pursuer yet the pursued. I ran and ran even though now I saw nothing white ahead of me. I ran, finding nothing but the path into the woods. It twisted and turned until I came to an open space and the old well. I stopped, exhausted, to catch my breath. My lungs ached and my legs were weak with fatigue. I leaned against the well, gasping for breath, my heart pounding in my ears, my mouth dry.

Caroline had been in the studio. I was sure. I didn't know where she had been hiding, in the closet or behind a curtain, but I knew she had been there and that she had led me a merry chase. She had slipped away like her laughter and the tune of the penny whistle.

It was silent here except for my breathing and my heart. My mouth was so dry I wondered if the water in the well was fit to drink. On the edge of the well sat a bucket. The rope and tackle seemed in working order. I picked up the bucket and reached for the rope. It was old and frayed but serviceable. I let the bucket over the side of the well, winding, playing out the rope hand over hand, and as I lowered the bucket I leaned forward to see how far the bucket had to travel down the well shaft to the water. I looked and I froze in horror.

I wound the rope over my hand and wrist to stop the bucket. I looked and saw it again. There, floating on the top of the water far below in the well, was Caroline's cloak. It was white, billowing out softly like the sail of a small craft that is becalmed and floating adrift in a fog.

I stared, my senses in kaleidoscope motion. There was the white cloak floating, the bucket dangling, the block and pulley swaying, moving gently in a semi-circle, the threads of the rope fraying. I was in a state of shock so that I neither heard nor saw whoever it was who came up behind me.

But I felt the blow on my head and the pain that followed. I felt myself falling as if into the bottom of a pit, into the blackness, down, down, down, never quite hitting the bottom but falling toward it, and as I fell I saw a brilliant white light, a light so bright that it hurt my eyes and blinded me.

I felt my wrist being burned, seared in a bracelet of fire in one small circlet of flame. It was painful being burned alive and I heard myself moan. I bit at my lip to keep from making any further protest against the outrageous fortune which I was heir to.

"That must hurt like hell," I heard him say. "A lump like that can't be good for your headache."

He had a grotesque sense of humor. Any fool should know that a bump on the head could not possibly be good for a headache.

"Can you open your eyes?"

He was really absurd. Of course I could. I just didn't want to because the sunlight would make my head hurt all the more.

"Can you hear me?" He was not going to stop until I made some response.

"Yes," I said. "I can hear you." I opened my eyes and looked at Mac, good, old, trustworthy Mac. One could always rely on Mac to be at the scene of an accident.

"I thought you were going back to the house to rest because you had a headache," he said severely.

I wished that I had gone back to the house instead of to the studio. I wished I was at home now in my own bed. I felt very poor indeed.

"What happened?"

"I don't know," I said weakly. "I was leaning over the well lowering the bucket. I must have swung the rope too sharply and hit my head with the pulley." It was as palpable a lie as James's trying to make me think Pompey had set fire to the library. Someone had hit me on the head, and the only person here was Mac.

"And what about this?" Mac demanded. He held up my arm and I saw an ugly, angry red weal around my wrist.

"It's a rope burn," I said politely, as detached as if it had happened to someone else. "My wrist must have caught in the rope."

"Yes," Mac said shortly. "It's a rope burn and there's a nasty lump on your head."

I reached up and touched the back of my head and I winced. It was a lump, Mac was right, and it hurt like hell.

"I found you halfway into the well." Mac seemed exasperated by my poor fitness report. "If your wrist hadn't been caught in the rope you would have been at the bottom by now. What were you doing here in the first place?"

"I went for a walk. I wanted some air. Please don't make me sit an examination. I have a pain, a really first-rate pain."

"All right," Mac said gruffly. "Last night I asked you to trust me but you wouldn't do that, would you? Instead you go running around getting your head squashed like a melon. If you know something, Martha, you must tell me."

"There's nothing to tell," I said, and there was nothing I could tell Mac, even if I had been sure of him, which I wasn't. What would I have said? "Today, when I left you and the girls I went down to the boathouse to look for Caroline who everybody says drowned in the sea but I know is alive. I saw her today but she ran away. I ran after her into the woods and now she's disappeared down a well." I couldn't say that. It made no

sense. Nor did Mac's being here without the girls when I had
left him to take them to the lighthouse for a memorial to dead
Pompey. I was suddenly in a panic for their safety.

"Where are the girls? What have you done with them?"

"I took them back to the house. They're with Mrs. Fairley."
Mac seemed not to notice my suspicion or to recognize my
concern. "You weren't there so I came to look for you."

"How did you know I was here? How did you know where
to look for me?"

"Fortunately Mrs. Fairley had seen you heading down
toward the boathouse."

"I see," I said. It was really laughable. It was too simple, too
pat. Everything about Mac was too simple, too pat. He never
failed to be on hand. He watched, he spied. He questioned like
an inquisitor. He pried, probed, demanded trust, when he
seemed to me if not suspicious at least suspect.

"I see," I said again, and Mac helped me to my feet. It was a
tentative operation. I found I had knees of jelly and my head
throbbed alarmingly. Mac's hands held me, gripping my
shoulders.

"I'd like to shake some sense into you," he said savagely. For
that instant I was afraid of him.

"Please," I said, "you're hurting me."

He let me go. "All right," he said. "I won't say any more. I
guess the best thing for you now is a little tender, loving care."

And he picked me up and carried me back to the house as
effortlessly as if it had been Miss Baby he had found battered in
the woods.

Mac was very nice to me for the rest of the afternoon. He
explained my accident to the girls and Mrs. Fairley so that it
sounded like a plausible thing to have happened to the inept,
careless Miss Raynor.

The girls hovered close to my bed. Mrs. Fairley bandaged my

wrist, salving it with some of the ointment and bandaging it with white gauze from the library medicine chest. After Mac had seen me settled in he said goodbye, promising to see me the next day.

"I'll be all right tomorrow," I said.

"I hope so." Mac seemed to be not so sure.

Before dinner the girls played nurse, taking my temperature by turns and rolling out bread pills by the dozen. Then Mrs. Fairley brought up supper for me on a tray. After supper the girls read me bedtime stories until they couldn't keep their eyes open any longer and went off to bed themselves.

I sat for a while when they were gone. My head was still aching and my thoughts were in a tangle. I sat staring at my wrist; the bandage masked something ugly and painful. It hid the truth from sight. It was a protection but also a concealment, the bandage that somehow was a link to Caroline.

Why would Caroline need a bandage? James had said that she had been afraid of fire but there were boxes and boxes of gauze bandages in the studio. A roll of gauze had been in the bathroom today beside a pair of scissors.

Was it Caroline who had hit me on the head or someone else? How long had Mac been there before I regained consciousness? Or was it Mac who had hit me? That seemed silly. Why would Mac want to hit me on the head and then carry me home? He had no reason and no cause. And what had happened to Caroline's cloak in the well? None of it made any sense.

I had tried to find Caroline. I had tried to handle things for myself without James's help. For my pains I had a lump on my head and a wrist that would be scarred for a long time to come. I was no nearer to finding Caroline than I had been before. There were now only two days until Emma's birthday and James was still in Boston. I missed James but I also needed him. I had to be sensible and admit that I needed help. James would have to know Caroline was alive sometime. I would have to tell him. But why would Caroline have hidden herself from James? Why?

I asked the questions but I didn't have any answers, only other questions. I must get in touch with James. It was too late for a letter. I would have to call him on the radio phone. Mac had invited me to use the radio phone whenever I wanted to. But this was a conversation I certainly didn't want him to overhear. An idea began to form and take shape in my addled mind. And, as even the longest journey begins with the first step, I got up, put on my robe, and took the tray down to the kitchen.

Mrs. Fairley was surprised to see me. She said, "Here, let me take that." She took the tray from me and put it on the counter by the sink. "Are you feeling any better?"

"Yes, thank you."

"That was a bad accident."

"It was my own fault."

"Maybe, but you're pale as a ghost. Don't you think you'd be better off in bed?"

"I would like a cup of coffee if that's all right."

"Please yourself." Mrs. Fairley put the coffeepot on the stove to heat and began clearing the dishes from the tray into the dishwasher.

I sat at the long kitchen table. I found I was too shaky to stand. My knees kept melting and giving way.

"What I don't understand," Mrs. Fairley said, rinsing the dishes, "is what you were doing down by the well in the first place."

I didn't know how to answer her, and so I told the truth. She had seen me going toward the boathouse. I couldn't deny that.

"I went down to the boathouse this afternoon," I said, "because I wanted to see Caroline's studio."

For a moment Mrs. Fairley said nothing. She went on holding a dish under the running water. Then she turned off the water, put down the dish, and came toward me. She stood facing me. She gave a short dry cough. It was a nervous habit of hers I had become accustomed to.

"If you wanted to go down there you should have asked me. It's her studio, you see, her place. It's been locked up ever since Easter. Since the accident."

"Yes," I said. "Locked." And I thought of the open door and then of Caroline at the foot of the stairs standing, looking back at me, laughing.

"If you want to go down there I'd be glad to take you. I go down there sometimes in the afternoon when you are all at the beach." She seemed troubled. Her eyes searched my face.

"Do you?" I said.

She looked away; her eyes left mine and were focused on something not in this room. She was lost in memory. She coughed again.

"In the old days," she said slowly, "it was where we used to go, the three of us. We had good times down there in the old days. This house was a ruin then. You couldn't heat it in the winter so we'd go off down there and stay. Caroline, her brother Miles, and me. I go down there now sometimes and just sit, waiting. I know she's dead but somehow down there I feel close to her. Sometimes when I'm there I think I can almost hear her laughing, the way she used to laugh."

I felt cold. I shivered as if someone had walked across my grave. And I heard Caroline laughing. The laughter echoed in my mind.

"We used to stay down there a month or more. We had to, to keep warm. But Caroline made a joke of it. She'd stand at the easel painting, smoking one of those French cigarettes, and Miles would play on his penny whistle flute. I'd sit sewing, looking at the two of them. The place was so warm. We had a big oil heater that kept us snug. The wind could blow all it wanted to when we were inside. She'd just laugh." Mrs. Fairley stopped, her voice unsteady with emotion. There were tears in her eyes. She seemed as worn by memory as she did by the rough life of the island.

"I can't believe she's dead in the sea like they say." It was almost a whisper.

I didn't want to cause her pain but I felt impelled to ask. "Mrs. Fairley, do you think there is any possibility Caroline could have survived the accident? Do you think Caroline could still be alive?"

"How?" It was a cry of anguish. "They say she's dead but . . . I don't know. I don't know what to think. I don't know what to think without her. I've never been without her to tell me what to do."

"You must miss her very much."

"I've known her all my life. They had advertised for a girl of all work. I got the job because nobody else would take it. They all said, 'You can't go off to that island, live there the whole year round. You're crazy. You'll be back on the mainland within sight of a month,' but I came and I stayed. The island was my home. We were like a family. She never made me feel like an outsider, a servant. She took me in. When there was no money to pay me she made a joke of it. Caroline said, 'You can be a poor relation to poor relations.' It didn't seem right that she was so poor when those other Fanners had so much."

"Why didn't they help her?"

Mrs. Fairley gave me a startled look. "You didn't know Caroline, did you?"

"No," I said. "I never met Caroline."

"She was too proud to take charity. She managed. She didn't have much but what she had was the best. She liked nice things.

She liked good food and good wine and those French cigarettes. She would have had more to spend on herself if it hadn't been for Miles."

Mrs. Fairley shook her head, then stopped herself from saying more and got me a cup of coffee. She put the cup on the table beside me. I didn't know if she would tell me anything else or not but she went on.

"Miles was handsome as the devil, but he was weak. He was always going off and getting into scrapes. She'd have to go and bail him out of it and then he'd come home all smiles and promises that he'd never do it again. But he always did. She loved him, you see. The way people loved her. She took care of him and me and the island. She always knew what to do."

Mrs. Fairley bit at her lip, chewed at it as if at a bitter pill. Then she coughed again and went on, she had made up her mind to tell it all.

"Then Miles did something Caroline didn't know about. He got a girl in trouble. She was going to have a baby and Miles was going to marry her. For once he was going to do the right thing. They were going to get the marriage license when he had the accident. The car crashed and he was burned."

There was a long silence. It was as if we were under a spell, the two of us. It was Mrs. Fairley who spoke first.

"Caroline made all the arrangements for Miles and the girl and the baby."

"What happened to the baby?"

"It was adopted. 'Best thing,' Caroline said."

"And what happened to the girl?"

Mrs. Fairly looked away. "The girl couldn't take care of the baby. She had to agree. It was for the best. But still it was hard on Caroline to know what had been going on all the time without her suspecting anything.

"After the accident she came back here. It was a lonely time

for her. You can't imagine what the place was like in those days.
Finally Caroline went to Boston to stay with her cousin Sara."

I remembered the time well, I had every reason to.

"Why hadn't she gone before?" I asked.

"Too proud, I guess. Too proud to need anyone."

For an instant I was almost sorry for Caroline.

"While she was there she met Mr. Hand and after Emma's
mother and father were killed she married Mr. Hand and she
brought Emma back to the island." For an instant I saw why
Caroline had decided to marry James for Emma's sake. It was
like a pyramid of tragedies.

"She had money then. She did over this house. She bought
whatever she wanted. Mr. Hand let her do whatever she liked.
He was grateful to her for what she had done for Emma. He
adored her. She said to me, 'You'll see, everything is going to be
all right.' She was happier than I had ever seen her. And it
seemed like everything was going to be fine at last. There was
Caroline and Mr. Hand and the Captain and me. When he
asked me to marry him I didn't know what to do, but Caroline
said it would be sensible to have two couples here on the island
and so it was all settled. She always knew what was best." Mrs.
Fairley seemed to find it an effort to tell the rest but she went on
hesitantly.

"Everything seemed fine, even for poor Emma. Caroline did
everything for Emma. She thought of everything. She got
Tibba as a companion for her. Nothing was too good for Emma.
No wonder Emma loved Caroline. You never met Caroline, did
you?"

I shook my head dumbly.

"Then you couldn't know what she was like. Caroline was so
alive.

"Then at Easter they went sailing, the three of them. When
they didn't come back I waited and waited. I waited until the

Captain came and he said that Caroline had drowned in the sea." Mrs. Fairley put her hands over her face as if to hide the events of that day from herself.

"It must have been a terrible time for you."

Mrs. Fairley nodded. "I didn't know what to do. I go down there now to the studio in the afternoons and I sit waiting. I know it's not possible but I think I hear her laughing. I think I can smell those cigarettes. I think she's there, in the room. In the old days she used to have seances. Pretend to talk with the spirits. It was a game we played, just the three of us. Caroline, her brother Miles, and me. When I am in the studio it's like a seance. I think maybe she will come back and talk to me. Tell me what to do." Mrs. Fairley looked past me, tears on her cheeks. "Sometimes I think I hear her but it's only me wishing."

"If she was alive," I said softly, "if Caroline was alive she would come back to the island, wouldn't she? She would come back to the studio."

Mrs. Fairley nodded and said, "If Caroline was alive she'd come to me. I'd know. If Caroline was alive she'd come here, I know she would."

"Do you think she hasn't come back before this because she was afraid?"

Mrs. Fairley gasped, her eyes wide. "Caroline afraid?" The idea was wild and fanciful to her. "Afraid of what?"

"Of something, or of someone?"

"Caroline was never afraid. Caroline was not afraid of the devil himself."

Mrs. Fairley stopped. Her mouth shut in a thin line. She was defiant now and unwilling to say any more about the past or Caroline. I had asked too much of her, I had demanded too much of her already.

So I was back where I had begun. It was all speculation. Layers and layers of questions wound round and round like the gauze. Only now I was more sure than ever that I must get in touch with James. I must call him on the radio phone and I wanted the conversation to be a private one. I wanted Mac out of the way.

"Mrs. Fairley," I asked, sure at last of what I must do and how to do it, "will you do something for me?"

"If I can."

"I'd like to ask Mac to dinner tomorrow night. I'm very grateful to him for finding me and bringing me home this afternoon. Would that be a lot of trouble for you?"

"No, why it would be good for all of us to have a nice evening together."

"Then it's settled," I said, and I rose to go and when I had said it was all settled, I had thought it was.

∽⫸ *Nine* ⫷∽

I thought it was settled because I had a plan of action. It was a very simple plan. I was going to get away and call James on the radio phone while Mac was here at the house for dinner.

Next morning after breakfast when I told Emma and Tibba that Mac was coming for dinner, they jumped up and down with pleasure. They eagerly agreed to my suggestion of writing him a formal invitation.

They made their first drafts in pencil. The invitation was written, altered, revised, and rewritten again and again until they sat surrounded by balls of paper puffed up like so much paper popcorn snow.

When they had the invitation properly written they begged permission to get pen and ink and paper from the library. I gave it, thinking that if I had used the girls for my private purpose at least I had given instruction in return. The writing of the invitation could be classified as penmanship and an English lesson all in one.

They came back with their treasures, black ink, a quill pen, and fine linen writing paper. They had even found some gold sealing wax with which to make the document more official.

When they sat down and began on the invitation itself they

were as careful as diamond cutters about to cleave a priceless gem. Emma wrote one word and Tibba the next. There were tiny beads of perspiration on the bridges of their noses. Tongues were held in a vise of clenched teeth. When it was finished they heaved giant sighs of relief. There was not a blot or a smudge to mar perfection.

Then they put the invitation in an envelope and wrote Mac's name on the outside, sealed the flap with wax and a signet, and sat back resting from their labors of creation.

It was Emma who thought of the complication. How was the invitation to be delivered? Their eyes rolled and their brows furrowed. This part was harder than the writing. There was no post office, no Western Union. The invitation would have to be delivered by hand. But in that case there was a further worry. If they slipped it underneath Mac's door a gust of wind might blow it away or it might be carried off by bad mice. No, the only solution was to deliver it by hand. Yes, that was the very thing.

They turned to me, all their hopes and expectations resting on my answer. I looked at those two pairs of eyes, the blue and the brown, and I had a pang of conscience. I had manipulated the girls into writing the invitation just as I had manipulated Mrs. Fairley into cooking the dinner. Now I had maneuvered the girls into asking if I would allow them to go to the lighthouse, to Mac's apartment, which was just where I wanted to be. I was the perpetrator of a plot, a stratagem, all because I wanted to get another look at the radio phone, and then while Mac and the girls and Mrs. Fairley were busy with a social evening I intended to get away and telephone James.

"Yes," I said, after a moment's hesitation. "That's the very thing. We can deliver the invitation in person."

We went to the lighthouse, the four of us, Emma and Tibba

and Miss Baby and I. We went out through the kitchen into the garden. We walked up toward the Widow's Look and the cliff path to the lighthouse. As we approached the Widow's Look I suddenly felt little tingles to the scalp and shivers to the spine when I saw the white scarf. It was Caroline's scarf wrapped around the door handle of the Widow's Look. It blew gently, swaying in the wind. It seemed a bizarre relic like the gloves and shoes one sees in the city put up on railings in case the owners should return to claim them.

"Oh look," Emma said, "it's Caroline's scarf."

She handed me Miss Baby to keep and Emma and Tibba went to the door of the Widow's Look. They stood there for a moment just staring and then Tibba reached out her hand hesitantly, timidly, to touch the scarf, but her courage failed her.

"How did it get here?" Tibba asked Emma. Tibba was frightened. I saw she was pale. Her eyes were magnified in her pale face. If the two of them had been calling up spirits then the scarf might seem a manifestation unforeseen.

"I don't know," Emma replied. She was as serious as Tibba was pale.

"It was Caroline's," Emma said thoughtfully. "I am sure of that."

It was the first time Emma had used the past tense in relation to Caroline. She quickly corrected herself.

"It is Caroline's," Emma said. "We'd better leave it."

"Yes," Tibba agreed.

"It might be a signal."

"What kind of a signal?" Tibba asked. She seemed stunned and shocked by the discovery of the scarf, more so than Emma.

"You know," Emma said, "like a distress signal, a sort of warning."

It made me shudder again to think what might have happened

if Emma had seen the light in the Widow's Look and she had come out to see what it was. She could have been killed. Emma could have been dead now, as dead as Pompey.

"How did it get here?" Tibba could not take her eyes from the scarf. She was fascinated, enthralled.

I interrupted briskly. "I am sure someone found it, Mrs. Fairley or Mac, and they might have left it here."

Emma and Tibba looked at each other. Then Emma said, "But if it was found Caroline must have dropped it. She must have been wearing it."

"No," I said as calmly as if one found Caroline's scarves all over the island every day, "it could have been blown along on the wind."

Emma looked at me. I knew she didn't believe me but I had the odd feeling that she would have liked my explanation to be the true one. I had the feeling she wished there was a simple explanation for the scarf.

"Maybe," Emma said, stiff lipped.

"Maybe," Tibba echoed Emma. And they both looked relieved of a burden. Yet the day had been clouded.

As we went on up and along the cliff path toward the lighthouse I was diverted from the reality of the white scarf by an attack of my vertigo.

I looked down over the edge of the sheer cliff straight down to the sea. Looking down made me quite faint and giddy. I heard a ringing in my ears. I tried to look away to the island, to the scrub oak and the *bois d'arc*, but I could not take my eyes from the sea. I had left it too late and I found myself going limp, losing control. The girls ran ahead of me skipping along the edge like young mountain kids at play. They were totally unmindful of any danger. I could almost see them. In one missed step they could both be over the edge. I froze in horror and was sick with the cold. I was chilled into focus but I found I had dropped Miss Baby. She hung teetering back and forth balanced on the edge of the cliff.

I had been given Miss Baby. She had been put into my care and I had let her fall into peril. I snatched her up and took a step back. I stood trembling, Miss Baby in my arms.

Miss Baby was only a poor thing of stuffed cotton, a toy creation. Her hands and feet were of china clay but she was as dear to Emma as the whole of the galaxy. It is wondrous indeed what we hold most dear. It is strange to consider how we select our love objects and with what violence we react when we are deprived of our beloveds.

Emma had been deprived of almost everything she loved. It would be the last straw if she were to lose Miss Baby as well. Yet as vulnerable as I knew Emma to be I felt that Tibba was the more fragile of the two and I didn't know why that should be.

At that moment neither of them seemed even remotely in the shadow of danger. They went skipping along together to the open door of the lighthouse. They gave a pull on the bell rope and then they started up the staircase.

I hurried after them, bounding up the stairs two at a time. I didn't want them out of my sight. Mac was at home. I could hear the keys of the typewriter as he hunted and pecked at them in the fox and hound school of typing.

The girls burst into the room before me and stopped. They were giggling, their faces flushed and dimpled with their shared secret. They forebore to throw themselves upon Mac bodily; instead, in honor of the occasion, they dropped him their best curtsies.

Then Emma thrust the invitation toward him. "Here," she said, "this is for you."

"It has your name on it," Tibba added for good measure.

"What's this?" Mac looked at the envelope and then at their faces. "Is it for me? Are you sure?"

"Yes," Emma said.

"Yes," Tibba said.

"Is it bad news?" Mac asked.

"No," they said together and shook their heads, giggling.

"Is it good news?" Mac asked.

"Yes," they nodded, still giggling.

"I know," Mac said, "you're getting married and you want me to come to the wedding." They had fits of giggles over the suggestion.

"No," they said, "guess again."

"I can't," Mac said. "I give up. You have to tell me."

"No," Emma said. "You have to open it." And she handed him the envelope.

Mac took it. He turned the envelope this way and that. He held it up to the light. Then, gravely and solemnly, he broke the seal and opened the envelope and pulled out the invitation.

As he read it the girls stood solemn and silent, waiting for his reaction. When he finished Mac looked at the two of them and said, "Are you sure this is meant for me? Are you sure this isn't a mistake?"

"No, no," they chorused.

"You are seriously asking me for dinner?"

"Yes," they shouted in delight.

"Well, what a wonderful thing," Mac said. "Just when I thought I'd be dining alone on sardines and cold toast here you have come and rescued me."

The girls gave a shout and began to chant, "Mac is coming to dinner, Mac is coming to dinner."

"There is one thing," Mac interrupted them.

They became silent and their smiles vanished.

"Is it black tie or white?"

The girls looked at each other in consternation. They were put to the test and they didn't know the answer. They looked to me for assistance. But it was Mac who kindly rescued them.

"Do you ladies want me to wear a tie at all?"

"Yes," Emma said. "Wear a tie and shoes, not sneakers."

"Okay," Mac said. "Tie and shoes, not sneakers, it will be." Then he paused. "Was this all your idea?" He asked the question of Emma and Tibba but he looked above their heads at me.

"Yes," Emma answered promptly. "It was our idea, all of ours, Tibba's and Mrs. Fairley's and of course Miss Raynor's."

I felt myself flush. Mac continued looking at me and then he said to Emma, "I accept your invitation with great pleasure and now since you're here at just the right time how would you like to feed the fish for me?"

It was something the girls loved to do. They ran to the cupboard to get the fish food. They measured it carefully and began rationing it to the fast and slow nibblers. They sprinkled a first serving on the water and watched the fast feeders spring from the bottom of the tank to the surface. Their brilliant colors and fins flashed about in the warm light of their world. They took the food and dived, darting in the green moss and weeds, while the second, slower, more timid set came for their food. It would be a comfort to find that the ocean depths were no more harmful than a goldfish tank.

I watched the fish while out of the corner of my eye I saw Mac take the piece of paper from the typewriter and carefully put it face down beside him on the desk. Whatever Mac had been working on he did not intend for me to see it. I didn't care, Mac could keep his secrets as long as I got a good look at the radio.

I moved down the desk unit away from Mac and his

typewriter toward the radio. It had ever so many knobs and switches. There were more than I remembered. It seemed a very complex instrument to me. Mac sat looking at me and at length he asked, "How are you, Martha? You look much better than you did when I left you yesterday."

Automatically my hand went to the bandage protecting my wrist and the still painful burn. "I'm much better, thank you," I said. Then I looked at the radio. I decided the best way of diverting suspicion was to be obvious and honest about my interest in the radio.

"This radio looks terribly complex," I said. "How do you ever manage to get someone on the radio telephone?" Mac rose and came down to me. He was more than willing to show me just how it worked.

"You use it like any other telephone. It's the same kind of mobile radio telephone unit that people have installed in automobiles and boats. It looks so complicated because it's all spread out on the table instead of being hidden neatly away in the luggage compartment of the car or below deck in a boat. Usually all you see of it is the instrument.

"It's just like an ordinary telephone. When you want to make a call you switch on the radio unit and let it warm up for a couple of minutes and then dial the nearest operator, who happens to be in Boston, just as though you were making a call from a car.

"When she answers give her your number and tell her the number you're calling. She dials it for you and patches you in directly and when they answer you talk just the way you do on a regular telephone."

"Do you get good reception?"

Mac thought for a moment before he answered. "Not always, but it's usually pretty good. Is there someone in particular you want to call?"

I flushed again. I felt trapped in my own deceit. Fortunately Emma picked that moment to announce that they had fed the fish and wondered if they might have an orange drink. While Mac supplied the girls with their Orange Crush I stored all the useful information I needed in my memory bank, including the number of the inshore operator in Boston. I ought to be able to make the thing work. After all, I only had one call to make.

By the time the girls had drunk their Orange Crush and were ready to go I had an exaggerated sense of well-being. I was in a secure state of euphoria. I asked Mac if he was coming down to the beach later for my swimming lesson. I thought he looked a little surprised by the question.

"Are you sure you're feeling well enough?"

"Oh yes," I answered blithely. "I'm feeling fine. Really I am."

"Okay," Mac said. "I'll be down about two or half past. If you're sure you're okay?"

And oddly enough I was okay and so was the swimming lesson. It was better than okay. I suspended all my fears and small neuroses. I put them in a holding pattern and, perverse as Eve, I floated, all on my own. Mac held my wrist out of the saltwater and then he swam, towing me far from the shore. Mac might be a mystery in many ways but he was a first-rate swimmer. In the water I trusted him absolutely. And he, not knowing I had a plot, a secret plan, was aware of nothing but my seemingly startling progress. Far, far from the shore I let him hold me in his arms, my arms around his neck, while he treaded water. I was nerveless, limp, relaxed. I was confident and I was surprised that I could so enjoy this game of double-down, black-hearted deceit.

"We could swim to China if you liked." Mac smiled at me and I smiled back at him.

"Not today," I said. "You must give me a rain check for China."

The euphoria continued. The world was suddenly full of hope. Tonight I would telephone James and everything would be all right. Somehow James would know what to do. James would make it all come out for the best. I floated, suspended in salty seawater, held from the deep only by the skill of Mac, Mac who was aware of nothing but his pleasure in what he believed he had taught me.

When we parted at the end of the afternoon Mac said he would see us all at dinner.

"See you at dinner," the girls chorused, "see you at dinner." And Mac walked up over the sand dunes waving. At the top he turned and waved again.

My euphoria expanded and continued. I bathed and washed my hair free of the sea salt. I took my time with my make-up and stuck on a false eyelash or two to give importance to my eyes. I picked out a lime-green linen dress to wear to dinner. My brown hair was silky and streaked from the sun. My skin had tanned to a café au lait. My figure was trim and my sandals were white. I looked, all told, as well as I had ever seen me look.

If I wanted James I should study witchcraft like the witch Tibba. I should burn codfish scales and Boston tea leaves and bits of hasty pudding and cast a spell over him. Instead I still mooned over him as if there were some hope that suddenly he might turn to me and say, "Martha, at long last will you be mine?" I looked at myself in the mirror and I saw a fool who would not speak up for herself, a nice-looking fool, but a fool all the same.

If I looked well the girls had outdone themselves. Emma and Tibba were in Liberty prints with smocking across the yokes. They wore Mary Janes and white socks. Their newly washed hair was parted just so and they had chosen hair ribbons to match their dresses. They were so ladylike and fine I almost didn't recognize them. Even Miss Baby was done to the nines. She was wearing a gown of flowing chiffon sewn by her personal dressmaker, Emma Hand.

"I would have made her a necklace," Emma said sadly, "but I didn't have any emeralds."

"Miss Baby looks lovely," I said, "she really does, and so do both of you." And I bent down and gave them each a kiss.

We were all making an effort to turn out in style. Mrs. Fairley had abandoned her apron for a navy blue dress with white coin dots and a white collar. I had never seen her look so nice; not even her Betsy Ross costume had done her full justice.

But the real knockout was Mac. When Mac arrived he was in a seersucker summer suit, a white shirt and blue tie, and shoes, not sneakers. His beard and moustache were trimmed neatly. He might have been a lawyer, a stockbroker, a banker, a professor. Mac might have been anything at all. I was not prepared to see Mac look so totally different. It was a small shock. I must have shown my feelings because he grinned.

"Do I look different to you?" he asked. "You put me in a suit and tie and I shine up real nice."

I flushed. It was just what I was thinking.

The dinner was as good as we all looked. There was clam broth, grilled fish, and then a roast of lamb, surrounded by vegetables, and a lemon sherbet. The first course of clam broth was set out on the table and then for the rest of the meal we helped ourselves from the sideboard. Dinner in the dining room was an event and Mrs. Fairley had done us proud.

Mac kept all his ladies in laughter. We responded to him like a harem to the sheik. I had never seen Mrs. Fairley laugh so much. Her eyes sparkled and made her look as soft and pretty as if she had had a week at Elizabeth Arden. She had a pretty smile and I could see that when she was a girl she could have been quite a flirt.

Emma and Tibba were astonishing. One could just imagine them in the future. If the girl is mother to the woman I could see what they would be like at twenty or even older.

I wanted to scoop Emma up and carry her far away from harm. I felt a sudden rush of rage to think anyone would want to harm her. Mac had said that Emma was in danger because of her money. I knew that Emma was vulnerable, no one knew that better than I did, but the danger was Caroline, not James, but Caroline, always Caroline. I could almost believe Caroline was here with us, invisible, watching, waiting, biding her time. At any moment she chose she could blow out the candles and leave us in the eternal dark.

But when we rose from the dinner table it was Mrs. Fairley who blew out the candles and it was Emma who suggested that we could play *Monopoly.* "It's such a good game," Emma said, "and since I thought of it can I be banker? Can I? May I?" No one objected to either proposal.

Tibba set out the board and Emma took over the business of counting out our stakes and I took my chance to get away to the radio telephone.

"Would you mind playing without me?" I asked innocently. "There are four of you and to tell you the truth I'm not feeling as well as I had thought. I think I've overdone it today."

Mac gave me a sharp glance. Once before I had told him I was going to rest and I had gotten hit over the head instead. He did not intend to be fooled by me a second time. But I had anticipated his reaction and I smiled at him and then at Emma and Tibba.

"Will you girls come in before you go to bed and say goodnight?"

That ought to convince Mac I meant to be in my own bed when the girls came upstairs. He didn't say anything but went on counting the paper thousands Emma handed him.

I thanked Mrs. Fairley for a lovely dinner. She seemed pleased and touched by my remark. For the first time this evening she gave one of her nervous coughs. "You rest well," she said. "You rest as well as you can."

I went out into the hall, up the front stairs and then, after a moment, down the back way and out of the house through the kitchen. It was as easy as falling off the well-known log, as easy as pie. It was dead simple. *Monopoly* was a long game. I had at least an hour before I had to be back in the house in my own bed ready for inspection.

Still I felt a sense of urgency. I took the shortest way between the two points. I cut diagonally up through the small thicket to the lighthouse. I didn't want to use the cliff path and neither did I care to be seen. There was a clouded moon, but if the clouds should clear then I would be a target. What an odd choice of words, target. I didn't think that Caroline would shoot me with either gun or bow and arrow but I didn't care for her to see me all the same, and I did not want to see her again until I had some advice from James and knew what he wanted me to do.

When I got there the door to the lighthouse was wide open, no locks or bolts. Mac might as well have left me an open invitation to come in. Well, in a way he had. Mac had told me I could use the phone whenever I wanted to, but I wondered if Mac always left the lighthouse open or if he was expecting someone. It seemed strange; as far as Mac knew we were all at the house.

On the iron steps of the spiral stairs my shoes made a clumping sound that echoed and reverberated up the round shaft. I found I was more nervous than I had thought. I was, in fact, in a high pitch of nerves. The door to Mac's apartment was

open like the front door; either Mac had nothing to hide away or
it was a trap baited with the cunning and guile of innocence.
There was a light on at his desk. It glowed soft and shaded
green, the light spilling out over his typewriter and papers. It
was all laid out for me on a plate. What could be easier or more
convenient? Perhaps too convenient. I must hurry.

I took the radio telephone manual down from the shelf above
me and checked the number of the inshore Boston operator.
Then I stood looking at the knobs and dials of the radio. What
man could build woman could operate.

I located the switch and moved it down to the on position. A
red eye glowed at me, the thing was alive. Then I dialed the
number and waited. I heard the electronic crackles and snaps
and pops. Something was happening, I had no idea whether it
was for the good or for the bad. I waited and then I heard a
voice only slightly distorted but definitely human say, "Number
please." I had gotten the Boston inshore operator. So far, so
good.

I gave the operator in Boston the number of the hospital and I
could hear her dialing, the digits semi-circling round their
sequential way. It was so simple, so easy, it was an example of
twentieth-century miracles. We might be about to pollute
ourselves into extinction but we'd be able to communicate with
each other about it brilliantly.

I heard the phone ringing and then the hospital answered and
I asked for Mr. James Hand. It was so very simple. In a few
moments I would be speaking to James. I would tell him it was
too much for me to cope with. I would tell him that I needed
him and James would come home and everything would
somehow be all right.

And then I heard the hospital operator's voice. She said, "I'm
sorry, but we have no patient here by the name of James
Hand." At first I was merely irritated. I knew what switchboard

operators were like. They were young and underpaid—they never looked things up properly.

"Please," I said, "will you look again? Mr. Hand entered the hospital this week." I gave her the date and the approximate time of his arrival, and I waited. I waited for the operator to apologize, to tell me she had found James for me after all but she said again that they had no record of a patient named James Hand.

"Please," I said. "Will you check again? It is urgent, a matter of life and death." I knew that sounded melodramatic but hospitals dealt in emergencies, in melodrama, and in tragedy.

But the answer was the same. She was absolutely sure there was no one there by the name of Hand, nor had there been. She was sorry but that was all she could tell me. She was sorry not to be able to help me.

I thanked the hospital switchboard. I thanked the inshore Boston operator. I sat for a moment staring at the radio's glowing red eye and then I switched off the set. It was like committing a little murder. I put the manual back in its proper place and I stood by the desk as if stricken. What I had just heard was neither believable nor bearable. Why would James lie to me? Why would he tell me that long sad story about being blind and having to go to the hospital? Why? It was beyond my comprehension.

I had gotten myself to accept the fact that I needed James's help. I had sent out a cry for help. But I might as well have sent that cry down a long, dark, empty tunnel. It had been as futile an exercise as calling down a well. My head ached as if I had been hit again. I had been stunned tonight by the news and now what was I to do?

"I had best go back to the house and think about it there," I thought. It wouldn't do to be found here in Mac's lighthouse. My own private game had been a dead failure. I didn't like the adjective I had chosen. I turned away from the radio and the desk, impatient now with myself and the rising tide of my old fears, and as I turned I saw Mac.

He was standing at the door. He was standing with his arms crossed in front of him, leaning against the door sill. He had, by the look of him, been standing there for some time. How long had he been there? What had he heard?

I stared at him, open-mouthed. At last when he spoke his tone was cutting and sarcastic. "How was the connection?"

"It was very clear," I said; my knees went suddenly weak. There was something about Mac's calm that frightened me. I walked toward him, my knees were melting. I hoped that Mac would stand aside and let me pass but he didn't move.

"You said I might use the radio phone. Remember?"

"Yes." Mac continued staring at me. "I remember."

"I thank you," I said. "And now I must go. It must be terribly late."

"Going so soon?" Mac spoke politely but his eyes chilled me to the bone. "Why not stay awhile? You won't be missed. The others are still playing *Monopoly*. It's a good game. It may last for hours yet."

"How . . . how did you get away?" I stammered.

"I went broke," Mac said, his face set in stone. "I had Boardwalk and Park Place. Things were going just fine but all of a sudden I got to wondering how you were and I made some unfortunate moves. I had to mortgage. I mortgaged too deeply and I was out of the game."

"I'm sorry," I said. I knew he was mocking me but I thought to keep on with the charade as long as I could for fear of what might happen when it was over.

"It doesn't matter," Mac said evenly; the edge of the words cut sharply into my conscience. "It wasn't real money, only paper money."

"I must go," I said, but still Mac would not let me pass.
Instead he shook his head slowly back and forth in a slow,
negative rejection of my small hope.

"Whom did you call, Martha?"

I didn't answer. I stood as speechless as if Mac were a lion in
the streets. I had hoped that my straight stare might cause Mac
to cringe and cry off but he would not give way or blink first.
He stared at me, an unremitting, uncompromising stare, and it
was I who blinked first, it was I who lowered my eyes.

"It doesn't matter whom I called," I said. "It's not important."

"It's important to me," Mac said quickly. "I'm a very curious
man. Let's see if I can guess who it was." He paused a moment
as if in deep thought and then said, "If I only have one guess I'd
say it was James Hand that you called. Am I right?"

I didn't answer.

"Am I right?" Mac's voice grew colder and harder. "Did you
talk to James Hand?"

"No," I said, and that much was true.

"Don't lie." Mac looked pained. "Martha, you are the worst
liar I have ever met. You called James Hand. I had that figured
out before I even got here. I was sitting there playing that stupid
game and all of a sudden I knew that you had set me up for this
evening. I knew that you had planned it all so you could come
here and call James Hand. What I don't know is why you
wanted to call him."

I said nothing. I didn't know what to say. I had called James
to tell him I was afraid and now I was more afraid than ever.

"Why did you call him?"

"I just wanted to talk to him," I said lamely.

"It must have been something important. What was it that
was so important that you had to call him to tell him?" Mac

probed. He might have been probing for the splinter in my hand.

"It was a private matter," I said stiffly.

"Something you couldn't tell me?" Mac looked at me and then he sighed. "Did you want to tell him that you still loved him?"

Involuntarily my hand flew up and I hit Mac full in the face. It was a hard, resounding slap. Mac hurt me and I wanted to hurt him in return. I was also hurt because of what I had learned about James tonight. I was hurt because of what I had learned about myself. I had learned that James had lied to me and I had learned that I still loved him without rhyme or reason, I loved him with as great a passion as Emma loved Miss Baby.

Mac reached up and with his hand felt his jaw and nose. I had hit him so hard he thought his nose might be bleeding but it wasn't.

"I'm sorry," I said and I was sorry that I had hit out at Mac. I was bitterly sorry for everything, including me.

"That's all right," Mac said, grinning wryly. "I had it coming."

I never thought I would be grateful to see Mac grinning.

"I'm sorry," Mac went on, "that you don't trust me. But I'll ask you again. Did you talk to James Hand?"

"No," I said. "I didn't talk to him."

"You didn't talk to him," Mac said slowly, "because he wasn't there. He wasn't at the hospital."

"But," I blurted out, still protecting James and my shattered belief in him, "he was there. You said James was in Boston. You said that James was at the hospital. You said that he had called from Boston."

Mac shook his head. "No, I said that Captain Fairley called me and said they were in Boston but I don't know where the Captain was or where James was. I'm sorry," Mac said again, and he seemed to be sincere. "I told you that you might get badly hurt in other people's dangerous games."

And I was hurt, badly hurt. I had thought that Caroline was the only enemy, the only danger, but now I was no longer sure.

"Martha," Mac asked. "Has James told you that he loves you?"

"No," I said, protesting too loudly. "I know that James doesn't love me. He loves Caroline."

"Poor Martha." I felt Mac's hands on my shoulders. He held me as tightly as he had when we had stood by the well. "You never met Caroline, did you?"

"No," I said. "I never met Caroline."

"Caroline was the most beautiful woman I have ever seen." His grip loosened. With one hand Mac reached up and touched my hair. It was a strangely gentle touch, almost a caress. "Poor Martha," he said pityingly. "You have two eyes like Caroline," and his fingers brushed at my eyelids. "You have a nose like Caroline." He traced the bridge of my nose. "You have a mouth like Caroline. But you could not be like Caroline no matter what you did, no matter how hard you tried. You could never be like Caroline."

I had rather Mac had hit me than to have been so brutally and so cruelly compared with Caroline. I was badly wounded. I wanted to run away and hide from him and from myself, but he would not let me go. Mac bent and kissed me on the forehead, a stigma of his pity for me.

"Poor Martha," Mac said. "Come on, I'll take you back to the house. You'll want to be there when the girls come up to say goodnight."

Ten

I wouldn't let Mac go back to the house with me. I went alone. I didn't fear now that only Caroline might be out there unseen in the dark. My fear was magnified to include James, but even if Mac had been with me I knew I had never been so alone, so on my own, in my life.

As I went up the stairs to my room I could hear, from the parlor, the sound of dice being thrown and exclamations of joy or sorrow at the outcome. The game of *Monopoly* went on, a harmless game for three, Mrs. Fairley and Tibba and Emma.

Tonight as I prepared for bed I didn't feel compelled to look out toward the garden and the Widow's Look to see if Caroline was there. The knowledge that James was not at the hospital in Boston had altered my feelings about everything. I was forced to view all that had happened on the island in a new and different perspective.

The first day I had come here, and it seemed a small lifetime ago, James had said he didn't want me to come, but I had come and I had been caught up and hurt in other people's dangerous games. I just hadn't known the name of the game.

Mac had said the object of the game was money. If that was true then the name of the game was the Fanner heiress. The game was Emma. I felt quite sick with dread. Tomorrow was Emma's birthday. Caroline had promised Emma she would appear. I had one day in which to take her out of the game so that she would not be "it," one day to keep Emma from being caught and sacrificed in a game of greed.

I got into bed and I lay in the dark staring at the ceiling. I lay waiting for some picture to emerge and show itself above me but there was no picture show, only a blank ceiling.

When I heard Emma and Tibba coming up the stairs I closed my eyes and pretended to be asleep. I hadn't the heart for small goodnights. I had been such a failure and Emma was in such danger, I couldn't talk to her until I had a way to save her.

Tibba and Emma tiptoed in quietly and hovered over me like a pair of angels, one dark and one fair. I felt their fragile breath on my face.

"She's sleeping," Emma whispered.

"She must have gotten tired waiting for us," Tibba said.

"Yes," Emma said. "Poor Miss Raynor, she was too tired to take off her eyelashes." I felt Emma's breath brush over my pathetic attempts at beauty as they stood looking down at me and then they tiptoed out again.

I opened my eyes when they were gone and went on staring up at the ceiling, projecting up a list of possibilities. It was no longer possible for me to believe in James.

If James was not in Boston he could have been here on the island all along. James could have used me to get something for him from the boathouse. James could have known who set the fire in the library and why. James could have wanted money badly enough to set a trap for Emma in the Widow's Look and James could have hit me on the head, and then my last thought was like a long, tearing scream in my mind. James could have known all along that Caroline was alive. James could be with her, here on the island.

The only possible objective for me now was to get Emma away from the island. I should have done it before but I had counted on James to come, like a god out of the machine, and save the situation.

I certainly was no deus ex machina, but Mrs. Fairley might be able to navigate a sailboat. There was one in the boathouse. It had looked small but seaworthy.

In the morning of the last day I would try to get us to shore, Mrs. Fairley and Tibba and Emma and me. I had no clear idea of what to do with Emma on the mainland but someone at the Fanner Foundation could work that out. Someone in authority could take over until after Emma's birthday. I slept, tossing in a sort of green seasick dream.

It was early when I woke up. I put on my clothes and hurried down to the kitchen. Mrs. Fairley was up before me. I could hear the radio in her apartment. I was on my way to knock on her door when I saw the reason for her early rising.

It was on the kitchen table.

It was Emma's birthday cake, an angel food cake iced in yellow lemon icing. It had eight candles and one to grow on ringed around the top and beneath the candles was Emma's name. The yellow icing shimmered before me. It seemed as brilliant and blinding as a burst of flame.

In the silence I must have cried out Emma's name, for it seemed her name echoed and reverberated in the still, sinister silence of that kitchen—Emma, Emma, Emma.

If I had called out there was no answer. Mrs. Fairley came from the pantry as if there had been no sound at all. I saw her lips move and form the words, good morning.

"Emma." I heard myself say her name as if I were a long way off.

"She's not here," Mrs. Fairley said.

"Where is she?" Each word was an effort.

"They've already gone down to the beach I guess. I haven't seen them."

"Gone already?"

"It's later than you think," Mrs. Fairley said.

In my hysteria I laughed at the cliché. It was so apt. It was later, much later, than I thought.

"The cake," I heard myself say quite distinctly, "it's Emma's birthday cake."

Mrs. Fairley nodded. "I've just finished icing it. It's Emma's birthday cake."

"You made a cake for Emma's birthday." It was not a question but a statement.

"That's right." Mrs. Fairley seemed pleased that I had noticed it. "It's Emma's birthday today."

"Yes." I felt faint.

"Is something wrong?" Mrs. Fairley looked at me. I was tempted to tell Mrs. Fairley everything, but then I stopped myself. If I could not trust James I knew I could not trust anyone.

"I don't have a present for Emma," I said. "I don't have anything to give her."

"Oh, don't worry about that." Mrs. Fairley seemed to be relieved to find me so foolishly concerned. "I'm sure Emma doesn't expect anything much from you, and I've got plenty of wrapping paper and ribbon so you can wrap up some little something for her. It's the thought that counts."

Another staggering but apt cliché; and all my thoughts were of Emma.

"Mrs. Fairley," I said, as calmly as I could manage, "can you sail a boat?"

"Of course."

"Could we sail into Fannerstown today, you and Emma and Tibba and I? It would be a change and we could get some shopping done. There is a sailboat in the boathouse. I saw it."

"Yes, it's there all right but she's in for repairs. The Captain was meaning to fix it when he went off with Mr. Hand to the hospital. I wouldn't want to put out to sea in that sailboat. It would leak like a sieve."

"What would happen if we had an emergency?" I pursued. "There must be some way to get to the mainland. What if one of the children were sick or had an accident? How would we get to shore then?"

"Why," Mrs. Fairley went logically to procedure. "We would get Mac to call Fannerstown on the radio and they'd send a boat."

"And if the radio didn't work?"

"But the radio does work," Mrs. Fairley replied, facts counting for more than fiction in her view.

"But, just for the sake of argument, what if the radio didn't work?"

"Why then we could run up a distress flag. The Coast Guard passes here on patrol every day."

"And if it were night?"

"We'd set a flare. My, Miss Raynor, you do ask a lot of questions. Is that because you're a school teacher?"

I nodded dumbly and asked, "Could we row to shore?"

Mrs. Fairley gave a nervous cough. "Row? Why yes, it's possible, but it would take a long time. Why would you want to row to shore?"

I had no plausible answer, only another question for Mrs. Fairley. "Last night did Emma say anything about its being her birthday today?"

Mrs. Fairley coughed again and then thought for a moment before she replied. "No . . . but . . ." She paused and thought again.

"But what?" I wanted the answer.

"Mac mentioned it."

"Mac? What did he say? Try to remember exactly."

"When he was going," Mrs. Fairley said slowly, trying to remember every word, "when he was going he said to Emma, 'I won't be seeing you again until your birthday.' "

"Did he say anything else?" I demanded.

"No." Mrs. Fairley bit at her lower lip, chewing over the answer. "No, not that I remember."

"Mrs. Fairley," I said as evenly as I could, "I'm going to look for the girls. In the meantime if they come back you keep them here. Will you do that?"

"Yes."

"Promise?"

"I said I would," Mrs. Fairley replied stiffly, as if I had in some way doubted her word.

"Thank you," I said.

I started out the back door and I heard Mrs. Fairley call after me. "You're welcome to the wrapping paper and ribbon any time."

I went out the back way into the kitchen garden. The sun was well up. I felt that the whole world around me had gone mad. I felt that I was in the midst of insanity but that wasn't true. The world was sane. There was no madness in the trees or the earth or the flowers. The madness must be in me. The confusion and the insanity must be in my own head. The only thing I was sure of was that I must not let panic rule. I must get a boat and get Emma to shore. And if I could I'd follow the accepted procedure so as not to attract suspicion.

I would go to the lighthouse and explain to Mac that I wanted to call Fannerstown and have them send a boat to the island. I would say I wanted to do some shopping and if he found that too trivial a reason I would pretend to have some strange and urgent complaint. I would say or do anything I had to to get

Mac to send for a boat and then after the boat was arranged for I would find Emma.

I would do one thing at a time. I would take one step and then another. That philosophy had not worked out too well for me before but it was the one hope I had. I started up toward the lighthouse cutting along the path I had taken last night. This way was becoming like a public thoroughfare for me but it was quicker than going past the Widow's Look or up along the cliff path. I went, walking rapidly. I had no time to lose. It was not philosophy that mattered today. What mattered was instant flight for Emma and for me.

When I got to the lighthouse the door was open. Mac and his open door policy. Mac had said I could trust him. Mac had urged me to tell him what had frightened me. Well, if Mac really wanted to help now was his chance to show himself friend or foe.

I went up the spiral staircase quickly and noiselessly. I was almost at the top of the landing and inside Mac's apartment before I heard the voices. At first I thought that Emma and Tibba had come to call on Mac. I thought that my problems had been cut in half, that I was going to be able to send for a boat and to have found the girls at the same time, and then I stopped. I heard the voices but they were two men's voices.

I stood frozen, listening at the keyhole, eavesdropping without shame or qualm. I heard Mac say, "She's found out. Martha knows that you weren't at the hospital."

And I heard James's voice say, "How did she find out?"

"She called you last night on the radio phone."

Then I heard James's voice again and he said angrily, "And you let her?"

"I couldn't stop her." Mac was equally angry.

There was a long pause then in which I could almost see James's face. I knew he was thinking, controlling his anger. I

waited, listening for whatever might come next. I was beyond
shock or horror, I was so numb to disappointment that I felt no
sensation at all. It was like a radio play. I was not a spectator,
only a listener.

"You should have told me what you were up to." Mac was
sharp and decisive. "I could have put Martha off the scent."

"I needed proof. You wouldn't have believed me without
proof." He paused and cleared his throat. "How much does she
know?"

"I can't be sure," Mac said slowly. "But I know she is
frightened of something."

I felt a sudden pain. The anesthetic of shock had worn off. I
felt my own anger like some powerful drug. It was not just
James and Caroline but Mac as well. They were all conspirators. James and Mac were in a plot with Caroline against Emma.
I might have known that Caroline could have both James and
Mac to do her bidding. All she ever had to do was ask and her
wish was a royal command.

Then I stopped thinking about Caroline because Mac asked,
"What about the Captain? Does he know?"

And James replied, "Yes. The Captain is down at the
Widow's Look now. He's fixing it so nothing can go wrong this
time."

It was the last blow but not a blow of grace. It was stunning
and sickening. I could not believe the Captain was a part of all
this. I could not believe that the Captain's kind face hid a black
heart. But why not? The Captain had always worked for James.
He had said he would do anything for James. If James had been
here all along then the light in the Widow's Look could have
been their doing. I had been as trusting, as unsuspecting, as
Pompey. Pompey would no more have suspected James or the
Captain of treachery than he would have suspected Caroline,
but Pompey had been wrong to trust or to love and Pompey

was dead. I didn't need to hear any more. I went back down the spiral stairs shaking so violently that I had to hold on to the cold metal railing for support.

When I was out of the lighthouse and back into the world of sun and sea and air I leaned against the lighthouse. I was gasping for breath, for self-control; I closed my eyes to stop the spinning of the universe that went round and round, too fast for me to follow. I didn't have any idea of how long I stood there. I made myself breathe slowly and regularly, I made myself open my eyes and what I saw made me wish myself as blind as James had said he was.

In the sea beyond the back of the island was the power boat. They had come to the island by the back door. The boat rode up and down in the swell of the sea. The Captain was obviously a part of it just as James had said. The Captain was in the Widow's Look making sure that nothing went wrong this time. That's what James had said, but where was Emma? Was she in the Widow's Look?

I ran. Panic drove me down the cliff path toward the Widow's Look. I was too frightened for vertigo to be of any importance. Vertigo would have been a pleasure in comparison to my present pain.

When I was above the Widow's Look I stopped running and came down slowly, silently, toward the little summerhouse. The white scarf was no longer on the floor. The signal, if signal it had been, was gone and the door was open, as open as the door to the lighthouse had been. They were all very bold, they were all completely confident that I could do nothing to stop them. I looked in through the open door and I almost screamed. I put a hand over my mouth as securely as Mac had done the night I had seen the light in the Widow's Look and had come out to see if Caroline was here.

Inside the Widow's Look I saw Captain Fairley. He was bent

down by the light socket and beside him on the floor was a kit of tools. The Captain was busy working on the socket. He was too busy concentrating on what he was doing to hear me behind him. He either was putting something to rights or was making another deadly trap.

It was for me to decide. The answer was at that moment in the eye of the beholder. Was the Captain doing something for good or evil? Should I ask him if he was friend or fiend? I had no way now of sending a radio message for a boat and the Captain had a boat. Would he take Emma and me to shore if I asked him? I thought not. The Captain had said that he had always worked for James. He had said he would do anything for James and so whatever the Captain was about it was for James, for Caroline, and for Mac. I should count it a blessing that I had not found Emma here.

I backed off into the thicket of trees and stood in the camouflage of protective leaves, shivering like a doe who has seen the forest on fire. I never considered that I might make more than a token friendship with the island, I always considered myself to be in a hostile terrain. But now the island was my only friend and somewhere on the island was Emma and I had to find her before the others did. Yesterday it had only been Caroline that I thought I had to fear; now it was Mac and the Captain and James as well.

I came out of the thicket well below the Widow's Look and started over the dunes to the beach. My single weapon was time, time to find the girls and to keep Emma with me. I raced over the last dune and looked down onto an empty beach. Emma and Tibba were not there. There wasn't a footprint on the sands. They had not been here. The hot sun blazed in my brain. Where were they? Where could they be? They were not with Mac at the lighthouse. They were not at the Widow's Look. I ran down the beach in hopes that they might be at the far end of the island shelling but I knew it didn't make sense. I knew it was not a logical hope if there were no footprints. Still I called out and called out to them but there was no answer. I hadn't expected one.

There was only one more place they could be. They could be in the boathouse with Caroline. I walked back along the smooth beach toward the landing and toward the beach house. I was too tired to run any more. Time was running out more swiftly than the sand and I had run out of strength. I went on, plodding and dogged, over the shale down to the doors of the old boathouse. I had no thought, no plan, no idea of what I would do if they and Caroline were there. I might be able to do nothing at all but I had to keep going. I had to try to find them. My arms and legs were lead. I heard my breathing, short and shallow, and I held to my wrist which throbbed, branding me as an inept failure. It seemed to be a fitting mark against my ability.

At the boathouse doors I had to pull hard against the swollen wood to get one of them to open.

Many of the shapes and terrors of the place had become familiar. I knew my way without doubt or fear. I took a look at the sailboat. I knew nothing at all about boats but there was a hole in the bottom of this one, even I could see that for myself—a jagged hole, a rent from a sharp rock. Mrs. Fairley was right. We would not be out in it long before we sank.

And as I considered briefly the possibility of asking Mrs. Fairley to run up a distress flag or fire off a rocket for the Coast Guard I heard the upstairs door of Caroline's studio close. I flattened against the wall of the boathouse. Down the stairs came a pair of feet. They paused on the steps toward the bottom of the stairs. Then I heard the key being put onto its hook and I saw Mrs. Fairley let herself out of the boathouse.

When she had gone I went to the third step, took the key, and quickly went up the stairs to open the door to Caroline's studio. I did not really expect to find the girls and I didn't. The place was empty, not a trace of anyone's having been there, no odor of Gitanes, no penny whistle, no background music, not even a seabird on the roof, all still, all calm, and empty as a tomb.

There was nothing left to do but to go back to the house and wait. I left the studio and locked the door behind me. It was a sort of final farewell. It was like saying goodbye to someone or something I had never seen or had. It was a parting and a last goodbye. The French have a saying, "To say goodbye is to die a little"; and it was a last, a final, little death.

Just because it seemed important to me to touch all bases on this point-to-point search of the unyielding island I went back to the house by way of the well but there was nothing there, nothing floating on the water's distant surface.

I let myself into the house by the front door and I climbed, heavy-hearted and bone-tired, up the stairs. I had just gone past Caroline's door when I heard the laughter of her mockery of me. I knew I heard Emma and Tibba laughing and that the laughter came from Emma's room.

I went to my own door and into the bathroom. I put some water on my face and dried away the dust that had accumulated in the long day. And then I went into Emma's room. Emma and Tibba were sitting on the floor. Miss Baby was beside Emma and in front of them were spread out open pages of dot-to-dot coloring books and scattered boxes of crayons. The crayons were from the jumbo boxes which contained every possible hue and bright color. They had seemed like riches to me in my own childhood. They were one luxury that had not palled, crayons, the one constant in a changing world.

They looked up when I came in. Emma's brown and Tibba's blue eyes fastened on me and Emma said, "Where have you been?"

The idea that they should ask me where I had been had its comic overtones.

"I've been looking for you," I replied. "And where have you been?" Question for question, fair was fair.

"We've been here," Emma said.

"All the time?" I asked pointedly.

"Mostly," Tibba chimed in defensively.

"We went out this morning," Emma said, aggrieved to have to answer to a full interrogation. "We didn't wake you because you looked so tired."

"You didn't go to the beach." It was not an accusation but a statement of fact.

"No," Emma shook her head. "It was too hot so we came in again. We never get to spend a day indoors unless it's raining. We get tired of always going out."

I understood her feeling and applauded her sentiment, but I knew it was not the whole truth.

"What have you been doing indoors?" I asked.

"We gave Miss Baby a bath and we sewed and we've been working on our dot-to-dot books. We've been coloring in the pictures that we've drawn. Look." Emma held up a page neatly worked for me to see and praise. On it was a picture of a large basket of brightly colored Easter eggs.

"It's very pretty," I said. "You've done very nice work."

Emma and Tibba beamed.

"When you were out this morning," I asked slowly so there would be no misunderstanding, "did anyone see you?"

They looked at each other slyly out of the corners of their eyes. "No," they said and giggled.

"Did you see anyone?"

They giggled some more.

"Yes."

"Who did you see?" It needed the skill of a Philadelphia lawyer to get the answers from these two.

"Well," Emma said as if beginning a story, "we saw James go into the lighthouse with Mac and we saw Captain Fairley go down toward the Widow's Look and we saw the boat. They've come back, James and the Captain."

"But they didn't see you?"

"No," Emma's giggles turned to laughter. "We hid."

"Were you frightened?"

"No."

"Why did you hide?"

"So they wouldn't see us, silly."

I felt very silly indeed. "Why didn't you want them to see you?"

"Because they are planning to surprise me. I didn't want to spoil their surprise."

"How do you know they are planning a surprise?"

"Well," Emma said in owlish delight, "the table in the dining room is set for a party."

"And," Tibba added without envy, "there are lots and lots of presents and paper hats."

"And," Emma went on in a near whisper, "there is a birthday cake hidden in the pantry with my name on it."

"Is it your birthday, Emma?"

"It must be," Emma said, "or why would there be a cake? It's all part of the surprise Caroline promised me. She promised she'd come on my birthday and bring me a surprise. I told you she was coming, remember?"

"Yes, I remember."

"You said she wouldn't come but she's here. I know Caroline is here. You'll see her tonight. Then you'll have to believe me."

"I believe you, Emma," I said, and I believed Emma more completely than she could ever know.

Eleven

I believed I had been outwitted today by Emma and her childish game of hide and seek. It was too late now to send for a boat from the mainland. It was too late to run up a distress flag and too late to fire off a flare even if I knew where they were kept.

I certainly believed that Caroline was here. I believed that Caroline was coming tonight to try to kill Emma for her money and I believed that James and Mac and the Captain and Mrs. Fairley were all a part of Caroline's plan.

I looked down at Tibba who a moment ago had seemed so open and generous in wanting Emma to have her presents and her birthday surprise; even Tibba was suspect in my eyes now. Miss Baby was the only creature on the island free of all suspicion.

"Well," I said, "if there is going to be a surprise party we should dress for the occasion. We should not go to it unprepared." And with that cryptic and empty remark I did the only thing which seemed positive and productive at the moment. I helped the girls to gather up the crayons and put them neatly in their boxes. Then I suggested they might take a bubble bath for two while I had my shower.

From behind the shower screen I listened to them chattering

and blowing bubbles. To me it seemed a ritual cleansing before sacrifice but they were in ignorant bliss.

I let the water run hot and healing over my tired body. I was tired from running up and down the island all day long and my body was in need of a rest but my mind was remarkably clear and tranquil. What was it wise old Dr. Johnson had said? When a man knows he is going to be hung in a few hours it concentrates the mind marvelous well.

And I was concentrated on my last defense of Emma. In that defense my only weapon was myself. I would not leave Emma. If Caroline or anyone tried to harm Emma they would have to do it over my dead body. I would not leave Emma. Let Caroline come. It would be a relief to see her face to face at long last. When I first came to the island I had been afraid that Emma's birthday would come and Caroline would not be here. I was afraid that if this day came and Caroline did not come back from the grave for the occasion then Emma would be shattered by her own guilt at being alive.

But then, and it seemed a long, long time ago, I had counted on James. I had been sure that with his love and understanding Emma would get through the crisis. I had thought I could count on James. But I had been wrong. I had been a fool. I had just not known how great a fool I really was. It had not occurred to me that everyone was a part of a well-planned plot to do Emma in.

Emma was going to get her surprise, of that I was sure, but what form the surprise would take I was not sure.

When we were all dried and powdered and dressed I helped the girls with their hair ribbons. Then I selected one for Miss Baby.

"Do you think we look all right?" Emma asked, the three of them standing a last-minute inspection.

"Yes," I said, with a large lump in my throat. "I think you look splendid."

Then the clock struck the hour. Emma put her damp hand in mine and we started down to dinner. I felt as if I were leading lambs to slaughter. We were on an irreversible road to the shambles with no way back. I felt Emma's hand tighten. I looked down at her face, excited and happy as any child anticipating a surprise birthday party. That's the way it should have been but it was not possible for the Fanner heiress, not for a child with that royal a fortune, it was like being an heir to the throne of England in Plantagenet times. It was as much as her life was worth.

We were a little crowded on the stairs, Emma and Tibba and I. Emma held to Miss Baby with one hand and to me with the other and being in the middle I held onto Tibba—Tibba who, because she was an orphan, was deprived of all of Emma's dangers. When we came to the bottom of the stairs we saw the door to the parlor was open but beyond, the double door to the dining room was closed.

"Should we go in or should we knock?" Emma asked.

"I think we should knock," I said. "They want to surprise us. We don't want to surprise them." But as we came up to the dining room door I was not so sure I hadn't given away some marginal advantage.

We stood before the closed door for a second and then Tibba leaned across me and whispered to Emma, "Since it's your birthday you do it."

"Okay," Emma said, and then since it was an event of such moment and circumstance Emma handed me Miss Baby who looked amazed that we were going to go in at all instead of running for safety. Emma dropped my hand.

Emma knocked and then we heard Mrs. Fairley say, "Come in," and I flung the doors open wide, ready to face a hail of arrows or Caroline, whichever was the more deadly.

But the tableau did not include Caroline. It was a still life. In the dining room the table was set for seven. On the sideboard there was a variety of good things to eat. The tea trolley was piled high with presents. I had forgotten to wrap up something for Emma. I had no present for her.

To complete the picture of a happy family occasion around the head of the table facing us stood James, Mac, the Captain, and Mrs. Fairley, friends and well-wishers, all assembled for the party. There was just one moment before the scene became animated and alive. Then they called out from their great distance of time and age and feeling, "Surprise, surprise! Happy birthday, Emma!"

It was really incredible. If I hadn't known better I would have sworn that they all meant their good wishes, that they were all focused with adoration on Emma, but I did know better. I was amazed at what good actors they all were and always had been, especially James.

I had not been looking forward to seeing James. I hadn't known what my own acting skills were. I had wondered if I could keep my face from betraying my rage. But then James would not be able to see, or would he? Was James really blind? Had he ever been?

As if in direct answer to that question James broke from the circle and started toward us. He walked without the Captain's aid, not holding to the backs of the chairs or touching the table. I watched James, fascinated. Surely he did not come to threaten Emma, surely it was too soon for that.

There was no way to tell from the faces he left behind him what James might be playing at. Mrs. Fairley looked the most solemn of the three but Captain Fairley was beaming in pink-faced pride on the scene unfolding before him and Mac was grinning as always and pulling at his moustache like a jolly walrus.

When James, who had not taken his eyes from Emma, came

up to us he dropped down on his knees to her level. He spoke to her softly, gently, as if she were his greatest joy, his dearest love, his cherished child.

"I told you I'd try and come back for your birthday."

"And you did," Emma said. She looked at James with a steady, noncommittal gaze. It was difficult to know how Emma did feel about James. I didn't think Emma had ever hated James no matter what he had told me.

"I've brought you some presents," James said.

"Thank you."

"I hope they are what you wanted."

"I hope so," Emma said. "I've got a lot of shells and nothing to glue them on and no glue either."

James looked up to me for a moment as if I might give him a grade for good or bad conduct. When he looked up I knew he saw me, I knew that he saw my face.

"When I was gone," James turned back to Emma, "I got a present for myself too."

"What?"

"I went to the doctors and I can see again." James looked at me again.

"It was a miraculous recovery," I said before I could check my tongue.

"No," James said. "No miracle. My sight is far from perfect, but I see shapes and some details. It's been coming back for some time. I'd been seeing light and shadow but I didn't want to say anything until I was sure."

"Did you have a lot of tests at the hospital?" Emma asked.

There was a pause. I held my breath and waited for James's answer.

"I didn't have to stay at the hospital after all," James said. "I was an outpatient."

"What's that?" Emma asked.

Well might she wonder.

I felt Tibba tug at my skirt; I had forgotten Tibba's existence. "What is it, Tibba?"

"Can Mr. Hand see Emma?"

"I don't know what Mr. Hand sees," I said coldly.

"Yes," James replied. "I can see Emma."

"Can you see me?" Tibba seemed to doubt him.

"Yes."

"Can you see Miss Raynor?"

James looked up. "Yes," he said. "I can see Miss Raynor." And I could see James. I could see him for what he was.

"Do I look different?" Emma asked.

"Yes. You look older."

Emma thought that over for a moment. "Do you see anything else?" Emma held up Miss Baby before her.

James smiled. "I see that Miss Baby is as beautiful as ever."

And Emma smiled at him. It was pathetic to see how James had charmed Emma into his confidence.

"I also see," said James, "that we are keeping everyone waiting for dinner."

We took our places in a flurry of small talk about who was to sit where and by whom. Emma was at the head of the table because it was her birthday. James was on her right and Mac was on her left like two wicked uncles who had made themselves her self-appointed regents. They were there to guard her fortune for themselves, not her person. Then came Mrs. Fairley and Tibba and then the Captain and I. At the foot of the table was an empty space. There was no place set for Caroline. She was, however, the unseen guest at the feast.

For dinner Mrs. Fairley had prepared all of Emma's favorite food. The clam chowder was a masterpiece. Then came meat loaf, whipped potatoes, and salad. The condemned child ate a hearty dinner. I wished I didn't have these gratuitous thoughts.

The company was very gay. First the Captain and then Mac toasted Emma in tumblers of cold milk. The others ate and made polite conversation but I wasn't hungry, not because I had eaten all that much today but because I had no stomach for the company. I ate little, picking up the fork and then putting it down again. I knew James was looking at me, as was Mac, but I could not look at them. I could not even look at Tibba.

If it had been any other night I would have noticed earlier that she was strangely silent and withdrawn. The Captain asked Tibba how she had been, what she had been doing, and she looked to Mrs. Fairley as if Mrs. Fairley might supply the answer. I gave it instead. I said we had spent most of our days at the beach. The Captain seemed to be fond of Tibba but he had never been as protective as Mrs. Fairley. Throughout all the meal I saw Mac glance down from time to time and his grin was knowing, or was that just my imagination?

"Know you're glad to see Mr. James home," the Captain said.

"Am I?"

"He's missed you." The Captain gave me a wink.

I was too angry to be polite. It was all too smooth, too jovial, too genial. It was not possible they were sincere. I knew that they were traitors all and the food choked me. I wondered why Caroline had not appeared.

Where was Caroline? I almost looked forward to her entrance. I wanted to get it over with. I was running out of patience. I wanted to meet the test and then lie down to rest. What hold could any one woman have on all these people to put them in her thrall, to make them all into such hypocrites?

When the meal was over and before dessert James suggested Emma open her presents. By now her face was shining like a moon of delight. All through dinner both Mac and James had been her admiring beaus and I saw that Miss Baby had been allowed to fall face down in the salad dish. If Miss Baby had been brought to the celebration as a sort of security blanket for Emma she had outlived her usefulness.

James and Mac had lulled and charmed Emma into a state of false security.

Mac wheeled over the trolley piled with gifts.

"I'll give you a hint," James said, "some of these packages all contain the same thing."

"What?" Emma wanted to know.

"You'll have to find that out."

By now I was willing to believe they all contained bombs. I glanced at Tibba, who was helping Mrs. Fairley to clear away the plates. Mrs. Fairley said something to her and Tibba turned pale.

When Tibba came back to her chair I asked her what she wanted for her birthday. "When is your birthday?"

"I don't know," Tibba said. "Not my real birthday. They gave me one at the orphanage. They gave me one that was convenient."

I stared. "How do you mean convenient?"

"There were a lot of children," Tibba said quietly, "and a lot of birthdays had already been taken."

It was a fault in me that I had not seen more often how precarious Tibba's life was here on the island. I had always found her touching but I should have tried to look at her more often, to consider her position. It was just that because of circumstance I had concentrated so completely on Emma.

Emma opened the first package. She felt it, and then when she thought she knew what was inside she gave a huge smile and tore away the wrapping to reveal a fine cigar box.

"Oh," she said to James, "just what I wanted. Oh thank you, James. Thank you."

James was very pleased to have given her pleasure, or so it would have seemed to a casual observer. To any stranger it would have been a scene of bliss.

"Just so you won't have to go on opening the same package again and again," James said, "there are several more cigar boxes. You can tell them now by the shape."

Emma laughed. Her eyes glowed. She was the center of attention and she not unnaturally liked it. She went on opening her presents.

The Captain had given her a ship in a bottle and Mac had given her a collection of different games, some with buckshot that rolled around and had to be put in a number of slots, and a nest of wire puzzles and a huge jigsaw puzzle.

"There," Mac said, when she thanked him, "that ought to keep you out of mischief."

Tibba had given her a hand-stitched sampler that had a motif of seabirds. When Tibba had had time to make it I didn't know.

The last presents were a doll trunk full of clothes to fit Miss Baby and not only one but three new wigs in different colors.

I felt badly that I had nothing for Emma but she seemed not to notice.

And now Mrs. Fairley said, "I've a little something for you too." She went into the pantry and in a few moments called out to the Captain to turn out the lights.

I had a sudden panic that in the dark Caroline would try to take Emma away or that when the lights went on there she would be at the end of the table.

The Captain turned out the lights and from the pantry came Mrs. Fairley carrying in the cake, all the candles ablaze. Her face in the candlelight was strange and distorted. I wouldn't have recognized her.

"This is from me," Mrs. Fairley said. "I made you your favorite cake. Now you make a wish," Mrs. Fairley said, "and blow out the candles. And if you blow them all out your wish will come true."

It had been said thousands of times at thousands of birthday parties as long as there had been cakes and candles and children to blow them out, but I felt a cold wind on my neck. I was terrified of what Emma's wish might be.

Emma shut her eyes tight and made her wish and then took a mighty breath and blew eight candles out in the first blast. One candle lingered. Then with the last of her breath Emma blew it out.

We sat in darkness. We sat in silence.

"Well," Mrs. Fairley asked, "did you make a wish?"

Emma said nothing. Then she turned to James. "Yes, I made a wish and I blew out all the candles so my wish will come true." There was silence again and out of the darkness I heard Emma say, "Where is she? Where is Caroline?" It was so silent in the room I heard the sea against the rocks.

"Where is she? Where is Caroline?" Emma asked again, her voice higher. She was shrill with anxiety. "It's what I wished. I blew out all the candles."

Mac and James exchanged a remark I could not hear. It was their signal, a knowing sign of knowing conspirators. Mac turned the lights back on. James was looking at me as he addressed himself to Emma.

"She isn't coming, Emma."

He might as well have put an arrow through her heart.

"But she promised."

"She isn't coming, not now or ever."

"Why?"

"Because Caroline is dead." Emma picked up Miss Baby and held her close.

James had done the cruelest thing I had ever seen one person do to another. He might as well have murdered Emma in front of me. He had murdered her dreams in one cut of the knife. He had severed her from hope.

Emma was in shock. Was this what they had planned all of them, to deal her this blow, to shatter her under one massive blow?

"It's not true," Emma said.

"But it is, Emma. Caroline died at Easter. You remember. We were all on the boat, you and Caroline and I. We had our lunch on deck. It was a cool day without much wind but there was a warm sun. You remember."

He spoke softly, soothingly; the venom of the most deadly viper could not have been more smooth than James's tongue. It was his way to crack and destroy Emma, to drive her mad and then have the keeping of her person and her fortune, a murder not of the flesh but of the mind.

"No," Emma said, her head shaking back and forth as if jerked on a line. "No. No."

"But you do remember," James said. "I know you do. You remember we had lunch and Caroline let you have a sip of her wine. You said it made you drowsy. And Caroline laughed at you. She said, 'Emma can't be tipsy on one sip of wine.' You said you were sleepy and wanted a nap. You curled up on top of the half-open hatch in the sun. You had on your life jacket. You were warm and drowsy but not asleep. You remember, I went down to the galley with Caroline to clear away the lunch things and then you remember what happened next."

"No," Emma said. "I don't."

I stared in openmouthed horror. It was like watching a Greek tragedy put into a New England idiom, made into a play by Eugene O'Neill. It was the Fanner tragedy and this was the third act. First Sara and Edward, then Caroline, and now it would be Emma. James went on.

"Caroline came up on deck and she moved you out of the

bright sun and toward the rail. She started to undo your life jacket, do you remember that?"

"I was hot," Emma said. "It was so hot in the sun." She did remember. I could almost see Emma there on the deck of the boat with Caroline bent over her. She remembered so vividly that I could see she had transported herself back again to that time, that deck, that place. I could see her there by the rail, Caroline bent over her undoing the fastenings of the life preserver. I could almost see Caroline's face. I saw her in Emma's imagination, her quick fingers undoing the fastenings of Emma's life preserver.

"Then," James said, "I came up on deck. I saw you and Caroline together. I thought she had you near the edge of the deck. I thought that you were in danger. I came over and pulled you away from the rail. Then Caroline and I went down into the hold. Do you remember that?"

"No," Emma said. "I don't remember. I remember being hot, that's all."

But she did remember it all too clearly.

"I left Caroline in the hold. I came up on deck and I closed the hatch. It had a plastic hood, remember? You could see through it down into the cabin.

Emma looked at James in horror as indeed we all did. Beside me Tibba sat, her large blue eyes wide with horror. She was trembling as if the story were hers, not Emma's.

"I started to fasten your life jacket," James said, "and then I heard the first explosion. It came from the galley. It must have been some fault in the cooker, that's what the court found at the inquest.

"And because I thought you'd be safer I pitched you into the sea, and then I went back to get Caroline. I tried to open the hatch. I tried, Emma, but I couldn't." James's voice shook. "And then there was another explosion and I was thrown into the sea.

Later, when Captain Fairley picked us up and took us into Fannerstown, we learned that Caroline was drowned. You remember, Emma, I know you do."

"No. No."

"You must remember, Emma. No one likes to remember bad times but that's what happened and that's how Caroline was drowned. Caroline is dead, Emma."

"No, she got away."

"How could she?"

"I don't know."

"Where is she now?"

"I don't know."

"Have you seen her?"

"No."

"You haven't seen her because she is dead. Caroline is dead. You remember the day she died."

"I don't remember. I was too sleepy. I couldn't keep my eyes open."

"You can't remember because it is too terrible for you, because you think you are to blame for what happened. To blame for the death of your mother and your father and Caroline. They all died and you are alive."

James had dealt Emma blow after blow, all shattering, all crippling, yet until now she had stood up to him. Now her face began to crumple, the eyes closed, the chin went slack, the lips began to tremble.

"But . . . but . . . she has to come. She promised she'd be here for my birthday. She promised me a surprise. I blew out the candles, all of them. She has to come back."

There were tears in her eyes, one great tear rolling down her cheek. James went on without mercy.

"Caroline is dead. She's not coming back. That is the truth,

Emma. It's the best present I could ever give you, Emma, the truth."

Emma opened her eyes, the tears streaming. She looked at James and then she looked at the presents James had given her for her birthday, presents she no longer wanted and could not accept.

"I don't want them." Emma picked up the presents. She began throwing them in every direction, stamping on them, breaking them. Glass smashed and china broke. The candles fell, the cake was smashed. In seconds the dining room became a scene of ruin and disaster. Emma made a wreckage of James's presents.

James reached out to try to hold her but she flailed against him.

"Stop it, Emma! Stop it! Please, Emma, stop. Listen to me."

But she would not listen. Emma ran from the room sobbing, leaving Miss Baby behind her.

The company sat for a moment stunned by the fury of Emma's passion and their faces betrayed the strain of the scene. Mrs. Fairley was white as a sheet. Then I rose from the table and went toward James.

"I don't know what you thought you were playing at but I hope you're satisfied." I looked down at James, his eyes could not meet mine.

"I tried." He said it more to himself than to me. "I tried."

"I see you did but you failed."

"You must go after her."

"I will," I said. "I will go after her and I will stay with her. But I warn you, leave her alone. All of you, leave her alone." I took Miss Baby out of the debris and I ran up the stairs after Emma.

I found Emma in her room. She was standing in a corner, her

face to the wall. She stood as if she were being punished. I didn't
know whether James had succeeded in breaking her spirit or
not; she was so quiet and still. I went over to her and I knelt
down beside her. I waited but she would say nothing.

"I've brought Miss Baby," I said.

There wasn't an answer, not a word.

"Don't you think we'd better get her ready for bed?"

Emma turned, her face was unreadable. She took Miss Baby
and carefully and slowly undressed her and put her into her
nightgown. Emma's silence frightened me far more than her
outburst of rage and hysteria.

Then, as slowly and carefully as she had seen to Miss Baby,
she put on her own nightgown and brushed her teeth and got
into bed. All the time I waited without a word from Emma. I
watched her sitting in the bed holding Miss Baby. She sat there,
her eyes straight ahead, her back not touching the pillows. Then
she took a deep breath and held it for a moment. I expected a
sign but instead she said, "She didn't come. Caroline didn't
come."

She rocked gently to and fro and while she rocked she patted
Miss Baby as if she were an ailing child.

"No, Emma."

"You knew she wouldn't come. You knew all along."

It was terrible to watch Emma stating the facts of her own
unhappiness. It was like watching her perform a sort of
open-heart surgery upon herself. Emma had loved Caroline. She
had transferred her love from her dead parents to Caroline and
that transference had been her therapy, a healing, a holding
pattern for her emotions. She had held her love in escrow with
Caroline until she was competent to handle her affections for
herself. And she was bankrupt.

"James thinks I don't remember," she said softly. "But I do. I
remember everything. I remember we were all in a ski lift and it

fell down. I remember being on the boat with James and
Caroline and the boat blew up." She stopped for a moment and
her hand stroked Miss Baby's back tenderly. "When you love
people they die."

I wanted to hold Emma in my arms and sit with her in a
rocking chair rocking her away from pain. Instead I said, "Is
that why you pretended not to love James any more? Because he
was the only one left? Were you afraid he would die too?"

"Why do people die?"

She had asked me a question and I didn't have an answer for
her. "I don't know, Emma."

"Is there anybody who doesn't die?"

"No, Emma, everybody dies sometime."

"Are you going to die?"

"Yes, but not right away. Not just yet."

"But you are going away. That's a kind of dying."

"It's a French saying. 'To say goodbye is to die a little.' " If
she would not ask me to stay then I would ask her. "Emma,
would you like me to stay?"

"Yes." She looked at me, her eyes wide and clear.

"Why?" I wanted some scrap of her affection but I was to be
disappointed.

"I've gotten used to you. I don't want to get used to anybody
else." I had to take what she offered.

"I could stay then for a while."

"For how long?" She challenged me for my answer.

"For as long as you needed me. I could stay and Miss Baby is
going to stay." I tried to sound matter of fact.

"She's only a doll. I want a friend. You were my mother's
friend."

"Yes. We could be friends. And Tibba is your friend."

Emma frowned.

"Do you like Tibba? I know she likes you."

"Tibba is paid to play with me." Emma was testing all her relationships to the limit.

"She likes you very much. Would you like Tibba to come up and play a game with you?" It was the best I had to offer by way of comfort.

"No," Emma shook her head. "I'm tired of games but you could stay and tell me a story if you wanted to."

I tried to think of a story suitable for the occasion. I decided on the favorite story of my class at the Mission. It was the story of an Indian boy who went on his first hunting party. I hadn't gotten very far when Emma interrupted me.

"I could hear you better if you moved closer."

I moved my chair closer to the bed and Emma settled down under the covers with Miss Baby in her arms. I went on with the adventures of the camp and the chase and the hunting party. When the story had come to an end Emma had gone to sleep holding my hand.

Hers was a very little hand. I did not intend to let it go. I did not intend to leave Emma, and as long as I held her hand they could not take her away from me. I was too tired to think properly. I did not know why James had told Emma Caroline was dead. I knew that I had seen her. She was here still, a very real threat to Emma and to me. Holding hands with Emma was my defense, my early warning system.

It was very still in the house. I sat listening for a sound that could foretell danger but I heard nothing until I heard the clock strike midnight. I relaxed then, put my head down on the side of the bed. I thought at last this terrible day was over but it was not so.

I dozed off, slept fitfully, and awoke holding tight to Emma's hand. But it was no longer Emma's hand that I held, it was Tibba's. She sat where Emma had been before. Tibba's great eyes stared at me, held open by terror. Emma was gone and so was Miss Baby.

"Emma, where is Emma?"

"She's gone," Tibba whispered.

"Gone where?"

"I can't tell you." Tibba was frightened to death.

"You must."

"I can't."

"Why?" I took hold of her shoulders. I would have shaken the answer from her but she was already trembling with fright.

"She told me not to tell."

"Who?"

"A ghost. She came. She came to my room. She was all in white. She gave me a note for Emma. She said I was to give it to her and that I was not to tell anybody else."

I wondered wildly if Tibba was so afraid because she and Emma had tried to invoke Caroline and she felt she had succeeded.

"Do you have the note?"

"Yes." Tibba nodded.

"Then give it to me."

Tibba sat like a statue.

"Tibba, you must give it to me."

"I can't," she said. It was like a cry of agony.

"Why not?"

"She'll send me back."

"What?" I felt I was removing fear from Tibba layer by layer.

"She said if I didn't do what she said she'd send me back to the orphanage. I don't want to go back."

I tried to stay calm, fighting back my own terror.

"Emma is in danger. Do you know that?" I too was using Tibba to my own ends.

"No." Tibba was near the breaking point.

"Then give me the note. If you are Emma's friend you will want to help her."

Tibba handed me the note. She might never have a harder decision to make or a more difficult thing to do again in her life.

The note was written on the fine linen paper from the library. It said, "I promised I would come for your birthday and bring you a surprise. I am waiting for you in the Widow's Look."

Caroline had won. She had beaten me. I looked out of the window and I saw the light gleaming, glittering in the Widow's Look. I had lost but I still had to try to find Emma. I had to go after her.

"When did she go?"

"A few minutes ago."

"There might still be time," I said aloud as if to reassure and convince myself. As I turned to leave the room I heard Tibba sobbing. I saw her face. She too had become a character in the Fanner tragedy.

"Now I'll have to go back to the orphanage. I'll have to leave you all and go back." She was stricken by a force too great to be coped with by a child.

"No, Tibba. No matter what happens you won't have to go back."

And I ran.

Caroline had come for Emma. Caroline was here on the island and Emma had gone to her. Emma's wish had come true and turned the night into a time of horror. I ran toward the nightmare. I ran down the stairs, out of the house. I ran as if my life depended on it but it was Emma's life that was in danger.

All of the evening had been a sham, a prologue performed for my benefit so that I would not suspect what Caroline was going to do. James had told Emma that Caroline was dead because it made her invitation to Emma irresistible. It was irresistible. But why would Emma go without telling me? It didn't matter, all that mattered was getting to the Widow's Look.

As I ran, I prayed, "Dear God, don't let it be too late." Ringing in my memory I heard James's voice saying, "The Captain knows what to do. He is in the Widow's Look making sure that nothing goes wrong this time." I ran toward the light, drawn toward it, repelled by it, magnetized to the power of the electric wires that could bring death as well as light.

I came to the door of the Widow's Look and burst in, ready to do whatever had to be done, ready for whatever had happened or was happening, ready for anything but the fact that the Widow's Look was empty.

There was no one there. It was empty—no exposed wires, no scarf, no sound, nothing. Where had Caroline taken Emma? Where could they be? My mind raced about a mental map of the island to the beach, the boathouse, the well. They were all possible. I had to choose, had to make a decision. It was like choosing between the lady and the tiger.

I went outside into the dark and turned round and round trying to decide; I turned until I was dizzy trying to divine the right path to take. It was a sort of frenzy and then as I turned I saw Miss Baby, or what was left of her. She was caught and held in a thorn bush on the path toward the cliff. She was left like a mark to blaze the trail for me. But if Miss Baby was a sign of what lay ahead I knew I could not bear it. Her doll's head was crushed. Her body was torn in a struggle she had not won. The stuffing had been beaten out of her by a maniacal hand. What sort of rage had possessed anyone to do this insane, wild act of violence?

Emma might have come out to meet Caroline of her own free will but I was sure she had not gone away from Miss Baby willingly. She had been taken up the path toward the cliff by brute force. Where had Caroline taken Emma? What did she mean to do with her? As I stood, undecided, I heard someone else coming up the path behind me toward the Widow's Look.

I ran up to the cliff. I ran toward the lighthouse. I ran and as I ran I saw the sea below and the moonlight catching on the rocks and I suddenly stood still, caught and frozen by an attack of vertigo. I stood on the path at the edge of the sea, and the bright moonlight caught and glittered on the waves. I stood transfixed, held prisoner by my fear of height and of the water.

I knew that I could not go back. I had no choice but to go on to the end of the path. I must go on until I found Caroline but I could not move. I was immobilized by fear. I waited, hoping for a sign, some miracle that would release me from my fear of the water. Yet all I could think of was the sea and the wet, jagged rocks gaping below like the teeth of a great sea monster waiting to devour me.

Then a little cloud hit and covered the moon. I was alone in the dark. I whimpered in terror of the dark above and the water below the way an animal whimpers in a troubled sleep before the fire. I heard from somewhere in the sea the toll of a buoy bell and it seemed surely that the bell tolled for me. It was the hour, the time had come and I must go on or it would be too late.

I began to make my way slowly toward the end of the path. In the dark I stumbled and nearly fell. The pebbles scattered loose from the edge and I heard them hit the rocks and splash into the sea below. Yet I went on, impelled. I began to run, wanting to have it done with. I ran and ran faster and faster in a sort of frenzy to find Caroline, to see her at long last. I knew she was there at the end of the dark and then, when I had begun to tire and to despair, the cloud sailed past the moon and I saw her at the end of the island, at the end of the path, standing on the point of the cliff.

She stood facing out to sea, dressed all in white from head to foot. I saw her clearly illuminated in the silver white of the moonlight. She stood tall and proud like the figurehead of a ghost ship, a specter shrouded for a burial at sea.

I was gasping, each breath a torment in an agony of survival, yet I managed to say her name. It seemed at first she hadn't heard me and then she slowly turned. As she turned her cloak billowed out and I saw to my horror that she held Emma captive in the imprisoning folds of her stark, white cloak. Poor Emma, such a little girl to be caught in such a terrible grasp and still I had not seen Caroline.

She was a flame of white, her dress, her cloak, her slippers and her face. Her face was swathed in a deathly mask of gauze. She was wound round and round with yards and yards of bandaging.

She took one step back and then another until one step more and she and Emma would have been over the edge and into the water. I had no choice, I reached forward and I wrenched Emma free from her grasp. As I pulled Emma free I cried, "Run, Emma! Run! Run!" And she ran but I couldn't follow for when I had reached out to pull Emma free I had myself been caught in the white cloak. It held and enveloped me. I was overpowered by Caroline. In our desperate struggle the bandages began to loosen and fall away from her face. One by one they fell until I saw her. It was what I had wanted. It was what I had wished for. Now I could not believe what I saw. It was not Caroline who held me. It was Mrs. Fairley.

We stood eye to eye. She held me gripped as close as if we were welded together in a lifetime bond. She stared at me, her eyes wide as if she were in a trance. Her pupils were dilated, her breath came in short, desperate gasps. Yet when she spoke she spoke softly like a conspirator who fears betrayal.

"Why did you come? Why?"

"I came for Emma. You had Emma."

"You've spoiled everything. You've made her run away. You shouldn't have done that." She seemed wounded, as if I had done her a great wrong, a grave injury.

"I tried to keep you away. From the first night you came I've tried to frighten you away."

"You?" I was stunned. "It's been you all along? You were in my room that first night? Why did you want to frighten me?"

"Why?" She seemed confused. "Because you had guessed. You must have guessed. Surely you aren't that stupid."

But I was stupid, very stupid indeed.

"Why would you try to frighten me? Why pretend to be Caroline if she's dead?"

Then she shook at me, as her rage shook at her, suddenly, like some wild wind had blown. She savaged at me as she had savaged Emma's doll.

"Caroline is not dead. Not dead. Caroline is too clever to be dead. Caroline can't be dead. I am Caroline."

I was sick with cold and horror. Her long cry had been the cry of madness. I had not imagined that there was madness here on the island. It had been here always, Caroline's madness. Now it possessed Mrs. Fairley and as she held me we swayed and teetered on the edge of the cliff, on the edge of madness and death. We were swaying back and forth on a hairline before falling into oblivion.

"No, she's not dead," she whispered again as if afraid of the force of her own fury. "No. I let them think that she was dead but I knew she wasn't dead. She couldn't be dead. I knew everything. Everything."

She looked at me, eyes widening but not seeing me, seeing only some terrible inner knowledge.

"What is it you knew?" I asked as gently as I could, and she began to tell me as if she were Caroline, speaking as Caroline must have told it to her in the past. What she told out now had been imprinted and blazed upon her memory forever.

"I knew Miles loved me." Even the timbre of her voice had changed. She held her head high and proud. She was chillingly like Caroline must have been in her arrogance. "I knew Miles loved me. He loved me. He went away with her but he didn't love her. He amused himself with her because he was bored. He went away because she told him she was going to have a baby. Did you know she had a baby?"

It was a question asked of me but she did not need an answer.

"She had a baby. Pretty, pretty baby." Her hands gripped at my arms with enough force to break my bones or break my heart.

"She wasn't fit to marry Miles, to have his baby. She was too stupid. If she hadn't gotten him to run away he wouldn't have been in the accident. He wouldn't have been burned. I waited and waited and waited before someone came to tell me there had been an accident. I went to the hospital. I saw him, my beautiful Miles, all burned, and it was her fault, her fault. She had done it."

She sighed, a breath of icy death blew against my neck.

"Why should I care about her baby? Miles was dead. Why should I care what had happened to the baby? I told her they took her baby away. I told her the baby was adopted. She cried and cried."

Her head shook back and forth as if she were trying to dislodge a pain too great to bear.

Then the head was lifted again, the chin defiant and haughty.

"I never cried. Never. I was generous. I was kind. I brought her back with me. We came back to the island and we sat together in the studio. It had been a game when I talked to the spirits when there had been the three of us, but now I tried to talk to Miles, to reach him. I knew there was some way to make him speak to me. I knew he loved me, but he had wanted money. He would have been happy to stay on the island if there had been enough money.

"That's when I went to Boston to Sara for money. She had money, my precious cousin Sara."

She spat out Sara's name as if it were a toad.

"She was as stupid as you. She was stupid and she was so happy with Edward and her baby and her money. But there was an accident. We all went skiing and there was an accident."

She began to speak more rapidly.

"James was Emma's guardian. James was Emma's heir. If anything happened to Emma he was her heir. I knew then what I must do. It was so simple. All I had to do was to marry James and when he and Emma were dead I would have the money. I would be his widow. I would be the Fanner heiress. Miles would come and talk to me then and everything would be all right. Miles would come back to me. It was so simple."

She began to laugh, her head back, her laughter brittle and shattering as glass chimes blowing in the wind. As she laughed she loosed her hold on me. One hand touched my face. I shuddered. It was as if she walked on my grave, my grave somewhere in the sea. I tried to run but she caught me up and now I was on the far edge of the cliff and I heard the little pebbles slip and fall into the sea behind me.

"So simple," she said, "except for you. I wrote you a letter." She seemed puzzled. "Do you remember I wrote you a letter?"

"I remember," I said. My heart was pounding, my lips were dry.

"I said I was going to marry James for Emma's sake. I said you had to give up James for Emma's sake. And you let him go just like that. You never questioned it because it was for Emma's sake. You were stupid, as stupid as James. He believed anything I told him. He believed everything I told him about Emma's being disturbed and having to be taken away from school and brought to the island. You were both as stupid as . . ."

She paused, looking behind me into the sea. "As she was. She did whatever I told her. She even married the Captain because I told her she had to if she wanted her baby back again. She had taken Miles and I had taken her baby. Fair for fair. I told her if she did what I told her to I'd get her baby back again and I got her Tibba, Tibba who looks so much like Miles."

The tears fell from her wide eyes and ran down her face. I pitied her as much as I feared her madness.

"I waited and waited for the right time for the accident. I watched and waited and I planned it all so carefully. At Easter we went out in the boat. Just Emma and James and I. I planned it all so carefully. No one would ever blame me for the accident. I set the fire. But I couldn't get out, couldn't get out. There was an explosion, and I . . ."

Her hands rose to shield her face from the invisible, all-consuming flames. And in the flames writhing and turning she began to laugh as she had laughed at James.

"I got to shore. I'm a good swimmer. I got to shore and she found me. I made her keep me alive. As long as I was alive she could have her child. She had to keep me alive. She salved me and wound me in bandages to keep me alive."

Shuddering she gave a sigh as if the worst were over, as if she lived, born again from the flames. She was herself again.

"Then you came and you guessed. You found the journal that told everything. You found it and you gave it to him. To James. You found it just as you would have found her in the well. But she is alive. She has to be alive, she has to live so I can keep my baby, my pretty, pretty baby."

And then as she reached out toward me there was a brilliant, blinding light which hit us both, illuminated us, there on the edge of the cliff on the side of the sea. And, as the light struck us from below, she was startled and frightened and she struck out at me with such force that we both fell over the edge and toward the sea.

In the long, long fall I began to scream, then we hit the water and together we went down, down, down. We were drowning together. I struggled against it. I knew it was a nightmare and that surely I must wake from the dream, for Caroline was already dead.

She had died before I had come to Fanner's Island, and now I was dying too, drowning in the depths of the sea. I fought to be free. I wanted to breathe. We struggled, tangled, caught, held together, I, fighting for the surface, for air. She was the stronger of the two but my desire for life brought us to the top. Our heads above water, I opened my mouth for air and in the moment before she dragged me under with her again I saw the light blazing, blinding, searching us out. The searchlight was from the boat. From the deck of the boat I heard the Captain's voice shout out into the night as sharp as the light, "There she is," and I heard the sound of someone diving into the water.

Then once more I was below the surface of the sea; fighting, struggling to free myself from her and as I pulled free in one great effort I felt other hands take hold of me.

I kicked out again toward the air, the blessed air. I was now caught and pulled in two directions. I was once again at the top. I knew it was Mac whose arms held me. I fought against him as he was shouting, "Stop it, Martha. Stop. Let me help you. Trust me. If you trust me we can get to shore together. If you trust me we can swim to China. Just do what I tell you. Just trust me."

But I could not trust him.

I fought with my last portion of strength. I went on fighting until Mac's fist came out of the water and hit me on the chin. It was a shattering blow. I felt as if he had broken my head. I would drown but it no longer mattered. I slipped under the sea. I slipped out of consciousness and I didn't know any more.

~ Twelve ~

I didn't know any more until I heard Mac say, "I think she's coming around now."

And then James's voice, "She's been unconscious for a long time."

And Mac said, "I had to hit her very hard."

I opened my eyes. It was a great effort to keep them open. It seemed that I was in my own bed and that James and Mac were standing, looking down at me, from a great height. I felt they were unreal. They must be figures in a fantasy. What was real was the pain. My jaw ached and my head felt the size of a giant melon. I had the bitter and sickening taste of salt water in my mouth.

I tried to sit up but I could not manage it. I sank back against the pile of pillows.

"Emma," I said. My lips were dry and cracked from the salt. "Where is Emma?"

"She's safe," James said. "She did what you told her. She ran until she found me. She's in her room. She and Tibba are asleep now. They've been taking care of Miss Baby. I'm afraid Miss Baby has had a bad time of it tonight."

It seemed an absurd remark to make considering the circumstances.

"I was behind you on the path," James said. "You must have heard me. Emma was too frightened to tell me much. All I could get out of her was that a bad ghost had hurt Miss Baby."

"It wasn't a ghost," I said weakly. And suddenly all the horror of what Mrs. Fairley had said to me rushed at me like the sea and I began to shake in uncontrollable fear. "Oh James, I thought it was Caroline who had Emma. I thought you and Caroline, all of you, wanted to kill Emma."

James seemed to find my statement incredible.

"I told you Caroline was dead."

"I know you did," I said. "But you had lied to me about so many things. About going to the hospital, about the fire. Then I heard you and Mac talking in the lighthouse and I thought . . ." I shook, my teeth chattering against the words.

"Oh my God." James reached out to me and then he let his hand fall without touching me.

"If I lied to you, Martha," James said, "it was to protect you. I didn't want you here. I didn't want you to come to this house full of ghosts. I never wanted you to come."

"I am afraid," Mac interrupted brusquely, "that you have me to blame for bringing you here. You see, we felt we had to have someone in the house that we could trust."

"We?" Mac had always talked in a code he seemed to think I could decipher.

"The Fanner Foundation." Mac took it for granted that this explained everything. "I have been with the Foundation and Emma for a long time. I'm responsible for Emma's security. I've been with Emma since she was born, always in the background. But I failed to protect Emma. After the accident at Easter I knew I needed help. The Foundation asked you to come because you were Sara's friend and because we knew you were absolutely reliable."

He made me sound like a home remedy.

"We knew there was something going on in the house but I couldn't very well walk in and ask what it was. I certainly couldn't ask James."

"Why not?" It seemed to me a reasonable thing to do.

"Because I was their chief suspect." James answered without anger. "They didn't believe the explosion had been an accident. They thought I had meant to kill Emma."

"And you knew Mac was an agent of the Foundation?" I asked James. I couldn't believe it was true.

"Of course," he said. "I was glad he was here to look after Emma since I couldn't."

"And you said nothing to me about it?"

"Not you or anyone."

I found the idea appalling. "If you brought me here to spy for you," I blazed out at Mac, "why didn't you tell me?"

"What you didn't know couldn't hurt you," Mac said. "If you had thought Emma was in danger we counted on your calling for help, to the Foundation." He stood for a moment pulling at his beard, which was a sort of disguise after all. "I had reason to believe you were still in love with James."

I flushed. I did not like Mac making a public declaration of my affections but James seemed not to have heard him. James was preoccupied with the past and with a disaster he felt he should have seen and averted.

"I knew the explosion had not been an accident. I knew it," James said, "but I couldn't prove it. What I told Emma and you tonight was the truth but not quite the whole truth. That day at Easter . . ." James looked away from us as if he could see the day and the boat and the time past. "There wasn't much wind but there was a warm sun. The three of us, Emma and Caroline and I, had our lunch on the deck. Caroline gave Emma some of her wine to sip and Emma said she was sleepy. Caroline laughed. I hear her now, laughing."

I had stopped shaking but I was cold, bone-cold in a chill so deep I might never be warmed again.

"Caroline said. 'Surely you can't be tipsy from that little bit of wine.' Emma yawned and said, 'I am, I'm sleepy and I want a nap.' Emma lay down on the half-open top of the plastic hatch. She curled up in the warm sun. I helped Caroline carry the lunch things down to the galley.

"In the galley Caroline smiled at me and she said, 'Why not finish the wine? There's not much left,' and she went back up on deck to get the rest of the lunch things.

"I had drunk my wine but there was some in Caroline's glass, the glass Emma had drunk from. I finished it rather than let it go to waste. It tasted bitter and I knew what Caroline had done. She had drugged Emma.

"I went up on deck." James's breath came quick and sharp as if he had been running. "Caroline had Emma by the rail. I saw her unfastening Emma's life jacket. I thought she was going to drown Emma. I got Emma away from the edge, and then I forced Caroline to come below. I didn't want to take a chance of having Emma hear what I was going to say.

"I told Caroline I knew she had meant to kill Emma. I said I would expose her. She let me go on and on until suddenly I began to feel groggy myself. My head began to spin.

"She stood there, beautiful and smiling, and she said, 'It doesn't matter what you know, James, because in a few moments there is going to be an accident. You and Emma will be dead and I will be your very rich widow.'

"I said, 'They will find you out,' and she said, 'Nonsense, it will look like an accident. Besides, who would suspect me, James? Everyone loves me. Everybody adores me.'

"I am not sure how I got up on the gangway or up the ladder onto the deck. I had to get to Emma. I closed the hatch after me. I left Caroline below locked in the hold. I was fastening Emma's lifebelt securely when I heard the first explosion. I put Emma over the side and I went back for Caroline.

"But I couldn't get the hatch open. There was too much pressure from the heat. She was there just beneath the plastic bubble. I saw her face, then there was another explosion. The last thing I saw was Caroline's face in the flames and she was laughing at me.

"Captain Fairley picked us up, Emma and me. He took us to Fannerstown and they told us Caroline was missing." James was silent for a moment, his eyes unfocused and staring at some far place.

"When the wound healed there was no real damage to my eyes but I still couldn't see. Perhaps it was a sort of self-punishment for having failed to see before what she had planned. I blamed myself for not having seen it all the time.

"At the inquest perhaps I should have told them about Caroline. But what good would it have done? I had to think of Emma and what that kind of truth would do to her. Besides, I had no proof, only my word for what happened and who would believe me? Caroline was right. Everyone had loved Caroline. Whatever I should have done at that time, I kept the secret.

"I couldn't guess that Emma would believe she was responsible or that she would hope Caroline was still alive and coming back again. It was another sort of punishment, one I could not escape.

"I sat here in this house alone in my self-punishing blindness. I sat in the dark and I thought about Caroline hour after hour. It seemed I could hear Caroline laughing at me. It was as if she were still here, as if she had never left. It seemed she was still in the house.

"When I learned the Fanner Foundation had sent for you I didn't want you to come. I didn't want you in this house. I didn't want you exposed to the danger and the evil I knew was here. But you came and you stayed out of loyalty.

"And all that time I sat, day after day, trying to outwit a dead woman, trying to outguess what she had planned to do. I knew it was not over, not finished. Caroline would not let Emma or me go. Caroline's plans went beyond her death. It was a form of madness. I wasn't sure that I was not mad. The blow on the head, the isolation of blindness, made me think I might have imagined half of what I thought was true. She haunted me. She was always there, laughing at me, looking at me through the flames. I knew she was dead yet I felt she was in the room in the house and I was alone with her in the darkness in a private seance.

"I had to know what had driven her. Little by little I came to think like Caroline. I saw with her eyes. At first I only saw shapes and shadows but what I saw was unspeakable.

"I knew no one would believe me without proof and if proof existed it had to be in the boathouse, in her studio where she and Miles and Mrs. Fairley had spent all those years together. I wasn't able to see well enough to go there on my own. I couldn't trust anyone else but you, Martha, and so I asked you to take me there.

"You found the journal and the documents. I wasn't sure of what you had found but when I was attacked for them and the house set on fire for them I knew I must be close to the truth. I didn't want to lie to you, Martha, but I did not want to involve you any further. I had done you enough harm. I said I was going to the hospital and I did, as an outpatient. The rest of the time I spent at my lawyer's having him read me the journal and the documents.

"It is, I suppose, a fortunate thing that the relationship

between attorney and client is a privileged one. But my lawyer
could not have enjoyed the privilege that day.

"Caroline had kept a faithful accounting. It was all there,
written in her own hand. As he read it it was like unraveling the
tangled web of Caroline's madness.

"Everything had been for Miles. Caroline had made up a
fantasy world for the two of them on the island where they
would stay forever.

"Miles did not share Caroline's fantasy. He had tried to go
away but Caroline had always brought him back like a naughty
child. When Miles went for the last time she suspected nothing.
She thought he had gone to Fannerstown for supplies. He didn't
come back. By evening she was worried. She went down to the
shore to look for him. She stood there watching and waiting,
looking out to sea. But he didn't come back.

"The Coast Guard came instead, to tell her there had been an
accident and that Miles was in a hospital near Boston. When she
got to the hospital she found her beautiful Miles unrecognizable.
Caroline's fantasy shattered like a looking glass.

"But there was more. He hadn't been alone in the car. He
had been running away from her with a girl, a girl he was going
to marry, a girl who was going to have his baby. The girl was
going to be all right. She had lost the baby but she was all right.
She had been thrown clear of the car. Caroline's world cracked
for a second time.

"At the hospital they all thought it was Caroline's kindness
that made her take care of the girl. But it was not kindness. It
was the beginning of Caroline's revenge. An eye for an eye, a
tooth for a tooth. When Caroline had seen who it was that
Miles had cared for enough to leave her, seen who Miles had
loved enough to get with child and to marry there was the third
and last crack in the mirror."

"Poor Mrs. Fairley," I said.

"Yes," James nodded absently. "Poor Mrs. Fairley. Poor, stupid Mrs. Fairley. Caroline made her life hell here on the island. She racked her with guilt and with Miles's memory every day. She made her believe the child had been taken from her because she was unfit to raise it. Only if she did whatever Caroline asked would she have any hope of ever seeing the child again.

"Tibba is not her child is she?" I knew the answer but I had to ask. In all of this twisted, tangled web Caroline might have been capable of any deceit.

"No, Tibba is not hers. I checked both the death certificate for Miles and for the baby. No, Tibba is just an orphan whom Caroline found who was the right age and coloring, a child who might have been Miles's."

"A convenient orphan."

"What?" James looked startled.

"Nothing," I said sadly. "Just something Tibba said about herself last night at dinner."

"Well," James sighed and shrugged, a gesture of finality. "You know the rest. I came back here and told Mac what I had found out. If you had stayed a little longer, Martha, heard a little more, you'd have known we were trying to convince Emma that Caroline was dead so that it would do her the least harm, cause her the least shock."

"I thought James ought to tell Emma flat out," Mac said. "It was my decision, my error. She had been so good about Pompey's death, and besides I had never bought the story about Emma being a neurotic and damaged child. So the scene she made surprised me." Mac glanced at James. There was a moment of indecision as to who should tell the rest of it.

"When Emma left the dining room," Mac continued, "you went after her. We all sat stunned, not knowing what to do. Then Mrs. Fairley began to clear away the broken dishes. We were going to talk to her later in the evening. We didn't suspect her of anything but we thought she might help us with some facts. She went into the kitchen and she didn't come back. We went after her but she had disappeared."

"We knew Emma was safe because she was with you, but there was no sign of Mrs. Fairley. We began a search of the island. James went down to the studio and to the well. The Captain went back to the Widow's Look to make sure the wiring hadn't been tampered with. I took the lighthouse and the beach but we couldn't find her. Then the Captain and I decided to sail around the island. We were back of the cliff when we saw the two of you. You and Mrs. Fairley.

"I'm sorry I hit you so hard. You wouldn't trust me to save you, to pull you to the shore."

"I thank you," I said. "You saved my life." It was something that had to be said but was so sobering a thought that we were quiet, caught in the short space between life and death.

Mac cleared his throat. "I still don't know why Mrs. Fairley chose tonight to pretend to be Caroline and try to kill Emma. If she had waited even a day or two she would have gotten away with it."

"I think I can tell you that." I sat up feeling painfully weak but determined to tell them the whole of it.

"You see, tonight, when James said Caroline was dead, he helped to set Emma free but it was a threat to Mrs. Fairley. She'd heard it said before, of course, but tonight it acted as some sort of trigger. She thought that if Caroline was not alive she couldn't keep her child. For her Caroline had to be alive, and she dressed up again as Caroline to prove it, at least to herself. And, in fact, Caroline was alive for a while."

James looked stunned.

"She managed to swim to shore after the explosion," I

continued. "She was badly burned and Mrs. Fairley took care of her."

"You mean that Caroline didn't die on the boat? That even when I had thought Caroline was dead she was alive?" His face was ashen pale.

"That's right. And little by little after Caroline died and Mrs. Fairley no longer had Caroline as her authority figure, she began to take on Caroline's persona. Little by little, because she could not function without her, she became Caroline. And tonight, as Caroline, she tried to kill Emma."

"I was so sure Caroline was dead," James said.

"When Caroline finally did die Mrs. Fairley put her body in the well," I said.

"And you got too close to her secret," Mac nodded, "and she tried to kill you."

"When was this?" James demanded.

"While you were away."

I couldn't meet his eyes.

"Did you think I had tried to kill you, Martha?"

I couldn't tell James I had thought him a villain, that he had been my chief suspect as well as Mac's.

"What will happen to Mrs. Fairley?" I asked Mac.

"She's been taken to the mainland."

"Already?"

"Yes. We called on the Coast Guard to send a doctor. The Captain went off with her, of course."

Poor Captain Fairley. In all of this perhaps the Captain was more to be pitied than anyone.

"There will be no charges against her. She's been taken to a hospital. The Foundation will see she has the best treatment and that she's well cared for."

"The Foundation is very thorough."

Mac looked pained by my remark.

"For Emma's sake it would be best to keep it quiet. Would you prefer another scandal, another sensation?"

"No," I said, "I'm sorry." I should have been grateful that the Foundation could afford to let it be ended in silence. As powerful as the Foundation was it could do almost anything within reason.

"Something must be done for Tibba," I said. "If it had not been for her I wouldn't have known Emma was gone or where to look for her. Tibba would like to stay. She's happy here. Surely the Foundation will let her stay."

"Of course she can stay." Mac looked puzzled. "We've taken it for granted that you'll be staying too."

I didn't know whether the "we" was Mac and James or Mac and the Foundation. Certainly I knew that I was taken for granted. That much I had already decoded. There was no point in making a fuss over it. I had promised Emma I would stay for as long as she needed me. The promise to Emma was a sop to my pride.

"Well, that's settled then." Mac turned toward the window and looked out toward the Widow's Look. The first grey light was turning bright. Yesterday was today, and the nightmare was over. No need for Mac to keep watch for a danger that was no longer expected nor coming.

"I'm going into Fannerstown this morning and on to Boston," Mac said. "I have to leave you for a few days till this business is settled. Do you two think you can manage on your own?"

I didn't know whether or not he was smiling. I never knew when Mac was joking and when he was not.

I felt James's eyes on me. I looked at him and I was trapped, mewed up. His eyes had always been able to catch me like a snare.

"What do you think, Martha?" James asked. "Do you think we can manage?"

I took time to answer so that my voice would be steady. And because I knew that if there was a last, final time when I could turn back this was it, the point of no return.

"We can try," I said.

"We'll be fine," James said.

"Good." Mac was all brusque and bustle. He bent over me and gave me a quick kiss on the forehead. "Remember what I told you. Remember I said you could never be like Caroline no matter what you did."

And he went away and left us to manage on our own on an island free of ghosts.